MADAGASCAR

a novel

Stephen Holgate

Blank Slate Press
Saint Louis, MO 63116

Blank Slate Press is an imprint of Amphorae Publishing Group, LLC
www.amphoraepublishing.com

For information, contact:
Blank Slate Press
4168 Hartford Street, Saint Louis, MO 63116
www.amphoraepublishing.com

Manufactured in the United States of America
Cover Design by Kristina Blank Makansi & Elena Makansi
Cover art: IStock
Set in Adobe Caslon Pro and Marion

Library of Congress Control Number: 2018940506
ISBN: 9781943075485

For John and Richard

MADAGASCAR

a novel

Stephen Holgate

Blank Slate Press | St. Louis, MO

1

I bring my fist to my ear and listen to the clacking of the dice, unable to shake the fear that I'm listening to the rattle of my own fate. The voices of the gamblers in this second-rate casino swirl around me like a river—eddies of French and Malagasy, whorls of variously-accented English, ripples of Italian and Japanese. Maybe these currents will carry the dice on their long fall toward the table and give me the nine I so desperately need. I close my eyes and blow, one last attempt to breathe on the dice some unearned quantum of good fortune, an overdraft on my depleted karmic account.

The croupier, a short, diffident Malagasy in an ill-fitting jacket, frowns at me and sighs. "Monsieur Knott."

"All right, all right," I tell him and grudge-flick the dice down the long green table, where they bounce awkwardly, skid to a stop, and thumb their nose at me—a three. Craps.

The croupier gathers in the dice like a mother retrieving her children from the attentions of a dubious stranger.

I might look for solace in the faces of my friends among the other gamblers, but I have no friends among the gamblers, have few friends of any description. Even those I have don't like me.

Working on my mojo as the Man Who Doesn't Care, I take a sip of tonic water, gone warm and flat, and stroll away from the table like an actor walking offstage.

I glance at my watch. Eleven o'clock. Only in Madagascar would this seem late. Nowhere to go but home. But I put the moment off, drift over to the tall windows at the far end of the room and gaze at the reflection of the tall fellow before me, still lean, though no longer athletic, hair flecked with gray. I flash myself an unpersuasive smile.

The Zebu Room is named after the humpback cattle that roam in every field, graze in every pasture, and stand on every street corner in Madagascar. The place sits like a boil on the top of the Hotel Continental, looking out over the vast darkness of Antananarivo, a city of two million souls—or four million, or six million, no one really knows—its shadowy expanse sprinkled with a few pinpricks of electric light and, out in the spreading shanty towns, the faint orange glow of oil lamps. Fourteen stories below, a gap-toothed string of streetlights edges the nearly deserted boulevard.

I try to pick out the distant lights of the country's main prison and feel relieved when I can't find them. Still, I can't shake the dread of tomorrow's visit to the crumbling penitentiary and its unhappy population of the brutal, the venal, and the luckless. More particularly, I don't want to think of the lone American rotting in his cell up there. Walt Sackett. Malfortunate sonofabitch. I picture him up there, gray, filthy and unwell, his life dribbling away in a hell hole beyond the reach of home or God or the American Embassy. I try to shake the image from my mind, rid myself of the corrosive conviction that his fate is not unlike my own.

I put my empty glass on the tray of a passing waiter and head for the door.

"Monsieur Knott, you are leaving so soon?" The voice cinches around my neck like a cowboy's lasso.

Even before I turn around, I recognize the wheedling tones of Jacques Razafintsalama, the Zebu Room's manager. He regards me with finely counterfeited regret.

"Just going down to put a couple more francs in the parking meter."

Jacques smiles at my little joke. We both know I'm more likely to find a unicorn on the streets of Antananarivo than a parking meter.

"The Colonel wishes to see you," he says.

I tap my watch like a man in a hurry. "It's getting late. Maybe another time."

But I'm not fooling anyone. We both know it isn't a request.

I fall in behind the Malagasy, who leads me toward a corridor at the far end of the room.

Maurice Picard, a fat, red-faced Frenchman in his fifties, gets up from behind his desk and offers me his meaty hand.

"Robert, how are you?" he asks in English and waves me into a chair.

A ceiling fan turns slowly overhead, purely decorative in the air-conditioned office.

Maurice insists his staff call him Colonel, out of respect, he tells them, for his former position in the French army. Occasionally he lets it drop that he made his stack as a soldier of fortune in Central Africa, fighting for a variety of dubious causes. Unfortunately for Picard, a string of defeats had, in the eyes of the victors, transformed his military adventures from a struggle for national liberation into a catalogue of war crimes. Chased by demands for his extradition should he ever reappear in his native France, Picard hopscotched from one unwelcoming African republic to another until he eventually landed on the island nation of Madagascar, the end of the line, a part of Africa and yet physically separate, as if it too had been cast out. There he bought the Zebu Room from a dying German who, like Picard, had run out of luck and places to run.

For years Picard tried to set the tone for his establishment by appearing each night in a dinner jacket, his diamond-studded cufflinks twinkling in the understated light, his heavy cologne speaking to a fat man's insecurity about his own excesses. Few of his gamblers heeded his call to elegance, continuing to come to the gaming room in street clothes until he finally traded the tux for shapeless khakis and a flowered shirt that bulged over his large belly, "to make this place less stuffy, give it a flavor of the tropics," he says. It really means he's given up, that despite the tally of each night's profits he is, like the German before him, losing whatever existential wager he has made on his casino. And on Madagascar.

"A drink?"

I wag a finger in a negative kind of way and pat a spot where I believe my liver to reside.

"Ah, yes, Robert." Picard's breezy familiarity and his insistent on using my Christian name sends a twist of unease deep into my gut. For all his outward affability, Picard has always struck me as the kind of man who could strangle you with a length of piano wire then walk into the kitchen and make himself a sandwich without even washing his hands.

With the grunt of a big man shifting his weight, Picard settles behind his desk and nods at Jacques, who backs out of the room, closing the door behind him. A photo of a young woman sits in a frame on the cabinet behind Picard.

"Pretty girl," I tell him, hoping the subtle compliment about his girlfriend might buy me a dram of grace.

The Frenchman turns and gazes at the picture. "My daughter. She lives in France." He might have been saying she lives on the moon. "You've told me you have a daughter too, yes?"

I don't much care to share anything about the sole issue of my loins with this thug, but I'm the one who started this conversation, so I say, "Christine. She'll turn seventeen this year."

"Christine," Picard sighs, as if it were the name of every daughter lost to her father.

With a swift pivot of his chair the big man turns his back to me. "You like the dice," he declares, like a sideshow mind reader. He folds his hands over his ample stomach and leans back in his chair. "Now, the Malagasy, they prefer the roulette table," he says, twirling his finger. "Round and round it goes. Like their sense of time. You know they don't see it—time, I mean—as a straight line like we do. We Europeans ride on a train going from the point of our birth toward"—the flicker of a smile here—"some unknown destination. Going immutably forward. For them ... Well, they're all on a carousel. All of them—and their revered ancestors—going in never-ending circles."

"Yeah, that's what I hear." The chair is hard, the air short of oxygen. I can't breathe and want desperately to be somewhere, anywhere, else.

Maurice, though, seems to be enjoying himself. "For an instant we run alongside each other, Robert, the Malagasy and us, and we think we're travelling together. But we're on entirely different tracks." He smiles philosophically. "It's like their sense of everything, elliptical, everyone talking in circles, dancing around what they mean. Very Asian. Never"—he brings his hand down like a cleaver, sending a shiver through what's left of my soul—"never coming at you directly."

"You seem to have picked something up from them."

Picard looks at me quizzically, then laughs. "Ah, maybe so." He clasps his hands together and leans over his desk, making the room feel smaller. "So, did you have a good night, Robert? Walking away with a little of my money, I hope?"

I manufacture a shrug. "My luck'll change."

"It's going to have to, Robert." Picard nods toward the gaming room beyond the door. "You signed for your chips again tonight?"

"I run a tab," I say, acknowledging what we both know.

"A large one, my friend, a very large one. Fourteen million Malagasy francs." He makes a low whistle at this weighty sum. "What is that?"

"I don't know. I forgot to bring my abacus." I lean back, clasp my hands behind my head. Just a couple of friends talking.

He squints at a piece of paper in front of him as if he hasn't already memorized the figure. "Twelve thousand dollars American, I believe."

"I'm good for it. The State Department pays us decently. Besides, what else am I going to spend my money on in Madagascar?"

Picard smiles and spreads his hands, a man laying everything on the table. "Yes. And you get paid in dollars, lucky boy. *Non?*" He slips into French as his smile fades. "Look at me. I rake in hundreds of thousands every night.

Millions. *Bouf!* All of it in Malagasy francs. Play money."
He mimes tossing a handful of it into the air. "Try cashing
it in for something real—euros, Swiss francs, dollars. The
banks won't do it. The Malagasy franc's a non-convertible
currency, they say." He flicks his hand and blows across his
palm. "And, as you say, Robert, what is there to spend it on?"
He cocks his head and winks at me. "How much longer are
you in Madagascar?"

"Almost seven more months." I try to make it sound like
so many years.

"Seven months." Picard grunts, ruminating on this. "And
you can pay me—what?—nearly two thousand dollars a
month until you leave?"

"You know I'm not allowed—"

"To pay me with any of the embassy's precious dollars.
Yes, I know." Picard leans back in his chair and stares at the
ceiling fan. "You're a diplomat," he sighs, "so I can't have
you arrested." He pauses a bit too long before adding, "Not
that I would want to. I can't even sue you." The injustice of
it creeps into his voice. He leans forward again, crowding
me, and asks, "And if I wrote a letter to the embassy—well,
what then? Private debts are private matters, no?"

With a soft *plonk* the pebble drops into the pool of our
conversation and I feel myself bobbing on its ripples.

Disgrace over gambling debts seems so old-fashioned,
like something from a Russian novel. But the Department
itself is as old-fashioned as hoopskirts, tut-tutting its way
backwards into the future. And in the mind of Diplomatic
Security large debts to foreigners are, like idle hands, the
devil's playground.

"You know, Maurice, I really haven't got much of a career
to ruin."

Picard waves his hand, trying to deny that I've taken his words exactly as he meant them.

"Look at me, Maurice. Twenty-two years in the foreign service. Forty-seven years old. And what am I? Political officer in Madagascar. And I only got this post because all the places farther from Washington are at the bottom of the ocean. My desk officer back at State never returns my e-mails. No one reads my cables. No one yearns to take my place. Why? Because no one cares what happens here."

"Ah, Robert, so much takes place here. The island is enormous. Madagascar—"

"Is like an old lady's private parts. Everyone knows it's down there somewhere, but nobody really cares. We've sailed over the edge of the world, you and me. What the hell harm do you really think you can do to me now?"

"Well, exactly, Robert, what harm *can* I do you?"

But the counterfeit colonel knows his man. After years dedicated to crawling up the treacherous slopes of the hierarchy, a foreign service officer can no more surrender even his most tattered ambitions than he can decide to breathe something other than oxygen.

"In a few years, I'll be past fifty. When I fail to get my next promotion—and I will—I'll be shoved into honorable retirement." I try to laugh at the punchline my life has become. "Retirement to what? I've spent most of my adult life overseas. The States are as foreign to me as they are to your average Malagasy. How many years have I spent in Africa representing a country I don't even know anymore? We're just alike, Maurice, you and me. Stateless. Professional foreigners." The little speech gains me no applause. "Okay. How's this?" I waggle my head like one of the island's Indian merchants offering a bargain. When

I go, I'll give you my car. A Peugeot. Worth at least eight thousand dollars."

Picard emits another loud *bouf!* "I already have a car. And even if I sell yours, I only get another pile of Malagasy francs. No, we'll have to make some other arrangement." He flashes a smile like a snake flicking its tongue. "I'm sure something will occur to us. Something to our mutual benefit." The big Frenchman stands and holds out his hand. The audience is over. "Always good to see you Robert."

We cluck a few affable words of parting and shake hands. Mine is sweaty and cold and I make for the door like a man with a fast-moving fire behind him. Standing at the end of the corridor, Jacques Razafintsalama bows politely and gives me his most ironic smile, the one he saves for those who kid themselves that they won't be back. I cross the gaming room, this time avoiding the view through the tall windows and their prospect of the distant prison.

2

In the unlighted parking lot of the Continental, I steady my shaking hands and wonder if Picard is standing at his window looking down at me, chuckling to himself. "Let him write his goddamn letter," I mutter. But my chest feels tight, and it takes a couple of tries to draw a good breath.

The night air tastes of exotic flowers blossoming in the dark and carries a promise of rain. In a couple of months, the jacaranda petals will fall like lavender snow.

I put the car in gear and drive along the small lake bordering the Continental. The boulevard leads through a tunnel that separates the upper town from the lower, and comes out along the sad and faded Avenue de l'Independence, the city's main boulevard, its shops shuttered and dark, the marketplace and its sea of white umbrellas folded up. The street is empty, deserted even by the children who crawl up to the cars at stop signs, begging for change, their faces eaten by leprosy or their spines deformed by congenital disease. More often than money, they ask for pens, at least from me. "*Donnez moi stilo.*" Sometimes, if I'm stuck in traffic—it only takes a few cars to make a traffic jam here—I take a government-issue pen out of my pocket and hand it to one of them. Mostly I keep going.

On the overbuilt slopes that rise above the rows of dilapidated colonial facades, dim lights glow in the tall, mud brick houses. I imagine their lamplit rooms crowded with ghosts. Most Malagasy believe their ancestors are always present, just over their shoulders, their spirits squeezing into every corner, tapping at the windows, haunting the doorways until there's not enough room for the living.

It only takes a few minutes to drive through the empty town and out the Route Hydrocarbure to the residential neighborhood of Ivandry where most of the embassy's Americans live. We have big houses, like our wealthy Malagasy neighbors, and, like them, we live behind high walls edged with the red blossoms and menacing thorns of Spanish Bayonet to persuade burglars to knock over less protected houses.

I turn up the short drive in front of my place and flash the headlights. The night guard, Monsieur Razafy—like a lot of Malagasy he has only one name—swings the gate open, touches the brim of his cap, and gives me a chin-up nod to welcome me home.

I pull into the carport of the large two-story house I merit as head of the political section. Funny, if I were head of the pol section in Paris, I'd have half a dozen officers under me and live in an apartment. Here, I'm the only pol officer and get a place that's practically a mansion. Costs the taxpayer a couple hundred a month.

For a moment, I sit behind the wheel and listen to the ping of the cooling engine. When I get out, I don't go inside right away, but wander into the back yard, dark and quiet at this hour, and take a deep lungful of the clean, thin air—the French describe the climate up here on the central plateau as pleasantly unhealthful—and try to exhale the tension built up by my meeting with Picard. I hear the snick-snick-snick of Monsieur Razafy cutting the grass with hand clippers in the front yard. I once bought him a gas-powered mower, but Razafy, a serious, solidly-built man, refused it. "I have always done it this way." I tried to tell him the mower would save him a lot of time. Razafy just looked at me with an expression that asked, "What is time—your kind of time—to me?"

As quiet as it is in the back yard, I know I'm not alone. Somewhere across the dark expanse of lawn and shrubs lurks Bobby, the resident chameleon, rough and beautiful as an uncut jewel. I swear I've never seen him move, but I've also never seen him in the same place twice. Sometimes I can't find him at all and I think maybe he's gotten through the wall somehow and moved on. Then, an hour later, there he is, sunning himself in the middle of the lawn as if he has never been anywhere else in his life. When I walk by he follows me with first one then the other of his bulging, turret-like eyes. Chameleons are considered bad luck and Razafy regards him with something not so dark as fear nor so benign as respect. They give each other a wide berth.

A gust of wind rustles the trees and I look up at the sky. Flashes of lightning reveal great thunderheads stacked to the east, the lightning bolts not striking the ground but leaping from cloud to cloud, blinking like some kind of celestial pinball machine. It's all silent, the thunder swallowed by the miles, the storm like a distant battle, weighted with unreadable portent. The sky here is big, and when I start thinking like this it's time to go inside.

As I come in through the kitchen door the snoring of my maid, Jeanne, rolls up the hallway from her small room at the back of the house. I grope my way through the dark living room, switch on a lamp and pick up the phone. Good, a dial tone—never a given. When the call goes through, the ringing on the other end sounds as distant as Mars.

"Hello?"

Even through the filter of miles and bad connections she sounds older, more mature. Sixteen. What does she look like now? I haven't seen her in two years.

"Christine?"

"Yes?"

"Hi, sweetheart."

A long pause, then her voice—flat, guarded. "Hi, Daddy."

"I was thinking of you earlier tonight, thought I'd call. How you doin'?"

Again, that pause. Maybe just the lag in the connection as it bounces off some distant satellite, perhaps the measure of my daughter's ambivalence toward me, the need to weigh every word she speaks to me. "Fine," she finally says.

"I'm calling you all the way from Madagascar."

"Yeah, I know."

"It's night here."

"I know."

"You just got home from school?"

"No school today. Teacher in-service." Her voice takes on a sudden note of urgency. "I have lots of homework to do. I need to get to it."

"Okay. I just wanted to call and say hi. Say hi to your mom. And to Howard."

"They're going out to dinner tonight. I get the house to myself. An evening without his lectures."

The pleasure of thinking she doesn't much care for her mother's new husband makes me indulgent. "Be nice to him, sweetheart."

"He's not my father."

I wait for her to say, "You are," but she doesn't think of it. I want to bring up the fact that Howard held off marrying her mother for over a year because it would end her mother's alimony, but it would make me sound cheap.

"Hey, sugar."

"Yeah?" she asks, a little breathless now as she sprints toward the moment when she can hang up.

"I'm staying sober. Four months now." I think of telling her I've replaced the alcohol addiction with a gambling addiction, but neither of us would be sure it was a joke.

Silence. Then, "Good, Daddy." She seems to know it needs something more. "That's real good, Daddy."

"Tell your mom about it."

"I will. Goodbye."

I fight the anger rising in my chest at how badly she wants to hang up on me. I stand with the receiver to my ear, hoping maybe she's still there. Finally, I put the phone back in its cradle, turn off the lamp, and head upstairs.

I undress in the dark and slip into the sheets. As I close my eyes I catch myself praying, the impulse as unconscious as leg twitches. Each night it takes me by surprise, and each night I stop before I know what I'm praying for.

I roll onto my stomach and, from the other side of the bed, pick up a bit of the fading warmth and a hint of perfume.

"Oh, shit."

I get out of bed, put on my bathrobe, and walk down the hallway. A bar of light shows under the door of the study. Tying my robe shut, I walk toward the light like a dying man.

Lynn lies curled up on the couch in her nightgown, watching a movie on the DVD player. No cable or satellite service stretches its reach far enough to take us in. More than anything else, that's what reminds me we're living far below the horizon of the connected world.

She glances up, her honey-colored hair down over one blue eye, and gives me a look meant to turn me to stone. Then she turns back to the TV.

"An old Errol Flynn movie." I say it as if nothing could make me happier.

"*Captain Blood*. It came in with the commissary shipment today. I'll put it out on the shelf after I've watched it. Gotta take some advantage from being the head of admin."

After that first glance, she doesn't want to look at me.

"Hey, Lynn. Sorry. I know it's late."

"I came over after work. Kept thinking you'd be home any minute."

Over the course of a stormy three-month liaison we've run the gamut—passionate fights, gut-wrenching remorse, ecstatic sex, soul-devouring doubt. We've never known peace. Her calmness at this moment carries the whiff of death.

"I was going to call, but—"

"But you forgot I was coming over." Her sigh is bottomless. "I heard you on the phone just now."

"I called my daughter."

"I should have known. You're always depressed after you talk to her."

"I'm fine."

"You didn't get in a fight with her again?"

"Didn't have time."

For ten years Lynn was married to a political officer. A guy named Dewey. I never cared enough to get straight whether that was his first name or his last. Two-career marriages are tough in the foreign service and they've been divorced for a couple of years now. No kids. A shame. Lynn would have made a good mom. Instead she's head of Admin, mom to the whole embassy.

"What time is it?" she asks.

Still thinking of my phone call, I ask, "There? Here?"

"Here."

"Almost midnight."

Ignoring the storm warnings, I sit on the couch and try to pull her feet onto my lap, make her think everything's fine. Without taking her eyes off the screen she curls into a tighter ball. I cup her feet in my hands. She relents, stretches out. Slowly, I run my hand up her leg, caress her thigh, trying to steer us away from these parlous shoals, back into open water. We've always been good in bed. Maybe that's all there's ever been between us.

"I think I'll go home," she says.

"Don't be ridiculous. It's too late to be going anywhere." I need her to stay. This isn't a night I want to spend alone.

She narrows her eyes at me. "What's eating you?"

"Nothing." I try to shrug it off. "I gotta see some guy in prison tomorrow."

"Is that so bad?"

"I mean, prison. In Madagascar. Sweet Jesus."

"You make it sound like it was you." I can't bring myself to answer. "But that's not it. You went to the casino tonight."

"For a little bit."

"You lost."

I try to fake a smile. "Hey, I always lose."

"That's you, isn't it? Pick a losing hand and ride it as far as it'll go. At the casino. At work. Us."

I laugh, hoping to convince her she's joking. Bad choice. It comes off as mockery.

"That's it, buddy-o," she says, "I'm going home."

She slides off the couch and walks down the hall, leaving me watching *Captain Blood*. I should probably follow her, remonstrate, plead, cajole, but I'm caught up in Flynn's sword fight with Basil Rathbone. Maybe I should grow a pencil-thin mustache like Flynn's. Sure. And take fencing lessons, too. The chicks'll come flocking.

Belatedly, I call down the hall. "Lynn." Nothing. "Lynn, it's too late to go anywhere." I hear her take her toothbrush from the cup in the bathroom. A very bad sign.

I get up and head down the hall.

Dressed in the clothes she'd worn from work, she walks toward the stairs without looking back. "Maybe I'll see you tomorrow," she says.

With that, she's gone.

A moment later I hear the gate swing open. She'll walk to her place. It's only three doors down the street. With an almost musical "clunk," the big metal gate swings shut again.

In the renewed silence, I hear Monsieur Razafy go back to cutting the lawn in the dark.

3

A shiver runs down my back as I peer through the car window at the stained and crumbling walls of the old prison. Choking on fear and loathing, I step out of the car. Before I take more than a couple of steps toward the gate, a wave of panic steers me back to the car. I lean in through the window toward Samuel, the embsasy-assigned driver I get when on official business. "For God's sake, keep the engine running. I may want out of here in a hurry."

Taking this for a joke, Samuel giggles and turns the ignition off. "I'll be right here, Monsieur Knott."

For a couple of reasons, there's no point getting sore at him. First, he's Malagasy and regards almost everything in a different light. I wonder what he sees in this situation. Whatever it is, he clearly thinks it's funnier than hell. Second, he's my only way out of here.

Muttering under my breath, I show my credentials to the guard, and the iron gate, groaning like the damned, slowly slides aside.

I step into the stone-walled compound and nearly retch at the overwhelming stench of sweat, shit, wood smoke, and death. Before leaving on vacation, Don Schiff, the consular officer, who normally handles stuff like this, told me what to do. "Just walk across the courtyard to the main guardroom and ask to see the American." Sure. Just take a stroll across the Valley of the Shadow of Death.

Memo to self: Kill Don Schiff when he comes back from vacation.

From the barred windows of the wooden cell blocks, clusters of brown faces peer down at me, their eyes aglow, their mouths murmuring, "*vazaha, vazaha*"—"stranger," "foreigner"—weighty words on this island-planet. In the eyes of the Malagasy an air of potent yet erratic magic clings to the unknowable *vazaha*—powerful, foolish people unable to distinguish good from bad, right from wrong, bringing fortune to the undeserving and disaster to the virtuous.

Prisoners idling in the courtyard stop talking to stare at me as I walk past. Most of them are bird-thin, their bodies wasted to bare essence, their souls protruding through thin layers of flesh. Yet a handful of them look startlingly healthy, round-faced, their clothes washed and patched. These are the prisoners whose families take care of them. A Malagasy prison, besides denying its inmates sanitation or medical care, clothes or dignity, gives them no food. The men live—or die—off whatever their relatives can provide. For many families, the inmate was their sole breadwinner. Without him they can give only enough to facilitate a prolonged starvation.

While I'm watching them watching me, I nearly trip over a man lying in the meager shade of a dying tree. His closed, sunken eyes, his shallow rapid breaths testify that he's preparing to slip over the threshold and become one of the ancestors.

I quicken my step, crossing the courtyard as quickly as dignity allows. On the far side of the prison's dusty square

I find the unpainted wooden door of the guardroom and push it open.

Inside, a dozen prisoners fill the small room. Some, their heads bandaged, wear bloodstained clothes and slump against those chained to them.

Two guards in faded cotton uniforms look up from their work of checking in the prisoners. The older of the two, a man with a graying mustache and large watery eyes, steps away from the line of newly matriculating inmates, takes me by the arm and hustles me back outside, shutting the door behind him.

He asks me my business.

"I'm here to see the American prisoner."

"Oh, yes, the American prisoner." He smiles. "Certainly."

Walt Sackett's cell smells of filthy clothes and unwashed bodies, of the slop bucket in the corner, and of a despair so profound as to render speech difficult.

"You're getting your mail?" I ask him. His face is gray and he slumps on the edge of his mattress as if he might fold up and die right in front of me.

"Beats me." Sackett hunches his sagging shoulders and lets them drop. "I don't s'pose they'd tell me if they was holding something back."

The American's flesh hangs off him in folds like something he's about to slough off. From Don's description, Sackett had, only a few months earlier, carried the vital heft of a guy who liked the long hours and hard work of a cattleman, one who knew how to reward himself at the end of the day with a fat steak and a couple of beers. Now, sitting in his dark cell, he seems hollowed out, as if it were the idleness killing him, not the uncertain diet and the filth of a Malagasy prison.

"You have any letters for me to take, Mr. Sackett?"

He grinned awkwardly. "Just call me Walt." He's from eastern Oregon, but his voice carries the twang of Oklahoma or Texas.

"Okay. I'm Robert." I sit across from him on the cell's other mattress. Like Sackett's, it rests on the floor and I talk over the top of my knees.

"Yeah, got a couple letters here." Sackett reaches under his mattress and pulls out two stained envelopes. "They're for—my wife."

I wonder about the catch in Sackett's voice. Estrangement? Shame? Or simply the loneliness and regret of living in a prison on the far side of the world?

The aging cattleman waves the envelopes and forces a half-smile. "I don't seem to have a stamp. I'll pay you back when …" He forces a thin smile.

"Forget it. We're good for a couple of stamps," I tell him. "I'm afraid I haven't got any mail for you. You telling everyone to write you in care of the embassy?"

"I sure am." Sackett takes a pencil from his shirt pocket and addresses the envelopes. "I 'preciate you taking care of these." He clears his throat but doesn't look at me. "Any chance I'll be getting outta here anytime soon?" He adds hurriedly, "I know you fellas have a lot more important things to do than get a broken-down cowboy out of prison."

"There's nothing more important to us than springing you out of here," I tell him. He knows I mean it.

The close air of the wooden cell makes me shiver even on this warm January morning, summer in Madagascar, where everything seems the opposite of what it should be. "How they treating you?"

"Oh, all right I guess." Sackett wheezes while he talks. Allergies? Bronchitis? Tuberculosis? It could be anything. "I dunno. I guess maybe most of the other fellas here have committed some kinda crime. Done something to land themselves in jail. But no one deserves this." He attempts a gesture to take in the prison and its inmates and the despair in which they lived. But there is no gesture for hell and he gives it up. "I seen 'em rot and die just waiting to come to trial. Me, I was stupid and ignorant. Maybe that's worse than being a criminal."

When I'd first heard of Sackett I figured I knew the type; one of those guys who seems tough and smart and determined, yet always needs to catch one more break to make it all happen. Frustrated at home, they think they can find that break in a foreign country, where they figure the rules that hold them back in the States don't apply. They never understood that they're going up against an entirely different set of rules, rules they know nothing about until they've broken them. I remember the American in Morocco, a sharp-eyed former ag exec from Missouri. He planned to grow aloe for skin lotion, but nothing went right, and he gradually spiraled into trafficking in kif, the local cannabis, and, like Sackett, ended up in prison. Or the guy from Louisiana I met in Mozambique, determined to make himself a player in the as-yet nonexistent 'oil bidness,' dropping names of men he knew with Amarada Hess and Shell and BP, walking with a swagger and standing with his hands on his hips. He started out sharing cigars with ministers in fine restaurants and ended up three months later filling out the embassy forms to borrow the eleven hundred bucks to get back home.

Sackett is different. For one thing, he's older. Sixty-four. I'd read his file and wondered what the old guy could be looking for so far from home. What was lacking in his life that he thought he could find here? The others I'd known were essentially con men. Not Sackett. He came here from a cattle ranch in eastern Oregon, ready to work hard. He'd done enough homework to know that Madagascar's central plateau has good grazing land and hardy cattle. He even had enough sense to pay "fees" to a powerful minister for permission to buy livestock and two thousand hectares— about four thousand acres—of good, well-watered land.

His run lasted six months. The ministry waited until he got his ranch up and running, with a few hundred head of the humped-back zebu cattle and his grassland in good shape before starting to send him notices for previously unmentioned taxes.

When he got the first bill Sackett drove the thirty miles into town to visit his friend the ag minister, a short man who wore cologne thick as a smokescreen. I can see him, picking at some imaginary lint on his lapel while he assures Sackett that "these little fees are nothing more than a bureaucratic inconvenience." He instructed Sackett to remit the taxes through him, in cash. After a couple of months of this Sackett told the minister that he couldn't get any more money until he sold some calves the following spring. A few days after that, three policemen and an official in a white shirt came out to his ranch with an arrest warrant for trespass and illegal importation of cattle. In his broken French, Sackett tried to explain that he had a deed for the land and that the cattle weren't foreign, he'd bought them locally. The man in the white shirt smiled. "But monsieur is a foreigner, so it is really the same thing."

The embassy first heard of Sackett when the Malagasy government transmitted the required notification that an American citizen was being held in one of its prisons. After hearing his story, the embassy lodged a formal protest with the Foreign Ministry. But the American aid program was too small to demand respect or afford us the leverage to get him out of jail.

Sitting on his thin prison mattress, Sackett shifts his weight from one tired haunch to the other. "When's Don coming back?" he asks.

"He's on home leave. A kind of extended vacation. It'll be another six weeks or so," I tell him. "I'm afraid you'll have to put up with me until then."

"I didn't mean …"

"It's all right."

On the floor of the cell someone has used a piece of charcoal to lay out the lines for a local game called "cops and robbers."

Sackett sees what I'm looking at. "Funny game, Robert. You ever play it?"

I've seen the rune-like patterns drawn in the dirt along the side of the road near my home, the guards playing it by the hour while keeping half an eye on the houses they're hired to protect.

"No, never played it myself."

With the toe of his shoe, Walt Sackett traces the lines of the playing board. "It's kinda like checkers. You take the other guy's pieces by moving toward them, or—now here's the real Malagasy thing about it—or by moving away from them." He laughs his broken laugh. "Just right for people

who don't know whether they're coming or going. I figure—"
The clanking of the cell door interrupts his thought.

A young Malagasy stands in the doorway, dressed in a ragged shirt and poorly patched trousers. He cocks his head to one side when he sees a stranger in the cell.

Sackett waves him in, and for the first time since I'd been there smiles naturally. "Speedy, how ya' doin'?" He grins at me. "My cellmate. I call him Speedy. Like Speedy Gonzalez."

"He's quick on his feet?"

"Nah. He just knows how to get around the cat."

The young man—I'd guess he isn't over twenty—nods at the guard holding the door open as if the officer were a bellboy and he, Speedy, has decided he'll take the room.

Despite his scarecrow appearance he bounces into the room like a man blessed by fortune. He offers me a smile and an outstretched hand. "I'm Dokoby Rakoto. Speedy. *Enchanté.*"

Enchanté? I can't keep from laughing with pleasure at this ragged kid with the manners of Fred Astaire. He laughs with me.

Sackett beams like a proud father. "My cellmate's all right, ain't he?"

I shake the young man's hand. "That he is."

Remembering something, Speedy snaps his fingers and in a sort of pidgin English says, "Ah, Monsieur Walt. Cigarette." From his shirt pocket he takes a pack of the cheap Pieter Stuyvesants favored by most Malagasy and tosses it into Sackett's lap. Then, with the smile of a magician performing his favorite trick, he pulls a mango from his pants pocket and hands it to his cellmate.

Sackett grins. "Speedy, you're o-kay."

Dokoby Rakoto flashes a smile at Walt then crawls onto the mattress behind me and lies down. "No, monsieur, don't get up," he tells me in French, then turns on his side to sleep.

Sackett says, "Speedy's just coming back from a long night's work."

"Work?"

"Yeah." Sackett chuckles and nods vaguely toward the guardroom. "How much do you figure the government pays those guys to keep an eye on us? Not much, that's what. So the guards have to find a way to make a little something on the side."

"And Speedy has something to do with that?"

Sackett indicates the young man curled up behind me. "Speedy's a burglar. Lot of burglars here. And the guards figure what's the use of all that talent goin' to waste? So they let 'em out at night to do what comes natural. When they come back in the morning, the guards take their cut. Speedy, he drops half what he takes with his momma and his sisters before coming back, and gives the other half to the guards." He juggles the mango in his hand. "Looks after me a little too."

"You're pulling my leg."

The cowboy holds up a hand as if taking an oath. "God's own truth."

"Why don't the burglars just run away once they're out?"

Walt squints at Speedy. "The police'd track 'em down again. And the guards know where their families live. They'd just be buying trouble."

"So most of the guys I saw in the guardroom are burglars?"

"In the guard room?"

"A bunch of prisoners, all chained together. Guards acted like they didn't want me to see them."

Walt Sackett frowns and shakes his head. "Funny thing. They been bringin' in lots of prisoners from the countryside. If I understand it rightly, they're havin' some sort of riots or something."

"Riots?"

"Something like that. Must be in the papers."

I give him the truth. "The chance of something making the papers in this country is in exact inverse to its importance."

Sackett squints uncertainly. "Well, my French ain't much. Maybe I'm not hearin' it exactly right."

"What part of the countryside are they coming from?"

"I'm not sure. Maybe from the coast. Some town there. Tommy-something."

"Tamatave?"

"Maybe that's it. But I think some of these fellas are from other places too."

Like a jack-in-the-box, Speedy pops his head over my shoulder and again uses his broken English, "Mister Walt. I see your woman at gate. I tell guard, let her come here." He points at his eye then toward the gate then, with his hands, suggests a set of curves.

The old cattleman glances at me, tosses his head a little too casually. "Just ... She's just a friend. She's the one keeps me fed. Nirina." There's something in the way he says her name.

"Nirina," Speedy echoes with a smile and lies down again.

The silence that follows tells me it's time to leave. I look at my watch. "I'll be back in a few days," I tell him. "I've got a meeting at the Foreign Ministry, then I have to—" I feel a worm of guilt squirming in my gut. "Sorry, I didn't mean to ..."

"It's okay. Probably good for me to remember there's a world out there."

"I'll see that your letters get in the mail this afternoon." I get up from the mattress and look at the envelopes. "You don't have the return address on these. You want me to—?"

"Nah." Sackett avoids my eyes. "Just send 'em the way they are."

If Sackett doesn't want his wife to know he's in prison, it's none of my business.

"I'll be back in a few days, Walt."

"Okay, Robert." Again, that half-smile. "I 'spect I'll be here."

I force a laugh and tap on the cell door. When the guard opens up, I find myself facing a tall young woman with long black hair. Her impossibly dark eyes look all the deeper against the sandalwood hue of her skin. I stand back in surprise. I wish I could coin the word "beautiful" right here, as if it had been waiting for her to appear.

In one hand, she carries a cloth-covered basket. Walt Sackett's lunch—and probably dinner. Likely breakfast too.

The old cowboy struggles to his feet. "Hello, darlin'," Sackett says. He has a hard time taking his eyes off her long enough to glance at me. "This is Nirina."

But I already know her, at least by sight. I can see by a slight widening of her eyes that she recognizes me too. A mask lowers over her features, demanding—assuming— my silence.

I try to remember if I've ever heard her name before. I've seen her occasionally with the party crowd in the bar at the Continental. In the midst of the laughing and drinking, she sits at the bar with a distant smile on her face—with the others, but somehow not of them. For a few months she'd been a frequent guest at the parties thrown by the embassy's Marine guards. Yet even there, the center of attention for a bunch of love-starved Marines, she gave the impression of being by herself.

About a year ago one of the Marines, a skinny redhead named Bud, had talked about marrying her. The gunny—gunnery officer, a sergeant—in charge of the six-man detachment sat him down and told Bud that he'd known lots of girls like her and Bud had better get wise. She just wanted the visa to the United States that came with being his bride, and would leave him as soon as she had her feet on the ground. He hadn't added, "Besides, she has way too much class for a guy like you," but everyone except Bud could see that.

I try to remember the last time I saw her. It had been about nine months. Yeah, about the time Walt Sackett came to the island.

For a moment we stand facing each other in the doorway—the American diplomat and the Malagasy party girl—then I step aside and, with a slight bow, let her into the cell, feeling her sexual gravity bend the light around me as she passes.

The girl allows Sackett a chaste embrace, offering her cheek to him while casting a sidelong glance at me. Behind her back, Sackett makes a gesture, indicating that I shouldn't let her see the letters.

Now maybe I understand the catch in Sackett's voice when he mentioned his wife. I tell myself that this, too, is none of my business. But, outside as I step into the sunshine, I can still feel the warmth of her breath on my ear, where she whispered as she passed, "Please. I need to see you."

4

Roland Rabary, head of the Foreign Ministry's Americas Desk, leans back in his swivel chair and skims the two-page *demarche*, his eyes occasionally darting at me, as if judging whether I'm serious in bringing this document to him, asking for his country's support on a matter before the U.N.

Rabary is an ugly little man on an island of beautiful people, the handsomest I've ever known. With his frog-like gash of a mouth and a nose that appears to have partially melted at some point in the distant past, Rabary has to know how far short he falls of local standards, further souring an already prickly disposition.

Frowning theatrically, he lays the two pages on his desk with a loud sniff. "So, your superiors in Washington want our United Nations delegation to support a condemnation of Iran's behavior." As if in compensation for his homeliness, he possesses a beautiful voice, resonant and deep.

"Washington has instructed—"

Rabary waves a hand like a man swatting at a fly. "Washington's instructions end at your desk, not mine." He hunches his shoulders in a Gallic shrug, an acquired trait. Like many Malagasy elites, Rabary's resentment of the French is aggravated by the fact that he can't break free of the compulsion to measure himself by their standards.

With a flick of his fingertips, he pushes the paper away from him. "Iran has been helpful to us on more than one occasion, while you Americans ignore us except when you want to tell us what to do. You know we can't support this."

I open my mouth to argue with him, but can see the futility of it. "Yeah, I was told the age of miracles had passed."

He chuckles. A sop to make me feel better.

It's a strange relationship we have. Required by our governments to seek support for policies we know the other side will never agree to, Rabary and I refuse each other's entreaties then fall back on professional expressions of civility. Over time we've formed a genial sort of bond, with each of us playing, in turn, the sadist and the masochist.

I offer a defeated sigh. "Well, I'll tell 'em I tried."

Rabary makes something like a smile and takes a cigarette from a box on his desk. "Tell them you really made me sweat," he says in English. Rabary spent a year at Cornell and likes to sprinkle remembered idioms into our conversations.

"I'll do that. The embassy will be impressed by how almost successful I am." I lean forward in my chair and clasp my hands on top of his desk. "Look, I need to talk to you about something else. You have an American in one of your prisons. A man named Walter Sackett."

Rabary exhales a stream of smoke through his unfortunate nose. "I know all about your Walter Sackett. He faces serious charges."

"All of them phony. You know that. He's been squeezed dry by the ag minister. There's nothing left. It's time to let him go."

Rabary swivels his chair away from the desk and stares out the window.

I can see him making a calculation on how to leverage this situation to his advantage. Somehow it doesn't add up and he shakes his head. "No. There's nothing I can do. He will have to wait for his trial. If he has done nothing wrong, he will be found innocent."

"He's sixty-four and unwell. He could die before he comes to trial."

Rabary continues to gaze out the window. "You are providing him with food?"

"He has a girlfriend who helps him."

The Malagasy stubs out his cigarette and swings his chair back around. "The Ministry of Justice has been known to re-examine certain cases—"

"He can't bribe anyone anymore. He's broke."

"Perhaps you misunderstand me."

"Perhaps I don't."

We glare at each other and recalibrate our positions.

"I have no patience with this sort of thing," Rabary says, fiddling with a pen. "If Sackett were French, his government would have paid to settle the charges weeks ago."

"We're not the French."

Rabary lets my comment hang in the air like the smoke curling up from his cigarette. "You're quite emotional about this Sackett fellow. It's not like you. Really, Robert, it's unbecoming."

"Knock it off, Rabary."

"It is much easier for us both when you, um, maintain a professional distance, Robert." The pleasing timbre of his voice cushions the cynicism. He leans back in his chair and changes the subject. "A diplomatic note crossed my desk the other day. I see you have a change in personnel at your embassy."

"Yeah, a new Public Affairs Officer. She comes in next week."

"Someone new to plead your case to the press. A woman this time."

Do I catch something in the tone of Rabary's voice? "And young enough to be your granddaughter, Roland."

Rabary smiles and waves away the unstated accusation. "You have less than a year left here, yes? Where will they send you next?"

"I don't know yet. I've put in some requests. And you? You're still hoping for Paris?"

The Malagasy diplomat frowns. It's his natural expression and seems to relax him. The Malagasy embassy in Paris will need a new political officer in the coming year. Rabary has for months been speaking of it with the dreaminess of a knight speaking of the Holy Grail.

He holds the pen between his forefingers, addressing it rather than me. When he's serious he has a hard time making eye contact. "One needs promotion to the proper grade to be considered for such a position. This year I did not get promoted, and ..." He lets the thought trail away and glances at me furtively. I think he feels ashamed of himself when he tells the truth. "Still, it is not impossible. Under the right circumstances." With the air of a man who has revealed too much, he stands up and holds out his hand to indicate our meeting is over, adopting a genial manner to cover his abruptness. "I haven't seen you around the Zebu Room lately."

"I leave early. It doesn't take long to lose."

"Ah, yes. You are becoming famous for it."

I wonder how long it will take for word of my ill luck to spread to the embassy. I try to smile. No point letting him know how much it bothers me. "And you always win."

I mean it as a joke but Rabary shoots me a sidelong glance freighted with suspicion. Out of curiosity, I poke a stick at the sensitive spot. "Picard must dread seeing you come in."

"Yes, our good friend, Picard." Rabary turns his head away, but his eyes linger on me, searching for something. Apparently satisfied he hasn't found it, he opens the door to his reception room. His pretty secretary looks up.

On an impulse, I switch back to French so that anyone within earshot can understand. "I hear you're having some unrest in the countryside. Maybe on the east coast. Tamatave?"

Rabary starts to close his door, as if to keep my words from escaping, but it's too late for that. So he smiles and makes a dismissive gesture. "Everything is fine in Tamatave—and elsewhere." He's a good liar but I've caught him off guard. "Who would tell you such nonsense?"

"I got it from a passing lemur."

Rabary laughs like a man gargling razor blades. "Lemurs are notorious rumor-mongers. I wouldn't want you to go around repeating this. You will only look foolish."

"Thanks for the tip." I take a couple of steps into his outer office before turning back. "Rabary, do something for me—don't forget about Walt Sackett. You and me, maybe we deserve to be stuck here. He doesn't. He needs to go home."

The Malagasy smiles and says nothing. With a nod, he indicates to his secretary that she should escort me downstairs.

We've barely stepped into the hallway when I spot a familiar figure shambling up the corridor.

"Well, Picard, so the rumors aren't true."

Maurice Picard scowls in surprise, looking as ill at ease away from his casino as a cockroach caught too far from the baseboard. "Ah, Robert, how nice to see you," the Frenchman lies to me. "What rumor is that?"

"No one's ever seen you in the daylight. Word was getting around you're a vampire."

The owner of the Zebu Room tries to look like a man who can have a laugh at himself. "Vampire. That's very good, Robert." He glances nervously at Rabary's door.

I detect a whiff of something untoward, some bit of business between Picard and Rabary that doesn't want the light of day. I remind myself that there's always something in the air here, and the quickest way to go crazy is to try to get to the bottom of it.

"So, Maurice"—the Frenchman winces at my unwelcome familiarity—"what brings you to the Foreign Ministry? Declaring war?"

He smiles as if it hurts him. "No. Just a personal visit." Picard glares at Rabary's secretary, his eyes demanding she get him out of this conversation.

I turn to the young woman. "Don't worry. I can find my way downstairs. The Colonel and I are just going to chat for a moment."

"As you say, Monsieur Knott." She smiles at Picard and retreats to her office.

With a frown that stops just short of a snarl, Picard acknowledges the obvious. "I am here to see Rabary."

"Having trouble getting an exit visa?"

Picard's frown deepens.

Bull's-eye.

"Robert, I would think you have enough problems of

your own without concerning yourself with mine." Picard sets his mouth like a man entirely in control of himself. But the pressure of suppressed aggravation breaks the seal of his lips and he bursts out, "Why do they insist on exit visas, except that it gives them one more way to put their teeth into you? This should be absolutely routine." He mimics an official putting his nose into things. "Suspected violations of certain unnamed laws, they tell me. They say they can't let me leave. I say show me the proof. And they know there is none." In his aggrieved state, Picard has said too much and knows it. He waggles his head to change the subject. "In most countries if you displease the authorities they throw you out. Here they make you stay." He gestures toward Rabary's office. "One uses what connections one has."

"One does," I assure him. I'm beginning to understand. "And in exchange, you allow Rabary quite a run of luck at your place."

Picard throws his arms out as if waiting to be nailed to a cross. "I tell him it would be easier to simply bring the money to him here." The Frenchman glances around to see if anyone has overheard him, then continues more quietly. "But no, he wants to play the role of the lucky gambler. Everyone oohs and ahhs. It makes me sick. Even that's not enough. Now he insists on taking his winnings in dollars. And I have none."

It still doesn't add up. The going price for an exit visa is a few thousand Malagasy francs—a few bucks—delivered to a mid-level hack. No, it's something else. Rabary has something on Picard and can insist the question of his exit visa be kicked up to him—and the price kicked up with it. Over what? Picard's claim that there's no proof he has broken any laws falls short of an actual claim of innocence.

As if riding the train of my thoughts, Picard says, "Why am I telling you all this?" The question is aimed more at himself than at me. "We are both white men exiled in Africa. We dance to the tunes they play. But this place used to be our colony, for God's sake." The aggravation turns his face a deep red. "We understand each other, Robert, you and me. You, too, have a daughter. You know what it is like to never see your child."

Picard's swagger has leaked away and for a moment I feel an unwanted pity for the old brute.

The Frenchman senses it and bridles. "Don't think I have gone soft, Robert. And don't forget your debts to me. I have not."

"Yeah, well, I'd love to stay and talk, but I have to get back to the office. Keep your chins up, Maurice."

The Frenchman mumbles something unintelligible and shuffles down the hall toward Rabary's office.

5

As it does at most hours, the broad tarmac at Ivato Airport looks like a deserted parking lot. The cavernous terminal, built in the '60s, echoes the shuffling steps of a ragged line of travelers burdened by woven baskets and boxes tied with string, making their way toward a door marked Departures. The high ceilings and vast interior swallow my sighs as I wait in the Arrivals section.

Given a moment of idleness, my thoughts turn, as they do too often, to my standing in the embassy. It's not good. I'm popular enough with the Malagasy employees that make up the great majority of our staff. But the American officers, embarrassed that someone with my years is holding such a minor post, expend little time on me and less respect. The Ambassador, Michelle Herr, a political appointee from Tennessee, regards me with a mixture of pity and disdain. In my worst moments of unhinged suspicion, I picture her and Lynn comparing notes about me, arriving at the same unflattering conclusions.

Herr's deeply bred Southern graciousness does not allow her to give me the sort of formal upbraiding I deserve for my unpredictable hours, sour disposition, and lack of productivity, so she lets her displeasure show in other ways, tasking me with unpleasant burdens such as making the long trek out to the airport today to greet the incoming Public Affairs Officer, a duty more appropriate to the head of Admin or one of the junior officers.

I get up from my hard, plastic chair and again check the Arrivals board mounted high on the wall, though it only lists the official ETA of each flight, no matter how late, early, or even non-existent the plane itself might be.

I ask the young woman at the information desk when the Air France flight from Paris might arrive. "It will come soon." Her smile is reassuring. An hour later she tells me the same thing with the same smile. I make a note to ask again in another hour. I think I'm falling in love.

Pushed by a sour gust of ennui, I go upstairs to the lounge and slide into one of the many empty booths, order a coffee, and replay my conversation with Rabary. I'd hoped to do better by Walt Sackett. And if I didn't already feel enough motivation from within, I'm being prodded from without. Sackett's girl, Nirina, has called my office three times this week. I don't take the calls and tell Cheryl, my secretary, to put her off.

What's in it for her? She's already lost her bet on one American, the red-haired Marine. Bud eventually went back to Camp Pendleton without her. She must see that Sackett is played out. So why is she calling me? Even if I spring him, he hasn't got the money to take her to the States. Maybe it's me she wants to take a run at. Sure, why not? Try a diplomat, squeeze what she can out of me in exchange for whatever she has to offer.

The thought stirs my imagination. I can almost feel her long black hair and see her dark almond-shaped eyes—her heritage, like that of most Malagasy, anciently Indonesian.

I think of how her skin might feel to the touch. I shake my head and blow out a breath, exhaling the succubus stealing into my vitals.

I distract myself by looking around the lounge for familiar faces. Usually, I run into someone I know at the airport, one of those like myself, whom the poor refer to as "the people who travel in airplanes." Like the rest of the airport, though, the lounge is nearly deserted, and the few faces I see belong to strangers.

I look at my tab and throw a couple of bills onto the plastic tray. I leave a large tip. No point making little economies now. How much did Picard say I owe him—twelve thousand dollars? Perhaps I can win it back, or at least enough to make repayment of the balance a realistic possibility. A mental reflex warns me of the danger in such thinking. Besides, Picard doesn't want me to win, not only for the obvious reason that it would cost him money, but because he needs me to remain in his debt, providing him leverage to—what? His predatory smile tells me we'll have to make some sort of arrangement. But what can I offer that would be of any interest to him? There had been desperation behind Picard's eyes. And, in Rabary, the Frenchman has his own wolf to feed.

Picard and Rabary. Both want out of here. Picard longs to see his daughter. And anyone who knows Rabary has heard him groaning like a lovesick schoolboy over his unrequited longing for Paris, his hunger for a life of good food, good wine, and a better brand of cigarettes.

Weighted with worry, stupefied by the sun beating through the tall windows, I let my chin sink to my chest and close my eyes.

"Patron, it's coming."

I nearly break my neck snapping to attention, trying to remember where I am.

"Ten minutes." Annibal, the embassy's airport expediter, stands in front of me. A long-headed man with dark, intense eyes, it's his job to know everyone at the airport, from the director to the baggage handlers, and, with a bottle of Johnny Walker here, a carton of cigarettes there, cut through the bureaucratic tangle that makes dealing with them such a nightmare.

I try to sound alert. "How do you know?"

Annibal smiles. He knows. He cocks his chin toward the arrival hall. "Come, Mr. Knott. We'll see if Miss Burris made the plane."

From the first, I don't like her. Short, young, and vibrating with energy, sporting a sexless pageboy cut, she comes up to me and grips my hand like she's running for office.

"Gloria Burris," she announces.

"Robert—"

"I need your help with those people in there," she interrupts, nodding over her shoulder toward the customs and passport desks. "They're holding up a crate of books for the library. They claim they don't consider them covered by diplomatic—"

Adopting my best old bull manner, I cut her off. "Our expediter can—"

"He's the one who helped me clear immigration? Are you sure he can clear—?"

"Annibal could clear a pork chop past a hungry wolf."

On cue, he strides through the doors from Immigration and Customs. "Everything's taken care of, Miss Burris."

The embassy's new Public Affairs Officer blinks in surprise, then gives Annibal what she no doubt regards as a warm smile. "Well done," she says.

A skinny young man with a camera walks up and snaps Gloria's picture.

She recoils and looks at me. "Who's this?"

"Jean-Francois." I shake the young man's hand and explain to Gloria, "Photographer for *Le Matin*. As a newly arrived diplomat, you're news."

"Really?" She allows herself to look pleased. "*Le Matin*. That's the morning paper?"

"Actually, it comes out in the afternoon. And *Midi* comes out in the morning. Legend has it that years ago they each got twelve hours behind schedule and never caught up."

"Here." She shoves her purse at me and strikes a chin-up Joan of Arc pose. "Tell him I'm ready now."

I don't want to tell her that the photo will, like most of *Le Matin's* photos, print up badly, showing only a black shadow against a gray background, like something from one of those charts that identifies airplanes by their silhouettes.

After the photographer takes his pictures, Annibal loads Gloria and her baggage into the embassy's ancient Land Rover.

"Welcome to Madagascar, Miss Burris," Annibal says and gives me a "she's your problem now" wave as Charles, the admin driver, pulls away from the curb.

I'm content to endure the ride in silence, but the new PAO feels like talking. "I came straight through from

Washington. Didn't overnight in Paris. Twenty-seven hours since I walked out of my apartment," she says, making masochism sound like a virtue.

I can only look at her and shake my head.

For a while she contents herself with gazing out the windows of the embassy car as it makes its way toward town, threading around the ever-present crowds that walk along the ragged margins of the road.

"Where's everyone going?" Gloria asks.

"Sorry?"

She nods out the window. "Where's everyone going?"

"Running errands, visiting friends."

"No, I mean—" Her eyes widen with sudden understanding and she claps her mouth shut.

I don't feel like letting her off easy. "Ah. You mean, why's everyone walking? No one can afford cars here, Miss Burris. They must walk. They are poor."

She turns away, embarrassed.

"Where have you been posted?" I ask her.

"I just finished a consular tour in Montreal."

"Well, you're not in Canada anymore." It's a cheap shot, but at this range I can't miss.

I look out the window at the mostly barefoot Malagasy in faded cotton clothes, regard their two-story mud-brick houses, some of them roughly white-washed, others the color of the red earth from which they rise.

Canada. Wouldn't it have been good to have gotten even one posting where I could drink water from the tap? But I've spent my entire career in the Third World, mostly in Africa, at first out of a sense of adventure, then for the quick promotions, lastly from inertia and the low cost of living that makes alimony and child support easier.

I look at Gloria Burris and for a moment see it through her eyes—everything foreign in the most profound sense, lacking any reference point to the familiar.

I remember my first day in Madagascar, arriving at my new house straight from the airport. After looking over the generously furnished yet somehow empty rooms, I stepped into the back yard and saw a knoll just visible over the top of the wall. On its crown stood a bizarre tree with wide branches growing in even rings, like a stack of rimless bike wheels with their spokes sticking out—as odd to the eye as something out of Dr. Seuss. It's a daily reminder of the unknowable world I inhabit now. Though my garden wall has a metal door to the outside, I've never walked through it to take a closer look at that weird tree. I prefer keeping it and, yes, the island itself, at a distance.

That was the same day I saw the chameleon for the first time, sunning itself in the back yard, rotating one eye to look at this parvenu who would occupy the building at the center of his principality, and with the other watching out for the dreaded Mr. Razafy. Right there, I christened him Bobby. I swear the thing winked at me.

Her head leaning against the window, Gloria suddenly looks worn out and drifting into shock, her long, sleepless travel beginning to catch up on her.

With a little start of surprise, I realized she's about to cry.

"You'll be home in a few minutes," I tell her. The last thing I want is to deliver up a weeping junior officer to her new house. Word will get around that I made a pass at her or told her I didn't like her haircut. "Take a nap, then call Lynn Brandt at the embassy. She's your sponsor. She'll come over with some dinner about—"

With a visible effort, the new PAO sits up. "I want to go straight to the office."

"You're out of your mind," I tell her, not without admiration.

Ambassador Herr sits on her couch and folds Gloria's hands into her own. "I'm so pleased to have you with us." Her soft Tennessee accent adds its warmth to her greeting. A major fund-raiser in the previous presidential campaign, the tall, gracious woman of sixty-two claimed as her reward the generally unsought prize of ambassador to Madagascar. It had something to do with reading a book about lemurs as a child. Though she occasionally makes career officers roll their eyes with her naiveté, she overcomes with enthusiasm what she lacks in experience, and things usually turn out all right. Though, as Steve Trapp, the Econ officer, put it, "But when they don't—well, my God."

She evidently sees a kindred spirit in her new PAO.

"We've been so long without a Public Affairs Officer," Ambassador Herr sighs. "And I'm so glad that you've had a consular posting. Our consul, Don Schiff, is on home leave and we've all had to pick up the slack."

"I'll be happy to help out," Gloria says, sitting on the edge of the Ambassador's couch, her back as straight as a sergeant major's.

"That's wonderful." The Ambassador realizes she's been neglecting me and forces a smile in my direction. "Robert, I guess we haven't spoken in a day or two. Tell me what you're dealing with right now."

Should I tell her I'm up to my neck in gambling debts,

my daughter hates me, my career is all but over, and Lynn Brandt has dumped me? Perhaps another time.

"I delivered that *demarche* to Rabary about the U.N. vote. It's a non-starter for them."

Ambassador Herr grips the arms of her chair as if it were my neck. "But you simply must persuade them. The Secretary expects me to have them on board."

I want to tell her I'm sure the Secretary expects no such thing, probably never thinks about Madagascar at all. Instead, I say, "The Ministry isn't going to budge, ma'am. You'll have to take it up with President Ramananjara himself."

"I certainly will," she says.

The hell of it is, despite my decades of experience and an understanding of political realities that runs even deeper than Michelle Herr's grasp of how to raise money, she just might browbeat Ramananjara into saying yes. If she does, her already shaky estimation of her political officer will drop even further. God, I want a drink. She has a bottle of cognac stashed away for special occasions. Maybe I could suggest toasting the new PAO. No. It isn't even ten in the morning. She'd see right through me.

"That reminds me, Robert, have you drafted that cable on the Chinese ambassador's visit with President Ramananjara?"

Of course she'd remember that. I promised it a week ago. "Not yet."

The Ambassador purses her mouth, more resigned than surprised. "What else, Robert?"

"I talked to Rabary about Walt Sackett, the American in prison. He didn't seem willing to help." Her frown sinks all the way to her chin. I hastily add, "But I'll keep working on it."

"Good. I'm sure Gloria, with her consular experience, can help us out on these matters."

Her experience? Jesus. I've got to do something to tip things back my way. "By the way, I asked Rabary about rumors of disturbances in the last week or so. Maybe on the east coast. Tamatave."

"Disturbances? What did he say?"

"Denied everything, of course."

"What do you think?"

"The way this government has screwed things up, the real surprise is that the whole country isn't going up in flames."

The Ambassador nods. "I'll talk to Alain," she says, referring to the French ambassador, Alain Jovert.

"If he doesn't know anything, I could go off to the coast to see what's going on."

Worry lines appear between her eyes. "Robert, if you go, do it quietly." She speaks like a grandmother who fears she has been overindulgent. "Stay out of the newspapers."

"I'm the soul of discretion, ma'am."

"Of course you are," she says, trying very hard to make me believe she believes it. "Oh, that reminds me. Do you know a newspaper called, *Notre Madagascar*, 'Our Madagascar'?"

"Yeah, vaguely. Sensationalist. Poorly written. Published irregularly. Printed on paper that looks like it was stolen from a men's room dispenser."

"Yes, that's it," Ambassador Herr says. "They've run an atrocious article, saying the United States Government is killing babies overseas to use their organs for transplants in the United States." She actually shudders. "It just makes me sick."

"It's an old disinformation scam, ma'am," I tell her. "The Russians pay some newspaper to run this stuff. Then they can write up their own story, citing this one. 'An independent newpaper in Madagascar reports, blah, blah, blah.' So no one sees their fingerprints on it."

"I'm sure you're right," she says, meaning she half-believes me. "When Gloria is settled in, you should take her to see the publisher and tell him how displeased we are with the story. Ask him to run a retraction." She turns to Gloria. "What a marvelous way to start your public affairs duties, talking with the local press. And you'll have Robert to back you up."

"I'd be happy to," Gloria says with an emphatic nod. If she sits up any straighter she'll blow a disc.

Ambassador Herr rises and once more welcomes Gloria to "our family."

I lead our new PAO down to the basement offices of the admin section. Lynn is talking to her bespectacled cashier, Annie Rabenarivo. Lynn's eyes turn toward me with an indifference that chills my blood.

The two women hit it off immediately, of course. Lynn gives Gloria a fat sheaf of papers to fill out. "Sorry. We live off forms like bacteria live off decay. Our political officer"— she gives me another bland gaze—"has taken you to meet the Ambassador?"

Gloria nods. "I've never worked for a political appointee."

"She's not bad. She may not know her way around the Department, but if the Malagasy need something big she can phone the White House directly."

I'm feeling neglected. "Hey, so can I."

Lynn bores a hole through me with her eyes. "Yes, but she won't get fired for it." She turns back to Gloria. "You'll like your house."

"A house? I only got an apartment in Ottawa."

"I had the General Services crew over to paint the interior

yesterday and generally clean up. The Boswell's medivac came on pretty suddenly and they left a bit of a mess."Lynn launches a ferocious smile in my direction, warning me not to add any commentary.

Fine, but gossip is the common coin of every embassy. Gloria will find out soon enough that her predecessor, Peter Boswell, was sent back to Washington on what was called a medivac—medical evacuation—because psychovac is not in the official vocabulary.

The strain of living in a foreign culture, especially one as alien as Madagascar's, affects people differently. Some thrive on the challenge. Most persevere. A few crash.

I liked Boswell. And he'd been a boon drinking companion. But here's the difference; after our late nights, I always managed somehow to get into the office the next morning and deal with my work, at least in a haphazard sort of way. Boz couldn't do it. His fall was quick. He became moody and missed work. With little provocation, he would launch into bitter tirades against all things Malagasy. When he began locking himself in his office during the day it was time to go. Ambassador Herr's fierce if occasionally misplaced loyalty to her staff led her to expunge any hint of Boswell's drinking problem from his annual evaluation, but gossip is relentless and the damage to his career was done.

Afterwards, I toughed out the killing looks I got from the other Americans, who blamed me for Boswell's disintegration. And I could see in their eyes that they expected me to be next. That's when I decided to stop drinking—just to prove the sonsabitches wrong. I was surprised how easy it was. I guess I'd never been an alcoholic, not in the classic sense. I just drank to fill the empty spot in my life, or at least have a few hours when I forgot about it.

I had hoped that the transformation from drunk to former drunk might elevate the regard in which I was held by my fellow Americans. If anything, though, they seemed more guarded than before, as if I were trying to put something over on them. And maybe I was—trying to pretend that I'm a consummate professional and a decent human being. But I'm neither, and they know it.

"I bought some groceries for you," Lynn tells Gloria. "You'll find them in the refrigerator. You can pay me for them next week. I'll come over this evening with some dinner."

Gloria turns to me, her previously flagging spirits thoroughly renewed. "This is going to be fun!"

6

The weekly meeting of the Country Team—the heads of the embassy's various departments—looks like a gathering of the recently dead. Sitting at the head of the table in the second-floor conference room, Ambassador Herr is pale with overwork. Her right hand, Pete Salvatore, the Deputy Chief of Mission, or DCM, and Steve Trapp, head of the Econ section, both have the ghostly and haggard look that comes with amoebas. The gunny, Sergeant Estes, has developed a cough and a weird rash and everyone wishes he would just stay the hell away from the embassy until he's better. I've been through this in other countries that are tough on your health. None of us will be entirely well again until we go home.

I understand the nature of their maladies. It comes from resisting Madagascar, attempting to lead their lives as if they were still back in the States, as if they were not foreigners in the most foreign of lands. They refuse to acknowledge limits to what they can understand, can't reconcile themselves to uncertainty. That, not the booze, is what finally got Boswell.

Me? I'm never sick. This worries me. Sure, after years in the tropics I've built up enough antibodies to resist anything short of a meteor. In fact, I possess in spades the one great necessity of the foreign service—I'm adaptable, flexible as a snake, able to bend, change shapes, speak in tongues, do whatever it takes to remake myself as needed. There's a downside. One of the hundred torments that makes me lie awake at night is the fear that my talent for adaptation has left me with no self to protect.

Have I accepted Madagascar better than the others? Is that why I remain preternaturally healthy? No, I think it's just the opposite. I don't even try. I just let it roll off my back. I'm not here. Maybe I never have been.

Pete Salvatore sighs with fatigue and waves a hand in front of his face, a tic he has acquired over the past few months. He's a pretty decent guy, but working for the irrepressible Michelle Herr has worn him down and he's seldom at his best. "Okay, we're getting vague stories in the papers about child kidnappings. Just something to be aware of. There's an article in *Midi* about some guy in a market town near Tamatave getting beaten to death over a child he couldn't prove was his."

I give Pete a lift of the eyebrows and he lets me speak. "I've seen it in other countries," I tell him. "When the economy tanks and the government looks unstable and things are really falling apart, you start getting reports of children being kidnapped. It works great as metaphor. The future is being stolen. Who knows? Maybe it's even true. Maybe when things start going to hell some people have this urge to start stealing children."

In the ensuing silence, I feel Salvatore's assessing gaze. He's trying to decide if I'm a prophet or a lunatic, with the betting going heavily toward the latter. Without comment, Salvatore's eyes slide from me and turn to Gloria. "You'll keep an eye on this story for us?"

"I will," she says with an emphatic nod. God love her because I can't quite manage it.

Ambassador Herr clears her throat. "Robert has mentioned something to me about disturbances in the countryside. I brought it up with the Foreign Minister yesterday. He said there was nothing to the rumors. But I'm thinking of sending someone down to Tamatave to take a look." She looks around the table, desperately searching for a volunteer. Anyone but me.

Normally, I'd have little desire to traipse off to the coast to chase down what might turn out to be no more than gossip. But this particular task is a political officer's job, and I have even less desire to suffer the humiliation of seeing it handed to someone else.

Besides, a tantalizing thought has occurred to me. Rather than regarding this task as another opportunity to get food poisoning in a roach-infested hotel, the trip might offer a way out of the professional purgatory into which I've sunk. Through a quiet gathering of facts and the drafting of the sort of incisive and succinctly drafted reporting cable with which I once made a reputation, I might gain a little taste of redemption. With some well-deserved props, maybe I can work up the mojo to start climbing out of the hole I've been digging for myself over the last how many years. Possibilities shimmer on the horizon of my mind like the Seven Cities of Gold. I can't let this chance slip away.

"I think the job is mine."

The Ambassador tries to smile but it looks more like she's stepped on a nail. "Of course it is, Robert." She looks around the table as if hoping for someone to contradict her. When no one does her this service, a pall of resignation momentarily clouds her customary graciousness. She quickly recovers and asks, "Any advice before he goes? Paul?"

Paul Esmer, the tall, dark-haired ex-cop who serves as embassy security officer essays a lop-sided shrug, a hint of his habitual bad Bogart imitation. "He should see Captain René Andriamana, head of the national police in that region." He squints at me. I'm sure he's about to say, "And how about all that money you owe Picard over at the Zebu Room." A cold sweat slithers down my back. Instead, he just asks, "You know him—Andriamana?"

He apparently knows nothing about my debts. I try to keep my relief from showing. "I've heard of him."

"Well, step lightly down there. He's the Prince of Fucking Darkness."

The worry lines between the Ambassador's brows grow deeper. "Now, Robert, you be careful down there."

"Don't worry about me. I've been around."

The Ambassador smiles, clearly asking herself what folly she has let loose in allowing me to roam outside the capital.

The only fun in the meeting occurs when Lynn mentions that the Ambassador's recently-fired protocol secretary, a Malagasy woman named Colette, has tried to make herself literally irreplaceable by putting a curse on her office, threatening with illness and death anyone who crosses its threshold. The problem, Lynn tells the Ambassador, is that the proposed remodeling of the embassy's ground floor will punch a new entrance through what was Colette's office. "Most of the Malagasy employees are saying that if the door goes there they won't come through it."

Michelle Herr slumps in her chair. "They actually believe in this curse?"

"Enough of them to give us real heartburn."

To anyone on the outside, anyone back home, this would sound preposterous. But this is Madagascar, and the Malagasy think the same of us and half the things we do.

The Ambassador sighs. "They never mentioned this sort of thing in the ambassadorial training course. All right, Lynn, come see me after lunch."

As the meeting breaks up I drift into the Ambassador's outer office, still anxious that word about Picard and the money I owe him might reach the embassy. I could make a hundred reporting trips to Tamatave, but they wouldn't help me survive that.

The room's empty. Sitting on her secretary's desk, I quickly riffle through the Ambassador's inbox.

"Looking for something, Robert?"

My internal organs fail. Still, I manage to look blandly over my shoulder at Alice, the Ambassador's secretary, standing behind me with the I'm-on-to-you expression she always uses with me.

"No. I was just … Say, did the Ambassador mention anything about following up on that UN resolution with the President? Maybe I should go back to the Ministry, try to bring Rabary around. With enough time, I think I could do it."

Alice's eyes narrow. Even if she can't figure out exactly what I'm up to, she knows bullshit when she hears it. I can already hear her gossiping with the Ambassador about catching me looking through her mail.

"She's decided this looks like a job for Ambo," she says, not bothering to add, "because the Pol officer can't get the job done."

"Great." I don't bother to add that the Ambassador should bring me along, because I know she won't.

I head back toward my office feeling the momentary relief of knowing there's no letter from the Zebu Room waiting for the Ambassador. At least not today.

It takes me so much longer than usual to lose ten thousand Malagasy francs that my night feels like a victory. Neither Picard nor Jacques, his manager, have shown any interest in me this evening. And, evidently, my credit is still good for now. Why? I can't escape the feeling that I'm a fish enjoying the bait while the hook digs deeper into my mouth.

It's nearly midnight before I head down toward the parking lot. The shortest way is through the hotel bar on the ground floor. Like an idiot, I take it.

I struggle against the riptide of the crowd as I squeeze my way toward the far door. Behind the bar, tall shelves of booze twinkle like Christmas lights. It occurs to me that I could demonstrate how I've beaten the stuff. All I need to do is take one drink, just one, then walk away. What better way to show that I've broken the hold of demon rum? I just need that one drink to prove my point.

I'm already veering toward the bar when I feel a hand on my arm.

"Monsieur Knott."

I turn toward the sound of the voice. "Jesus!"

"I've been trying for a week to reach you, Monsieur Knott." In the press of the crowd I can feel the warmth of Nirina's body against mine. I try to step away, but the crowd pushes me back. Does she know what she's doing to me? Of course she knows. Beautiful women always know what they're doing to men. "I've called your office, Monsieur Knott, but your secretary . . ." She puts a hand on my arm.

"Yeah, I've been busy." I try to brush her hand away, but she tightens her grip. "Okay, you got lucky and ran into me."

"I know you come here often. Everyone knows about the *vazaha* with no luck."

So, I'm a legend, am I?

"I need to talk to you about Monsieur Sackett. About Walt." She says it "Wolt."

"I have no time for that tonight."

For a moment I can see myself as if from a great distance. And what I see isn't a man trying to fend off an importunate young woman, but someone who doesn't trust himself enough to talk to her. I mutter some excuse about talking with her later in the week and push through the door.

Once outside, I breathe a deep lungful of the clear night air, panting like a rabbit who's just escaped a trap. Then I hear the noise of music and voices momentarily spilling through the door behind me, and I know she's followed me out.

"Monsieur Knott." Something in her voice—not pleading, only insistent—tells me I won't get away. "Walt has been very kind to me. Now I have to help him."

Can she mean it? The thought bothers me. I want her to be a gold digger preying on Sackett. Instead, she may be what my instincts tell me she is—a good woman who's trying much harder than I am to get Sackett free.

"Look, the embassy is doing everything it can," I tell her. The words sound feeble even to me.

"Are you?"

Before I can tell her to shove off, a young man pushes through the door open behind us. He's dressed in a thin shirt and shapeless slacks, clothes that belong in a village byway rather than at what passes in Antananarivo for a glitzy nightspot.

"Nirina," the young man calls.

She turns and says something in Malagasy that clearly means, "Go away."

I maybe see a way out of this. "It looks like your boyfriend doesn't want you standing out here in the parking lot talking to a *vazaha*."

"He's not my boyfriend," she snaps back at me. "He's my brother." Again, she speaks sharply to the young man in Malagasy, and this time waves him back inside.

The boy stands his ground and calls to me, "You should not listen to her, m'sieur." After her precise but unfussy French, his sounds poorly formed and heavily accented. "Her father wants her to return. Her father does not want her to be like this."

What the hell does that mean?

Flicking her arms at the young man like a farmwife shooing a chicken across the yard, she finally impels him back toward the bar. When the door has closed behind him, Nirina turns again to me. "I'm sorry. He … Well, you know how we are about family."

If I've learned one thing during my time in Madagascar, it's the importance of family—the living, certainly, but especially the dead. The ancestors hover over the shoulder of every Malagasy, judging their every move against impenetrable layers of *fady*—taboo—formed by timeless custom into webs so complex that even the Malagasy can't master their intricacies, leaving them unable to propitiate the silent but exigent dead. I once asked a Malagasy friend, a European-educated civil servant, how he knows when he has offended his ancestors. The friend replied, "Things go wrong." In Madagascar, where so much has gone so wrong, the pervasive sense of melancholy owes no small part of its burden to the half-conscious realization that the endless demands of the ancestors prove that even death does not release the soul from the torments of life. Over the course of my two years here, I've come to understand why the Malagasy call their land the Island of Ghosts.

"Yeah, I know how you are about family."

"They are rice farmers from the coast, near Tamatave," she says, as if this explains everything.

"I guess everything's happening in Tamatave." Her puzzled expression tells me my little joke has missed. "I'm going down there soon to figure out what's going on in your hometown."

She looks at me uncertainly. "What is it you hope to do there?"

The question takes me by surprise. "Do? I'm a diplomat. I don't do anything. I just see what other people are doing and write about it."

She's standing close enough for me to touch, to smell. I detect a faint hint of perfume, an earthy hint of sweat.

"You like Walt," she says.

"That matters?" There's no escaping her eyes. "Yeah, I like Walt."

"And you think I don't, that I'm after whatever I can get."

"Your relationship with Walt, or anyone, is none—"

"I want you to believe me when I say I will do whatever I can to get him out."

"Okay, I believe. Now tell me, what is the point of this conversation?" I point toward the bar. "It's late. Why don't you go back inside and talk to your brother. It sounds like your family wants you to be a good girl and go home. Take their advice."

She lowers her head and crosses her arms over her chest. "Home? I no longer have a home. We are both foreigners here, Monsieur Knott, you and me."

I don't want to hang around long enough to find out what she means. "You're going to have to sort that out for yourself." I feel physical yearning collide with what's left of my desire not to make a fool of myself. "And whatever you want to do for, or to, or in spite of Walt Sackett is your affair. In the meantime, I'm doing what I can." I try not to look into her eyes. "Believe me, I have enough problems of my own tonight, and I don't have any more time for this."

"You must help me, Monsieur Knott, I know you're a good man."

"Like hell I am." With that, I walk away.

I'm shocked at what a week has done to Walt Sackett. More than simply losing weight, he gives the impression that some psychic or spiritual store has run dangerously low. Thin and pale, he lies on his prison mattress, his eyes darting restlessly around the room as he speaks.

"I got food to eat, but I don't feel hungry," he says, his voice thin and reedy. "And I've really got the sh—" His eyes move to Gloria. "Everything's goin' right through me."

Gloria sits at the foot of Sackett's thin mattress, unable to hide her revulsion at the prison's squalor. When we first entered the cell and the door clanged shut behind us she gave a sort of moan. Scared or just horrified, I don't know. But it isn't doing Sackett any good.

She takes out a notebook and manages a smile. "So, Mr. Sackett, is the medical care here adequate?"

"About the same quality as the maid service." A wheezy, rattling laugh escapes his throat, more painful to watch than any attack of fever.

"Or the staff at the front desk," I throw in, trying to add a little lightness to this dismal place. I'm sitting on the other mattress and start to lean back, forgetting that Speedy is curled up behind me, sleeping soundly after a long night of police-sponsored burglary.

Sackett stares at the ceiling, "Robert, what do you hear from the ministry?"

"I'm working on it, Walt. I promise you."

"Thanks, I 'preciate it. Why you would do this for a broken-down old …" Walt lets his words trail off before self-pity can steal into his voice.

I want to tell him, "I'm just one broken down son of a bitch trying to help out another, because if I can get you out maybe things will change for me." Instead, I say, "It's all right. It's my job. But they're hanging tough on this one."

The old cowboy nods. "I'm out of money, or I'd try to put together a bribe."

"And I'd figure out who to send it to."

Gloria looks at Sackett in surprise, and glares at me. "You'd assist him in bribing a government official?"

"Damn right I would."

I give her what I trust is my most maddening smile.

I'd thought her estimation of me couldn't drop any further, but the look she gives me tells me there was a little room left at the bottom. To Sackett she says. "If there is not adequate medical care here I can bring Dr. André to see you," she tells him, speaking of the Malagasy doctor the embassy keeps on retainer. With a two-can-play-at-this-game glance at me, she adds, "It's not within the regs, but I don't think it will be a problem." She writes something in her notebook. "And I think, rather than trying again to get the ministry to free you based on the questionable legitimacy of the charges against you, we will make a case for humanitarian release."

Sackett raises his head and grins at me. "That's something we hadn't thought of, Robert. I think I like this girl."

I want to tell him I don't, but get distracted by a movement behind me. Speedy is peering over my shoulder.

"Monsieur Walt is very sick. I should steal some medicine for him," he says in French, then adds in English. "Rob medicine for Monsieur Walt."

"Speedy, you're o-kay," Sackett sighs.

I flick a hand in Gloria's direction. "Thanks, Speedy, but Mademoiselle Gloria is sure she can take care of it."

Speedy smiles at Gloria. "Ah, Monsieur Walt has a new girlfriend."

For the first time the French term, which translates literally as "little friend," strikes me as funny.

"No, she's with me."

Speedy raises his eyebrows. "Then Monsieur Robert has a new girlfriend."

Gloria tries to scowl, but she's too shocked. I can't help but laugh.

"No. We work together. She's new here."

Speedy nods, takes it all in. When he turns his smile on Gloria again, it carries a new warmth. "Mademoiselle." He says the word slowly, tasting its possibilities. "How do you find our beautiful country?"

She reacts not so much to the question as to its tone, sitting up straight and tucking in her chin like a turtle retreating into its shell. "I like it just fine." She drives each word home like a nail.

"Tell me what kind of flower you like and I will steal one for you."

Even in the dim cell I can see her face redden.

"What's he in for?" she asks me in English.

"Not what you're probably thinking."

Gloria's expression turns to ice. Is it possible that she's never been hit on? She's taken a lot of trouble to build this unassailable wall around herself. Anyone can see it unless— it suddenly hits me—you're from another culture. If Speedy manages to get around her defences it's because he doesn't even see them.

"Speedy is one of nature's gentlemen," I tell her, adding a quick explanation about how he is one of many imprisoned burglars the guards let free at night to ply their trade. I don't attempt to square the circle of how this makes him a gentleman.

However weak his English skills, Speedy understands we're talking about him. He gazes at Gloria, his eyes glowing. "I will show you all around Madagascar," he tells her. "I will take you to the rain forest and we will see the lemurs together."

Without taking her eyes off Speedy, Gloria asks me, "When does he get out of here?"

"Every night."

"No, I mean … Oh, never mind."

Irritating her is just too easy.

Sackett lies on his bed, smiling. Our visit is doing him good.

"You got any letters for me?" I ask him.

Sackett grunts affirmatively, raises himself on one elbow and takes an envelope from under his pillow. This time he doesn't apologize for the lack of stamps. Again, the envelope has no return address. "You getting any mail here?" I ask him. "There's nothing coming through the embassy."

Sackett shakes his head. "No. That's okay. I don't really expect her to—" He stops himself. "You can get that letter out today?"

"Sure."

"I 'preciate it."

Gloria stands, closes her notebook. "I'll send Dr. André here tomorrow. He'll bring some medicine and let us know what you need to be eating."

The smile on Sackett's face makes him look almost healthy again. "I tell you, Robert, I like this girl."

7

January brings the monsoon to the central plateau. The mornings break soft and pleasant but as the day marches on the sun feels closer, heavy as a hammer. Towering thunderheads build throughout the long afternoons, glowing a dazzling white in the sub-tropical sun until, by five-thirty, they can no longer hold back. Long thunderclaps shake the air and rivers of rain instantly fill the streets. In the market, the crowds run for shelter, people laughing at their slower companions, who are hit by walls of water thrown up by passing cars.

The drive home, normally twenty minutes, takes twice that long in the rain. When I arrive, I honk for Monsieur Razafy, who opens the gate, gives me that chin-up nod and, as always, touches the brim of his cap as I drive in. I can never decide if it's a gesture of deference or mockery. Or maybe his hat doesn't fit. All I know is that it makes me feel vaguely uneasy.

In the kitchen, Jeanne is checking the roast, a rare treat she cooks only when guests are coming. Though she doesn't quite look at me—she almost never looks at me directly—she nods politely as I come in the door and with her usual ambiguous smile says, "*Valoma topko*," to me. Good day, sir, the one phrase of Malagasy she has managed to teach me. She picks up a wooden spoon and stirs a vegetable dish on the stove. "You are going to Tamatave tomorrow."

I can't remember having told her. "How did you know?"

She waggles her head and says, "I have packed your bag and put it in the hallway."

"You're too good to me."

"That is the truth of it, Monsieur Knott."

How can I scold her for agreeing with me? I mutter, "It's dark in here," and flip on the light switch. Nothing happens.

"The electricity is out, sir."

A friend once told me that anyone can carry his part of a French conversation simply by saying "ah, bon" in different intonations. Now it's my turn and I sigh, "Ah, bon," as I drift into the living room and pick up the phone to make a call.

"The telephone is also out, sir," Jeanne calls from the kitchen.

"Ah, bon."

She comes in to light the candles on the dining table, already set for eight.

Gloria was to have hosted tonight's dinner at her residence, her first social event in Madagascar. She'd invited an American Fulbright scholar, a Malagasy professor and his wife, and Steve and Julie Trapp. But on Wednesday she fired her cook for theft and told Ambassador Herr she would have to call off dinner. Rather than see her cancel it, the Ambassador asked me to host it at my place. My only change has been to add Roland Rabary to the guest list.

As evening approaches, I stand at the window and listen to the rain drumming on the metal roof, producing an agreeable melancholy that wants only a warm brandy to feel complete. But no.

No doubt Bobby Chameleon is sheltering under the bushes, or wherever it is he goes when he doesn't want to be seen. I imagine him hiding in the shrubbery, goggling at the downpour. I wonder what he's thinking. Probably nothing. Or something as elemental as "there is rain." That's the ticket. Keep it simple. Don't try to understand, simply accept.

I pick up the box of matches where Jeanne has left them and go through the house lighting the slow-burning coils whose acrid smoke repels the mosquitoes trying to come in out of the rain, carrying with them their dram of malaria or encephalitis or god-knows-what.

Where can I find similar incense to ward off the dread that builds in me throughout the day like the afternoon thunderheads?

Over the noise of the downpour I hear a faint banging and see Razafy trot out to open the gate, his shoulders hunched against the rain. It's Gloria's guard. He hands a note to Razafy, who takes the paper and jogs back to the kitchen door, where he hands it to Jeanne—he would no more consider coming into the house to deliver the note himself than she would think of going out to cut the lawn. The elaborate transaction deepens my conviction that I live within the gears of an elaborate machine that I don't understand.

Who are these people? Where am I? What am I doing here? From one posting to another, one culture to the next, I have adapted with professional ease, or at least given its appearance, changing to meet every new demand, diving in without leaving a ripple. In my obsidian heart, though, I've never really committed myself here, in Madagascar. The gift of adaptation has deserted me, or something in me has rebelled against it. I've never wanted out of a country so badly, nor ever before felt that it would not let me go until I've surrendered myself to it.

Sitting in some airport, my provenance and destination now forgotten, I once read a newspaper article on modern physics. Its author was speculating that the universe contains countless unseen and overlapping dimensions. Perhaps Madagascar exists in a dimension beyond my ability to perceive. I'll never understand the place because I can't really see it. It remains irremediably foreign, holding me at a distance. And that damn tree on the knoll, alien and unapproached, is its talisman.

Jeanne comes out from the kitchen, breaking my melancholy train of thought. She stops in the middle of the living room, holding in her hand the note Razafy has given her, and says with the grave formality of an English butler, "Monsieur and Madame Trapp called Miss Gloria just before the telephones went out. They regret to say that their road is flooded and they cannot get beyond their driveway." She stops, but remains standing stiffly in the middle of the room. Clearly, there's something more.

"And ...?"

"And Miss Gloria also says that she is sick and won't be able to come, sir."

"Ah, *bon*."

I pass the remaining hour hoping everyone else will cancel, too.

Yet somehow the dinner goes well. Good food and good conversation, the warmth of the candlelight and the sound of the rain on the roof draw the five of us together as if we were members of the same tribe gathered around a campfire.

The Malagasy academic, a professor of anthropology, begins the evening as Dr. Adrianansoa, but after a couple glasses of wine insists that everyone call him Didier. His wife, a shy, fleshy woman who covers her crooked teeth whenever she speaks, further warms the table with her humor and her loving regard for her husband.

Only Rabary holds himself apart, saying little, while his unfortunate features simmer with amused detachment at the conversation.

If every successful dinner has a center that holds, it proves this evening to be Tonja Adams, the Fulbright scholar, a slight, square-shouldered young African-American woman from Colorado who has spent the past year in a village on the northwest coast, studying Malagasy folkways.

"I can't imagine a greater tedium," Rabary says when she describes her project. "These villagers are in thrall to fear and superstition. The men are brutes and the women servile." He looks around the table as he speaks, happy to play the provocateur.

The young Fulbrighter nods thoughtfully, the candlelight playing shadows across her face. "Maybe so. But the world's villages are like our early lives. They tell us who we were— and who we still are underneath. As for the women, what you say has some validity, but the truth is far more complex. And, in any case, some of the women have found a way out of their condition."

"Explain," I say.

Tonja lays down her fork and takes on a professorial air. "Monsieur Rabary is right. In their daily lives the women defer to the males, taking what comfort they can from knowing they are following the path set out by the ancestors." She looks around the table. For the moment, she is back in the university classroom and we are her students. "Yet some of them, a few, will suddenly break away—opt out of their lives, if you will—and become someone new."

I look around the table at the Malagasy guests and realize I'm the only one who doesn't understand what she's talking about. I raise my eyebrows in curiosity, requesting her to continue for my sake.

"They literally take on another identity," Tonja says. "They claim to be someone else now—often someone related to the old royalty. Overnight, they change from docile and silent creatures to wild women, drinking and smoking, talking back to everyone, refusing to submit to their husbands or fathers. Many of them go off to live by themselves, usually just outside the village. They give themselves a new name and refuse to answer to their old one. From that day on they are seen by the other villagers as spirit-possessed, almost holy. Maybe it's the connection to royalty that gives them this new status, or the awe in which we hold those who live on a different plane from ourselves. They become *tromba* women."

Rabary snorts. "They have simply gone mad with the unbearable pressures of life in a backward village."

"I'm not so quick to make that judgment," the young scholar says.

Listening to her carefully weighed words, I feel I'm hearing the first draft of a lecture she will be giving for years.

"All right, if they are not themselves, who are they?" I ask. I understand that the conversation has become ostensibly for my benefit, but I can see that Tonja also wishes to test the reaction of well-educated Malagasy to a discussion of this ancient and atavistic side of their culture.

She hesitates before answering. A candle flickers, its crackling hiss gives an exclamation mark to the growing silence. The young Fulbrighter's dark eyes widen and her professorial air falls away. "That's the oddest part," she says "As I say, these women come up with new identities, new names. But a few claim they are from some other village, sixty, maybe eighty kilometers away, a place no one from their own village has ever visited."

Rabary opens his mouth to speak, but the young scholar raises her hand and continues. "Yes, I know what you're going to say, that choosing an identity from some faraway place makes it easier to carry off their fraud. No one is going to check out the woman's story." We all lean forward to catch every word. "So, I decided to do it myself. There was a woman in the village, named Lalao, a woman no longer young, who had become one of the possessed, a *tromba*. She left her husband and children and abandoned her village for a little lean-to she made near the creek. She claimed her name was Rina now and that she came from a village far away. Rina, she said, had died before she was ready and so had come to live in her body for a while."

As the rain patters on the roof, Tonja leans forward, her face only inches from the candle, its dancing flame chasing light and shadow across her face. "I decided I would research this phenomenon of the *tromba* woman objectively, as I would any other. I should add that when the villagers realized I was there to study them, to understand who they were and what they believed, the initial welcome they gave me faded. I was regarded with increasing suspicion. It's as if they feared that if I came to understand who they were, their beliefs would lose their potency, as if they lived within a dream from which I might wake them, leaving them with nothing. Over time, as they got used to me, I entered into the life of the village, established my own role, and their guardedness eased. But I'm a scholar, a servant of the truth. I knew I would have to follow this idea of *tromba* wherever it led." She gave a us a crooked smile. "And it might lead straight into trouble."

She took a drink of wine and continued. "What I did one morning was to walk a couple of miles to the nearest road and catch a bush taxi to the village Lalao-Rina had named, which was more than forty kilometers away." The young American laughs shyly, aware that everyone around the table, even Rabary, is hanging on her every word. "I was quite the sensation when I arrived in this other village— just as I had been when I first came to my own village. I'd thought that being black would help me to blend in, be accepted, but it didn't. It gave me a special status, perhaps, but I was still a *vazaha*, a stranger. I was a little disappointed. But I reminded myself that the people here aren't African, they're not exactly Asian. They are the Malagasy, and there is no one like them.

"Anyway, the villagers surrounded me as if I were a rock star. People wanted to touch me. They asked me where I was from. When I told them I was an American they were amazed. It was quite a while before I could work things around to asking them if they knew a woman by the name of Rina." Tonja raises her eyebrows. "That was a conversation stopper. Everyone fell silent and stared at me. Finally, an old man, a village elder, told me that, yes, there had been a woman by that name, but she had died a couple of weeks earlier. Now it was my turn to be amazed, because that was about the time Lalao had broken from the village and taken on her new identity. Despite their initial shock, the villagers didn't seem surprised that a woman in a faraway village was claiming to be the repository of another woman's wandering soul. This was common, they said. They couldn't understand why I was so curious about it.

It was getting late and they wanted me to stay the night. But I told them I had to return to my village. It was way past midnight before I got back. When I finally came stumbling in, the couple I was staying with got up and asked me where I'd been. They told me they'd been worried. I told them where I'd gone and what I'd learned. They seemed very upset. They had been telling me for weeks that I shouldn't be asking about things like this, about these *tromba*, and they were offended that I had ignored their advice.

"I just wanted to go to bed, but the couple insisted on making dinner for me. I figured it was their way of showing me that everything was still okay between us. I was exhausted and only ate a little bit. They encouraged me to take more, but I said I couldn't and went to bed. By morning I was sick. Vomited all day. I began to suspect they had poisoned me. All that day they made me more food. But I wouldn't eat it."

Tonja looks at us one by one, fearing judgment. "I know this sounds crazy, or paranoid, or whatever you want to call it. Now that I'm here, away from the village, it sounds crazy to me too. But things look different in a village. Life follows a different set of rules.

"So, I waited until the couple left the house late that afternoon. Then I managed to get up and grab my notebooks and a few of my things. Sick as I was, I somehow made it to the road and flagged down a bush taxi that took me to Mahajanga. For a few days I holed up in a cheap hotel, until I felt strong enough to head for Antananarivo." She shrugs and smiles her shy smile. "And here I am."

The silence that has fallen over the table deepens as she finishes her tale. As the only foreigner in Tonja's audience, I know it's up to me to ask. "So, what do you think? About *tromba* women and all that."

After a pause, Tonja starts to speak slowly, as if she knows she's on the verge of making herself sound credulous, naive. But her voice builds as she goes, increasingly sure about what she's saying. "I decided that in most of these cases the *tromba* women, much as Monsieur Rabary suggests, take on an assumed identity to give themselves a chance to break free. For a few of them, I believe it's a conscious decision, a ruse allowing them to gain a new status and take a sort of psychic vacation. For others, it might be a form of temporary psychosis, a mental breakdown aggravated by personal problems and the suggestion laid down by previous examples. I think these latter women believe in the roles they have taken on. Eventually, as they recover, they say that the spirit has left them and they go back to their old identities."

I look at her through the candle flame, her image flickering and glowing, as if she herself were only half real. "You say this explains the majority of these cases. What about the others?"

She takes a moment, lowers her head, working herself up to say what she needs to say. When she's ready she raises her head. "I see myself as a scientist. I form my conclusions based on an objective analysis of the evidence." She purses her lips. This is difficult for her, and I admire her willingness to risk our dismissal of what she says. "I would never have imagined a year ago I would be saying this, but now I can only explain what I've seen by insisting that in a few cases these women have truly been possessed by the spirits of others."

I feel the hair on my neck stand up.

Rabary blows out a breath. "Miss Adams, I have heard these stories since I was a little boy and have never known any of them to be true."

Before Tonja can reply, Dr. Adrianansoa, the Malagasy professor, pushes himself back from the table. "Yes, it all seems too fantastic, literally unbelievable, especially for those of us who have enjoyed the privilege of a European education and become fully civ-il-ized." He draws out each syllable for maximum irony and his smile takes an impish turn. "As her adviser, I have asked Mademoiselle Adams, as I have asked others in the past, to observe what is in front of her and to analyze clearly what she has seen. But after something like this we may feel highly unsettled by what we've seen. We try to escape from our inescapable conclusions." Dr. Adrianansoa folds his hands over his stomach. "Now it is my turn to tell you a story. In the northern mountains, deep in the rain forest, there is a legend of a village, a village that countless people claim to have actually seen, situated on the crest of a steep hill, almost hidden by the forest. In certain lights, particularly after a rain, some say they have, from a distance, witnessed people walking its paths, men plowing its nearby fields. But when anyone goes into the forest to find it, they become lost and climb up the wrong hill. Through a gap in the trees they find that the village they seek is actually on a neighboring hill. So they plunge back into the rainforest. But—ah!—

when they climb to the top of the next hill they find they are again mistaken. And so they continue thrashing around in the jungle, from one hilltop to another."

"You're saying no one ever gets there, to this phantom village?" I ask.

Dr. Adrianansoa waggles his head ambivalently, a skilled storyteller enjoying himself. "Oh, it is said that a very few have actually found their way into the village—and never come back." Here, he thrusts out his lower lip and shrugs. "Now, do I believe this story? I wish to assure you that I do not." He smiles slyly. "Yes, that is what I wish to assure you. But can I do so honestly? I'm not so sure. Could it be that here in Madagascar—a place so distant from the rational shores known to Descartes and Voltaire—that there exists a last primordial portal to the fantastic, to that bygone epoch when the shape of the world was still in flux, before mind and spirit had taken their separate paths? Is it possible that things can still occur here that are no longer possible in the modern world—a world made not in the image of God but of Europeans?" He tips his wine glass in my direction and addresses me genially. "The problem might lie less in our urge to let go of superstition and magic than with the inadequacy of our imagination. We lack the courage to believe differently from what others have taught us to believe, to see what they tell us is not there." The professor waves his hands gracefully. "It is said of many places that 'anything can happen here.' In Madagascar we must take that a step further. Not only can truly anything happen here, it must. We must stipulate that here, in our beloved island-world, the implausible is not only possible, it is mandatory." He pauses for effect, lets his words sink in. "I suggest that we should remain willing to accept the possibility that some forms of the supernatural are in fact perfectly natural, but lie beyond the range of our understanding."

I feel a shiver down my back, a frisson of unease at the possibility that the spirits I had been reflecting on earlier that evening might somehow prove real.

Dr. Adrianansoa appears to sense my discomfort. His eyes sparkle with amusement. "I speak of course as a scientist." He throws back his head and laughs.

Rabary twitches his prodigious nose. "I remain skeptical." He looks at me. "And I think our host agrees, though he is too polite to say so."

Dr. Adrianansoa cocks his head to one side. "And yet, Monsieur Rabary, I am sure that, despite your expressions of skepticism, even you follow our traditions in ways you are reluctant to acknowledge. Do you not, every few years— what is it for your Merina tribe, every seven years?—disinter your dead, speak to them, tell them jokes, scold them a little for the troubles they have given you recently and then wrap them in new shrouds and return them with honor to the family tomb?"

Rabary snorts. "We all feel compelled to observe these customs, no matter how little credence we give to the beliefs behind them."

"Of course we do," the professor allows. "I'm sure you spend lavishly for the burials and the reburials of your most revered ancestors, yes? Do you not, at the very least, find the means to buy a couple of zebu to be killed in order to mark this ceremony and provide a great feast for all who come?"

The Malagasy diplomat works his mouth, ending up somewhere between frowning and smiling. "You know how our families would regard us if we did not. Even the most civ-il-ized among us find it more convenient to acquiesce."

Gracious in victory, the professor spreads his arms wide. "Yes, you're right, Monsieur Rabary. I, too, do what is expected. I honor the old customs, take part in the disinterments, spend money I can't really afford for the reburials of my parents and grandparents. I speak to their bones and tell them jokes." He leans back, closes his eyes and sighs a deep sigh of contentment. "And afterwards I feel clean and good inside. I have done what is required of me. What greater freedom is there?"

As he says this, Jeanne comes in with coffee, breaking the mood set by Tonja's story, steering the conversation toward the safe trivialities of the rain and the condition of the roads. I watch Tonja and see that she, too, appears relieved at the change in topic. I wonder if, after she has returned to the clear skies and mountain air of Colorado, she will dare say in her scholarly paper the same things she has said to us this evening. Once back at the university she will likely be inclined to dismiss her own ideas as she would a too-vivid dream, one that seems so real in the moment before awakening.

That's what I'd do.

When we have exhausted the limited and comfortable scope of our chit-chat, have thoroughly broken the spell woven by Tonja Adams and Dr. Adrianansoa, my guests begin to leave.

Rabary says goodnight and departs with the others. But I see that he has left his umbrella behind and I know he will contrive to return and fetch it.

After everyone else has left, he knocks on the door.

I pick up a candle and let him in.

Rabary ambles into the living room.

"I'm off to Tamatave tomorrow," I tell him.

Rabary emits a signifying "hmmmmm."

We both know why I'm going, and Rabary understands there's little point in trying to persuade me to stay home.

"I'll make the usual calls," I tell him, trying to make it all sound routine. "The mayor, a few others. I'm told I should visit the head of the police down there. A guy named Andriamana." Rabary's eyes widen, and I can't help but smile. "Funny, everyone looks at me like that when I mention him. Horses must whinny every time his name is spoken."

Rabary betrays nothing but a faint smile.

I wave him into an armchair. "I won't ask how you know him. Operators like you always know each other." Rabary still says nothing. I picture him as a cat, slowly twitching his tail while his eyes never move from my face. I take a seat on the sofa. "I'm told he's ambitious. Maybe he wants to be head of the national police?"

Rabary doesn't rise to the bait. He rests his chin in his hand, one finger curling up to tap at a tooth, as if my question has irritated a nerve residing in one of his incisors. Finally, he speaks. "This is a critical moment in the Captain's career. Opportunities present themselves—for advancement or for ruin. He will want no distractions now."

I swear I'm about ready to punch him, just to get an uncalculated reaction. "'Opportunities present themselves.' I've read fortune cookies clearer than that."

Rabary looks amused. "Robert, you have managed to make your life here exceedingly difficult. You wander around like a blind man. At times you seem to yearn for your own destruction."

"Fine. But this would go easier if you'd speak a language I understand."

"Perhaps there is none," Rabary says. "Just to talk with you, to communicate in French or English, we Malagasy must take on another way of thinking, must drop the subtlety, the depth of our own language and substitute for them Western bluntness. We stop being Malagasy in the very act of speaking to you."

"Don't lay this 'Mysterious Island' bullshit on me, Rabary. You're not some rogue *tromba*, or whatever the male equivalent is. You're whiter than I am."

Rabary chuckles and shakes his head. "No, Robert. There you are wrong. Neither of us likes to acknowledge how Malagasy I am. But let me speak with the unseemly bluntness of a Westerner. If you go to Tamatave to see if there's unrest, you will be looking for trouble—and you will find it. Things are connected in ways you don't understand. Don't look too far below the surface. You'll regret it."

"This is a warning?"

Rabary closes his eyes as if I'm a child trying his patience. "A caution, Robert. A caution you will want to heed."

Rabary rises and I follow him to the door. The rain has stopped. We both look up at the glistening stars, their light distorted by the wind and the heavy rain-washed air.

"Good night, Robert." Rabary walks toward his car.

"When I get to Tamatave, Roland, can I tell the Captain hello for you?"

The Malagasy stops and looks back at me. "No, I shouldn't do that, Robert. I shouldn't do that at all."

8

The Chinese built the road to Tamatave years ago and, except for the bit of highway between the airport and the capital, it's the best road in the country, which isn't saying much. Narrow and bumpy, it twists like overcooked spaghetti as it rises into the hills east of Antananarivo, leading to the coast.

Sitting in the back seat of an embassy car, I look over my shoulder and draw an easier breath as the city disappears behind me. For the next couple of days I can escape the reach of Picard's vague threats, Rabary's vaguer warnings, Nirina's wholly obscure designs, and Gloria's clear-as-glass ambition. Among the thousand cuts of which I'm dying, the one that stings the most, though, is the thought of Walt Sackett still rotting in a Malagasy prison.

For the hundredth time, I remind myself that this trip represents my last best hope for redemption. A short, focused visit might reveal the discontent seething under the sunlit surface of Tamatave, show the storm building under its limpid skies. Gathering these tangled threads, I'll weave a cloth of vivid patterns and stark outlines, drafting a cable that will make clear what the events in Tamatave presage for the people of the island nation and its beleaguered government. With this cogent, insightful essay, I'll shake off the shackles that the Lilliputians of the goddamn State Department have twisted around me, rehabilitate my moribund career, and restore to me a decent sense of myself. My chest expands in contemplation of these happy prospects.

Unaccustomed to so much oxygen, I lapse into a coughing fit.

"Are you all right, sir?" Samuel asks.

"Yeah, yeah. I'm fine."

We motor east through Moramanga, climb past Andasibe, drive deep into the warm and humid rain forest, alive with lemurs and lizards. We pass through thick canopies of palms and rosewood, past thick tangles of orchid and vanilla. From the forest's shadows echo the cries of unseen birds and the roar of distant waterfalls. Occasionally I'm still moved by the wonders of the places I've been favored to live.

After a couple of hours, we top the summit of the hills and descend their eastern slopes, skirting a fast-moving river that leads to the sea. A few miles on, we emerge from the forest and drive through hills denuded of trees, their lower slopes terraced with rice paddies that spill down the rugged ravines and spread across the coastal plain. Many of the neatly-diked paddies are dry and empty. In others, men and women—who look more African, less Asian, than those on the central plateau—stoop to their labor amid the emerald-green shoots. In the distance, a young man drives three zebu toward a wooden pen. The identical scene must have rolled out on these same fields five hundred years earlier and may do so five hundred years from now.

Not everything speaks to the quiet continuity of un-counted generations. As we speed through a village on the coastal road, I catch a glimpse of burned-out shops. In another there are signs of looting—broken windows and smashed chairs. Women and children poke among the wreckage lying in the puddles left by last week's rains.

The paved section of the coastal road ends at Tamatave, Madagascar's main port. We drive through the outskirts and into the city past low huts and wooden shacks. They eventually give way to stuccoed buildings and a view of the Indian Ocean. Diffused by the humid coastal air, the tropical sunlight makes even the dullest colors glow with disturbing intensity. Equally disturbing is the heavy, hu-mid coastal heat—like a sauna, except that you have to wear all your clothes.

Close in to shore, a few rusting cargo ships lay at anchor off a crescent-shaped stretch of beach, the water so crystal clear that the ships appear to be floating in the air.

I check into the Parador, a whitewashed three-story hotel a couple hundred yards from the beach. Like most of Tamatave, it gives the impression of having seen better days. In my room I put on a fresh shirt. I'm sweating through it before I've come back down to the lobby.

Samuel waits for me in the car. I climb in and tell him to drive me to the *mairie*, where I have an appointment with the mayor.

After sweating for nearly thirty minutes in a sweltering outer office, I'm about to tell the mayor's secretary, "I get it already. He can make me wait," when a door swings open and a thin, dapper man in a well-cut suit appears. He smiles and holds out his hand. "Monsieur Knott? Gamini Ravalisona. Sorry to keep you waiting. Please, come in."

Except for the photo of President Ramananjara behind the mayor's desk, the spacious office, served by a gasping and ineffectual air-conditioner, is free of decoration.

The uniformed man sitting in a straight-backed chair, his back to the door, certainly doesn't count as ornament. Even seen from behind, he emits sparks of malevolent energy.

"Ah," the mayor says, "This is Captain Andriamana, the local commander of the national police."

The notorious captain turns in his chair and shoots me a look like an ice pick to the heart.

People seldom look like what you think they will. Captain Andriamana does. Though seated, he appears tall, with a neat black mustache that frames a thin down-turned mouth. Trim and tough, his olive skin and dark eyes give him a Latin appearance.

I brave a smile, hold out my hand. "I didn't think I'd have had the pleasure of meeting the Captain until our appointment later today."

Andriamana looks at my offered hand as if it were a dead fish. "I have a busy afternoon. I've canceled your appointment."

A pretty girl—there is no lack of them in the offices of government officials—brings in coffee and cookies, and we pass fifteen minutes chatting about the recent rains, the current blue skies, and the many points of interest along the road from Antananarivo. Or at least the mayor and I speak of these things. The Captain, who has made it clear he doesn't much care for me, or for the mayor either, adds an occasional grunt.

When I judge that we have laid down the requisite bed of polite conversation, I steer us toward the dismal state of the economy and the hardships it works on the residents of Tamatave. "It must be tough to keep a city running, to bring jobs in."

For an instant, the mayor appears to forget the presence of Captain Andriamana, raising his eyes toward the heavens—or at least toward Antananarivo—and speaking candidly. "You have no idea. In the big ministries back in the capital it is all statistics and finger pointing. As a mayor, I must live in the real world, do what I can to make things better. But I have so little to work with."

I know better than to take notes. A pen and notebook can make even the most expansive personalities clam up.

"It's the same thing in an embassy," I say and shake my head in sympathy. "The stuffed shirts back in Washington aren't satisfied with telling you what to do. They also tell you how to do it, with no understanding of the realities you deal with. Enough to drive you crazy. I suppose people here occasionally want to express their frustration, too."

Even after the endless preamble, I've broached the subject too soon, too directly. The Malagasy prefer indirection to bluntness, metaphor to clarity, and I've blundered. Behind his desk, Ravalisona stiffens, casting a nervous glance at the captain.

There's no going back now. I plow ahead. "In the capital, I hear rumors of unrest."

The smile has disappeared from the mayor's face. He leans forward and steeples his fingers on his desk. "Unrest? I cannot speak for other regions of the country. Only for my small corner. While people's lives are hard, they do not consider violence an acceptable recourse."

He throws an anxious glance at Andriamana to see if this is an acceptable response. We all know the mayor's words stop short of an actual denial.

I try to make the next sound as bland as possible. "You know, on my way here this afternoon I passed through villages where I saw some shops that looked as if they'd been burned and looted. And I wondered if—"

"You saw no such thing," Captain Andriamana breaks in. It's the longest speech he's made since we exchanged greetings.

"No?"

The Captain's voice holds the edged mildness of a man whom no one contradicts. "You saw damage from last year's storms," he says, referring to the cyclone that nearly destroyed Tamatave last year. "Regrettably, we are not a rich country like America," he sneers. "Some of the effects are still visible."

On the way into town, I'd noted roofless houses and abandoned commercial buildings, the tropical undergrowth slowly pulling them back into the earth. But the damage I saw on the road that afternoon was fresh.

"Some of the buildings I saw had been burned," I say.

The policeman shrugs. "Abandoned buildings catch fire."

To atone for his earlier burst of candor, the mayor appears anxious to agree with anything Andriamana says. "Yes. As the Captain says, there is still much damage from the cyclone. We are a country rich in its people, its beauty, its spirit. We are poor only in money." He makes a little throwaway gesture. "Yet money means so much."

I think of the debts hanging over me, of Picard and his need for dollars, of Rabary's yearning for money and what it can buy.

"So it does," I whisper.

"Listen." Andriamana shoots out the word like a bullet. "I know what you will do. You will go back to your embassy and speak of how poor our city looks, amuse your colleagues with stories of the backward Malagasy. But do not tell them there is anger directed toward the government here. No. Our people are heroic and understand that our development will take time. If there is righteous indignation, it is justly directed at foreigners, Indian merchants, who profit from the people's suffering. I enforce the law as best I can, but under the circumstances there are limits. Tell your people that." The Captain raises his chin, daring me, or the mayor, to disagree.

My first meeting of the day, and I've screwed things up already. I could talk with these two all day and get nothing more from them. The mayor is cowed by the Captain's presence, and Andriamana, if it suited him, would deny gravity. Shadows are falling over my previously clear path to redemption. I give it one more try, just for self-respect. "I hear reports of children being kidnapped near here. Are these all being done by one criminal, or has this phenomenon become general?"

With a nod, the little mayor defers to Andriamana.

The police captain eyes me as if measuring me for a coffin. "There have been reports. We are looking at suspects," he says. "I'm sure we will make an arrest very soon." His lips compress in resentment at his need to give credence to anything I say. "I suppose this sort of thing never happens in your country." He barks a mirthless laugh. "We both know of the deviants and criminals in your society. Even you, Monsieur Knott, have your vices, yes?"

The elevator of my soul drops ten floors. Can he know about my misadventures with Picard? Who would have told him—and why would they have bothered? Or maybe it's only a chance remark that my guilt has blown out of proportion.

"Yeah, I like to gamble," I tell him, leaning back in my chair, and smiling, hoping it will irritate the policeman. "I recommend the Zebu Room in Antananarivo, Captain. I'm sure they'll treat you well."

My little act of bravado has a remarkable effect. The Captain leans forward in his chair, his face red with anger. Yet behind the rage, his eyes betray a flicker of unease. It vanishes so quickly, I could have missed it, but I know what I've seen.

He sees it, too, and goes on the attack. "We know the sordid ends to which men turn themselves. You can be sure that here, at least, they will be dealt with as they deserve." He raises his hands, to forestall any further conversation, then slaps them against his thighs, loud as the crack of a pistol.

I slide into the back seat of the embassy car and tell Samuel, "I want to visit a shop."

"Are you all right, sir?"

"I'm fine," I tell him, but after my unsettling talk with Andriamana the hand I run through my hair is shaking. "Just find a shop for me."

"What shop, sir?"

"Any shop. It doesn't matter."

After fourteen years of driving for the embassy, Samuel knows every town in the country as if it were his own. A five minute drive brings me to a dirt street lined with unpainted houses and small stores, most of them closed, a strange thing for a late afternoon. I spot a small grocery with its door open, and tell Samuel to stop.

Idle rickshaw drivers sit in the shade of the trees, watching us. In my present state, I'm sure that among them is one of Andriamana's spies.

I take a deep breath and walk into the little shop. Its unpainted shelves rise to the ceiling, sparsely ranged with a few canned goods, some spices, and cartons of long-life milk. Two large bags, each with a little rice at the bottom, take up a large part of the floor. Baskets of mangoes and papayas hang from hooks.

Standing behind the counter, the shop's owner—like so many small-time merchants in Madagascar, a man of Indian descent—greets me with silence.

I pick out a packet of batteries and a carton of milk from the shelves as the opening bid to conversation. "Business is good?"

The man behind the counter looks at me, his eyes giving away nothing. Indians make up the merchant class in most cities along the rim of the Indian Ocean, and are almost universally despised for their prosperity. It makes them suspicious of everyone but their own.

I want to appear as if I know more than I really do. "It doesn't look as if you've suffered any damage. You're lucky."

The guy hears my accent and switches the conversation to English. "The others are afraid to open. I'm not."

I look out at the nearly empty street. "Why? Things seem pretty quiet here."

The merchant scoffs, and I know he's seen through me.

Though his tone testifies to his reluctance to talk, I'm a fellow foreigner, which makes me relatively safe, and he needs to tell someone what's happening. "It's at night they come. That's when there's trouble."

"So you close at night."

The man blows out a breath and turns his head away. He has no words to waste on the obvious.

"Your neighbors stay shut even during the day."

"To avoid trouble at night. Me? I need to make money."

"And people have very little money?'

The Indian looks past me and into the street. "They haven't got rice. That's worse than not having money. Rice is the only thing they believe in."

"I passed the rice fields today. They looked good."

"Then you don't know how to look. These days the government tells the farmers how much they can charge for their crop. But the farmers can't grow rice for that price. So they abandon their paddies. People go hungry."

"Why do they attack you and not the government?"

The man glares at me as if I'm deliberately aggravating him. A thin man in a ragged shirt comes in and pretends to be considering the papayas. The shop owner makes a show of puttering with items on his shelves until the man leaves.

I figure I've lost him, that he's going to clam up tighter than the mayor, but his anger overwhelms his reticence. "They started out by protesting against the government. Then someone"—with a flick of his dark eyes he indicates the hostile world outside his shop—"told them it was our fault, the Indians' fault, and they turned on us. The police come, but they stand aside long enough to let the mob beat one of us up and take everything from the shelves. Then they step in and make a couple of arrests. But the same men they arrest are in the crowd again the next night."

"So the government won't protect you."

Now he turns his anger on me. "Who do you think tells them to attack us?"

"You want me to understand this. To take it back to Antananarivo."

"I want you to know these things. What you understand is up to you. Now I want you gone. I'm closing up."

9

The tepid water dribbling out of the Parador's crusted showerhead only adds to the humidity, giving little relief from the weight of the coastal heat. After getting out of the shower, I lie on the bed without drying off and drift into a troubled and unrefreshing doze.

By the time I wake, the sky has dimmed and the vivid colors of the day have faded to an hypnotic glow. I go down to the hotel dining room and have a surprisingly good meal of grilled fish and rice, then walk the two blocks to the guest house where Samuel is staying.

I'm surprised not to find him in the front room, waiting for me. He's the most conscientious man I know. The woman who owns the place directs me to the back of the house, where I find Samuel lying on a cot in a darkened room.

"Samuel, you all right?"

"I'm fine, sir." He doesn't move. "I was just sleeping."

I don't buy it, but tell him, "I need you to drive me to a place out of town this evening. Have you eaten?"

"It's all right. I don't need to eat." But he makes no move to get up and his eyes gleam unnaturally in the dim light spilling through the door.

"Are you sick, Samuel?" It's impolite among the Malagasy to use the French word for "ill." Far too direct. So I say *fatigué*, which more literally means tired. It makes the question ambiguous, and the answer even more so.

"It's only the heat, sir. I am not used to it. I am good to drive."

"It's all right. You can stay here. Just give me the keys and tell me where the car is."

Samuel stirs uneasily. "Don't go without me, *patron*. There may be trouble tonight."

I see the keys on his nightstand and pocket them.

Samuel responds to the telltale jingling like a prizefighter to the bell. He rolls off the cot and staggers to his feet, swaying slightly in the dark room. "You can't go without me," he insists. "I won't tell you where the car is." For good measure, he adds, "I've hidden it."

"You've what? Oh, for crying out loud." I throw him the keys and he smiles. "Okay, let's go."

In the gathering dusk we drive north along the coast road. On one side of the road the light from kerosene lamps flickers in the huts set among the palms, on the other side the Indian Ocean lies as quiet as a great gray stone.

As night falls we turn up a rutted drive toward an unlighted stone building. I tell Samuel to park near the front door.

He squints at the stone structure. "We are going to church, sir?"

"What better place for a couple of sinners like us?"

Samuel smiles. "I am strong with the Lord tonight, Monsieur Knott."

"We may need that."

I leave Samuel with the car and knock at the church door but get no response. A few yards away a house stands almost hidden among the trees. I cross the open ground, walk up on the porch and tap at the door. A heavy tread approaches and I feel a shaft of lamplight across my face as a tall man opens the door.

"Yes? Who— My gosh, Robert!"

"How are you, John?"

The tall man with curly red hair opens the door wide. "What a blessed surprise. Come in, come in."

John Barrow and his wife, Sarah, have been in country for several years. We first met at the embassy's Fourth of July picnic in Antananariv and struck up an unlikely friendship. John had been dispatched by a Bible society in Tennessee to serve as an administrator and occasional preacher for several churches near the capital, but he soon came to understand that for many of his flock the local brand of Christianity formed only a whisper-thin veneer over the age-old framework of animism, fady, and ancestor worship. Despite this, John adapted to his new parishioners and they to him. After a year he asked for a church farther from the capital where he thought he could accomplish more. Since their move, I haven't seen him much.

"Sarah's at a women's Bible study. She'll be very happy to see you." We both know this is too generous. Sarah doesn't like me. This is the basis of my respect for her.

John settles into a wooden armchair. An open Bible lies on the armrest next to a tall glass of beer. Barrow follows my gaze and gives me a sidelong glance. "Can I get …?"

"It's all right, John. I think I've quit."

The tall man smiles and gently places his beer on the floor, out of my line of sight. "I'm glad to hear it, Robert. I've prayed for it many times. Maybe I could fetch you a mango juice?"

"No. I'm fine. I'm only here for a few minutes." It feels good to speak to someone with whom I can come to the point. "The embassy has sent me down here to check out some talk of unrest. I was in town today talking to the mayor and the police chief. They tell me that nothing is happening, nothing has happened, and nothing will happen."

John clasps his big hands before him and leans forward in his chair. The strength of his faith and his deep commitment to the truth make him a blunt-spoken man. "They're lying," he tells me. "Ravalisona, the mayor, isn't a bad sort. He's trying, though the government doesn't give him any resources to work with, no real budget, and he's going mad with frustration. In public, though, or with visiting dignitaries such as yourself, he toes the government line. The police captain, Andriamana, is another story. An evil man. I say that without hesitation. Smart. Capable. More complicated than he seems. I've been in a few meetings with him over the last year and I've never sounded his depth. But I believe he's capable of anything."

"Tell me what's going on."

For half an hour the churchman describes the coastal people's growing resentment toward their government, the impoverishment of the local farmers and their abandonment of the fields. He draws a clear picture of his demoralized congregation, adding that policemen have broken up peaceful demonstrations in town and arrested several of his parishioners. "After that, gangs of young men took to looting. Some of them see it as a form of protest. That makes it easy for Andriamana's goons to deflect them into attacking foreign merchants, take the heat off the government. The Indian's are everyone's favorite enemy, and there's no one to stand up for them. The Malagasy are generally the most peaceful people, but they store up their anger—against their government, against their poverty, against their ancestors—and when they reach the breaking point they explode. You're taking quite a risk just being out tonight."

"Yeah, I think my driver was trying to tell me the same thing." I shift a little uneasily on the sofa. "These gangs come out after dark?"

Barrow nods. "And the police, too. They may have uniforms, but they're undisciplined and untrained. They see everyone as their enemy. They're very dangerous."

"Do you think this sort of thing is happening in other areas of the country?"

Barrow spreads his hands wide. "How could it not?"

He's made things clear for me and I thank him for it. We speak for a couple of minutes of life in the capital. Barrow asks after a couple of mutual acquaintances and I rise to go.

"You might do better to spend the night here, Robert," John says. "I don't like the idea of you out on the road at this hour."

"Thanks, but I've got to leave early and my things are at the hotel. I'll be fine."

He gives me a penetrating look. "How are you doing these days?"

"I'm okay."

"Your face tells a different story. It looks like five miles of bad road. Do you want to tell me about it?"

"Too long a tale. Another time."

"Have you spoken to your daughter lately?"

"A few days ago. She's fine."

"And you've been working on your resentment toward her?"

"Resentment? Why should I feel resentment toward her?"

"Because you're so angry with yourself—and your love for her is so strong."

Like I say, the man goes straight to the point and speaks the truth. "I'm— We're fine."

"I'm glad." He stands and looks at me, waiting for more. When I say nothing, he doesn't insist, but grips my hand. "Do you want to take a moment to join me in prayer before you go?"

I smile, embarrassed. "Have I ever?"

"No. But I keep asking."

"Say one for me."

"I will, you know."

"You don't know how I count on it."

We walk together out to the embassy car. The heavy night air hasn't let go of the day's heat and I feel a prickle of sweat on my back and arms. As we walk past the church I notice masonry has fallen from the building. Cracks line the mortar between the bricks.

John Barrow reads my thoughts. "I look around me," he says, "and I don't know whether I'm seeing an ancient way of life crumbling to a sad end, or a new and better one being born."

I want to tell him that I wonder the same thing about myself.

Barrow looks at the car. "You don't have a driver?"

"He's lying in the back seat. Says he's not feeling well."

At the sound of our voices Samuel sits up, his eyes dull and his shoulders sagging. Barrow leans into the car and speaks with him for a few moments in Malagasy. He puts a hand to Samuel's forehead and frowns. "He's burning with fever," Barrow tells me. "Says it's malaria. Comes and goes. I tried to convince him to stay the night. I have a little clinic. The Bible Society gives us a bit of medical training before we go overseas. He says he can't stay. He has to take care of you." He lets that sink in for a moment. "I have some pills I could give him. It should start bringing the fever down."

Barrow goes back to the house and returns with the pills, which Samuel swallows. The tall preacher turns to me. "If you insist on going back to Tamatave tonight, I think you'd better drive. Be careful."

"You know me."

When it all goes wrong, it goes wrong very quickly. Though I can't remember passing through any villages on the way out of Tamatave, I find myself coming into one, and am sure I've taken the wrong road. At the edge of the village a signpost indicates the route to Tamatave lies somewhere behind us. Unable to make a U-turn on the narrow dirt road, I take a rutted track that appears to loop back and should point us again toward Tamatave.

It doesn't. After twisting around, it brings me back into the same village from another direction.

I turn to Samuel lying in the back seat. "I think I've gotten us lost."

The Malagasy props himself up and peers out at the

village. Its few dark lanes appear deserted. No life shows from any of the buildings along the road.

"Where are we?"

It seems to take him a long time to decipher the question. "I think we are in Adilazana, sir."

"Is that good or bad?"

Out of the corner of my eye, I see dark forms flitting between two buildings. When I turn to look, they are gone.

"It depends, sir."

It would. "Which way do I go?"

From a dark side street I hear shouting and the pounding of running feet, like the sound of heavy rain.

"I'm not sure, sir." Samuel pauses, his mind working slowly against the fever. "I think we should turn around and go the other way."

"That's the way to Tamatave?"

Samuel shakes his head. He looks very uneasy. "I don't know, *patron*, but I think we should leave this town."

From somewhere in front of us comes the crash of shattering glass and a loud whoof. I look up to see blue flames burst against a row of shacks, the fire flowing like a waterfall down the wooden walls. Silhouetted against the flames, a group of young men run down the street toward our car.

"Turn around, Mr. Knott! We need to leave this place."

I try to make a quick U-turn, but the dirt lane is too narrow for the Peugeot and I hit a wooden post I hadn't seen. I back up, the steering wheel shuddering in my hands. The right front wheel whirs loudly against its crumpled fender. Another shack bursts into flames in front of me. Half a dozen young men throw their hands in the air, shouting in triumph.

Out of the darkness comes a flat *pop-pop-pop*. The young men scatter.

"That is gunfire, sir," Samuel says from the back seat, his voice tight. "Get out of this town, Monsieur Knott."

"I'm doing the best I can." Fighting the balky steering wheel, I manage to back the car around and point it down the street.

I realize later that the police must have been waiting in the shadows for the fire bombs to explode, ready to crack down against the violence they knew was coming and had probably provoked. Now they run into the unpaved street, dragging two metal barriers after them, and set up a roadblock. One of them lights a couple of flares and throws them into the road, illuminating the scene in an intense red light that give the policemen the lurid appearance of apprentice fiends.

I drive slowly toward the barriers and hope I appear to be exactly what I am, a befuddled *vazaha* who has taken a disastrously wrong turn.

Two policemen, one with sergeant's stripes on his arm, stand at the barricade. As I drive toward them the one who isn't a sergeant fires a burst into the air from his AK-47, orange flame flaring from the muzzle.

I involuntarily duck my head but continue to creep forward. My hands are slippery with sweat. My foot hovers over the accelerator then the brake and back to the accelerator. I'm afraid that if I stop the car they won't let me pass. I'm equally afraid that if I don't stop they'll shoot me.

As we approach the roadblock, the sergeant spots the car's diplomatic plate. After a moment of hesitation, he waves me through.

I roll into the narrow gap between the metal barriers. As I do, a movement in the rear-view mirror catches my eye.

Two policemen are running toward us in the dark, shouting and waving their guns. One of them stops, pulls back the bolt on his assault rifle and braces to fire.

With my car blocking their view of the barricade, these two apparently haven't seen the sergeant wave me through. They think I'm running the barricade.

From the back seat Samuel lets out a cry. "*Patron*, they're going to shoot!"

The chatter of the rifle, the crash of the breaking glass, and the whir of the bullets passing through the car come in one single, terrifying roar. I stand on the accelerator and the car jumps through the barricades, scattering the policemen in front of us.

They jump out of the way and bring their weapons up to fire. I turn sharply down a narrow dirt lane. The rattle of automatic rifles breaks through the chaos of burning buildings and running men.

I curse as the unpaved lane quickly ends in a T formed by an intersecting footpath. My foot falls off the clutch as I slam on the brakes and the car dies. That's when I hear Samuel groan.

Shouts and the thud of approaching boots come from the direction of the roadblock. I doubt they're running up to apologize.

I jump out of the car, throw open the back door, put my hands under Samuel's arms and drag him out of the car. "Are you hit, Samuel? Samuel?" I feel something warm and sticky on my hands and hear him groan.

Half-dragging, half-carrying Samuel, I stumble down the footpath, which runs along the back of a row of wooden shacks. I look up an alley that opens to my left. I see the glow of burning buildings and hear the popping of gunfire.

Where the path and the alley intersect, I lay Samuel in a sitting position against the wall of a hut. A dark stain has spread over his shirt.

"You've been hit."

Samuel rolls his head back. "Yes, sir," he says, his voice thick with shock.

I tear his shirt open, but can't see much in the dark. When I draw my hand back it's covered in blood. "Where are you hit?"

"My arm, I think, sir. I am sorry, sir. I did not mean to get hurt." He blinks like a man warding off sleep.

I hear someone approaching along the alley. Against the light of the flames I see two women running toward us. Behind them, a policeman stops maybe fifty yards away and raises his rifle. Flame sputters from the barrel. The report echoes off the walls of the wooden huts.

The women scream. One of them falls to the ground. The other turns away from us down the footpath and hides behind a hut. From its shelter, she peers back at her fallen companion, who now jumps to her feet and, shouting unintelligibly, gets to the end of the lane and runs up the footpath in the opposite direction, going by without seeing us. The first woman starts to run after her. When she comes into the open, the policeman fires again.

Bullets whiz around us. I hug the ground, pulling Samuel down after me. The woman has stopped in the middle of the lane, frozen in fear.

"Get down!" I shout in French and grab her by the arm. She falls in a heap across Samuel and me.

Crying out in Malagasy, she tries to scramble to her feet.

"Stay down!" I yell at her.

I hear the running boots growing closer. A flashlight plays off the walls of the wooden shacks. Again, the woman tries to get up. I'm sure the policeman will fire again if she runs, and at this range he won't miss. So I hug her close, try to keep her from getting up.

The wandering beam of the flashlight falls across her face for an instant, and I see her clearly for the first time.

"My God!"

Nirina stops struggling, her eyes wide in astonishment.

The shadow of the gunman falls across us. I see a silhouette pulling back a rifle bolt and bracing to fire. I put an arm around Nirina's shoulders as she buries her head against my chest. Eerily calm, I close my eyes and wait for the man to shoot us dead.

"*Non!*" The voice comes out of the distance.

Over the distant cries of running men and the crackling of flames from the main street, I hear a heavy tread advancing up the lane.

"Put a light on them," the voice orders. The flashlight shines in our faces, and I can't see anything against its glare.

He must see the blood on my hands, because he says, "You've been shot." Something about the voice sounds familiar.

"No," I tell him. "It's my driver."

"Get on your feet."

Holding my hands away from my body, I let Nirina slide to the ground as I get to my feet.

"That one is your driver?"

"Yes."

I sense the mind behind the voice, feel it assessing the situation, making a decision.

"*Bon*. Get out of here and take him to a doctor."

"He's bleeding. Don't you have a medic with—"

"This isn't a medical mission." He says something to the group of policemen around him. Two of them grab Samuel and pull him to his feet. He screams in pain.

"They will get him to your car," the voice tells me.

"My car's all shot up."

"You shouldn't have tried to flee. You think as a Westerner you are above the law."

Now I've got it, the voice.

"I was lost, Captain Andriamana. One of your men waved us through the barricade, but when I drove through, others started shooting at us."

The Captain grunts in scorn. He appears even taller than I remember and looks at me like Death its own self. "Now I understand why you sneered at me when I told you it was the foreigners causing our troubles. You're one of them."

I want to tell him that I wasn't the one sneering during our meeting with the mayor, but decide it's wiser not to bring that up. As with most bullies, there's something defensive, an insecurity in Andriamana. It makes him sense disdain in anything said to him by a Westerner. I remember the look the Captain gave me when I mentioned the Zebu Room. I have no idea what that was about, and this doesn't seem like the moment to ask. Right now, I'm hoping that even he doesn't have the nerve to shoot a diplomat in cold blood, at least with witnesses present.

Lowering my hands slowly, I tell him, "I didn't come here to cause trouble. I told you, I was lost. I turned up here by mistake."

Andriamana snorts in disbelief, then gives a long, appraising look at Nirina, still lying on the ground.

"The girl comes with me," he says.

Nirina rises, her face slack with fear. She looks at the captain and his men and senses her fate.

"No. She stays with me." I struggle to breathe normally. The Captain could still shoot me and call it an accident.

Andriamana pauses surprised. "You know her?"

"Yes." I take Nirina's arm and speak quietly into her ear, "My car is in the next lane. Find it and get in."

She starts to walk away, but it will require her to walk past Andriamana, and I can see her lose her nerve. She stops and backs into me.

A twitch of uncertainty clouds the policeman's gaze. He looks at me, looks at the girl. Makes some calculation of risk and reward. Then he laughs to cover his retreat. "You're a lucky man, Monsieur Knott. I promise you, the next time, I will not see you so clearly in the dark. Now get out. Both of you." With a soft exhalation of contempt, Captain Andriamana turns on his heel and walks away. Before he's taken two strides, he stops. "I wouldn't go toward Tamatave, if I were you. The roads are full of trouble tonight. It would grieve me to hear you were hurt."

What he means is that it would be a nuisance he doesn't need if one of his men should kill me.

Two policemen drag Samuel by his arms, the driver groaning as he struggles to stay on his feet. Nirina and I follow.

Out of the sight of their captain and in the presence of an evidently important vazaha the soldiers are happy to help when I ask them to pull the fender off the front tire. They lay Samuel across the back seat. One opens the door for Nirina, like a valet. I think of tipping him, but figure he'd shoot me. You can only push things so far.

Broken glass litters the car's interior and the smell of blood turns my stomach. The back window is blown out, the front one starred and cracked. Bullets have punched holes in the trunk and rear fenders, but apparently not the gas tank. To my surprise, the car starts at the first turn of the key. Heeding the Captain's advice, I take the road leading away from Tamatave. I ask Nirina, "You know the American church near Panandrana?"

She nods.

"Okay, tell me how to get there."

Once we're clear of the village, Nirina crawls into the back seat. I hear the tearing of cloth as she rips away a part of her dress to make a bandage for Samuel. As she gives me directions she tells me she's been in Adilazana visiting family. I remember her brother outside the bar of the Continental, telling her that her father wanted her to come home.

The girl I saw her with is her cousin, she tells me. "She'll be worried about me. I should go back."

"Andriamana and his men won't let you get away a second time."

She doesn't argue.

Fifteen minutes later we pull up to the little church set in the trees.

"Go to the house and bring the minister here," I tell Nirina.

A moment later I hear John Barrow letting out a low whistle at the sight of the riddled car. "Man, who did this?"

"Andriamana's goons. My driver's been shot."

Barrow gives me a look that I hope I never see again. He glances at Nirina, her dress torn and stained with blood. He leans into the car door and looks at Samuel lying across the back seat. "Let's get him inside where I can see what I'm doing."

We pull Samuel from the back seat, get our shoulders under his arms and carry him into the small clinic at the back of the house.

Once inside, we lay Samuel across a narrow table. Barrow tears off what's left of the driver's shirt and cuts away Nirina's makeshift bandage. He points to a lantern and tells me to hold it close while he examines the wound.

While he works, he speaks quietly to Samuel, who lies on his back, his eyes staring and unfocussed. Barrow swabs the wound—it isn't bleeding much anymore—and dresses it. "The bullet went straight through his upper arm without breaking the bone. The bandage stopped the bleeding." He looks at Nirina. "Well done."

When he has finished dressing the wound I tell him, "Maybe I'll take you up on that offer to stay the night after all."

The minister smiles grimly.

Barrow gives Samuel an injection. The driver's eyes close and his face goes slack.

The preacher sees the look on my face. "Don't worry. I just gave him some morphine for the pain. He's fallen asleep. I don't think he's lost a great deal of blood. It's a clean wound. As long as it doesn't get infected, he should recover well."

Throughout the procedure, Nirina has stood against the wall of the small room, her hair disheveled, smears of blood on her face and arms and on her torn dress. I feel a little spasm of self-revulsion at finding her more alluring than ever.

Barrow speaks with her in Malagasy. "She says she's a friend of yours, Robert."

"Not what you're thinking." I don't blame him for being skeptical. "I know her from Antananarivo." I explain our chance meeting in the village.

"She says you saved her life."

She looks straight into me, unblinking.

A few minutes later John's wife, Sarah, comes home from her meeting. Her face grows increasingly stony as she listens to her husband's narrative of my misadventures. She glances daggers at me, then finds Nirina some clean clothes and leads her off to the bath.

Too wound-up to sleep, I sit up talking with John for a while, explaining in more detail what happened in the village. When I finish, he makes a low whistle. "My guess is that it's all a set-up. Andriamana probably hired a couple of young men to throw the fire bombs so that he could make a show of looking tough. For all the gunfire you heard, I'd be surprised if anyone but your driver was hurt. But there will be a row of burned-out shops in the morning."

Sarah makes up the sofa with clean sheets. For her husband's sake, she remains civil.

I lie on the couch wishing I had a ddrink to stop the trembling in my hands. Anyone would understand. I get up from the couch and tiptoe into the kitchen. In the dark, I run my hands among the cupboards, tapping like a blind man for the bottle of brandy John keeps for special occasions.

Muffled voices come from the back of the house. Barrow calls from the bedroom, "Robert, is that you?"

I work to make my voice sound normal. "Just getting a drink of water."

"You know not to drink out of the tap."

Barrow thumps out of his room and opens the refrigerator door. He pours a glass of water and hands it to me like a parent giving his child a drink in the middle of the night.

"John, I really need a drink," I tell him, shame and craving choking my voice.

He looks at me not unkindly and says softly, "I just gave you one, Robert."

Could he really have misunderstood me? Or was he granting me a favor by pretending we were only talking about water? The ways of a good man are mysterious to me.

10

I wake at first light, the day already warm and muggy. At first I attribute my morning stiffness to sleeping on a too-short couch, but realize that my aching shoulders, tight jaw, and sore legs represent the hangover from the fear and tension of the previous night. Whether awake or dreaming, I had spent the night replaying the sound of bullets shattering the windshield, the sight of the burning huts and of Samuel wounded and in shock. Most of all I relive the moment when I held Nirina in my arms as we waited for the policeman to shoot us.

After breakfast Barrow and I clean the worst of the blood and glass from the car. Sweating pleasantly in the tropical sun as we work, the night's terrors gradually release their hold, and I begin imaginging the outlines of the cable I'll file when I get back to the embassy, still hoping it will impress the deep breathers back in the Department and resurrect, Lazarus-like, my moribund career. Yet, while I toss shards of glass into a tin can and wipe smears of blood from the car's upholstery, premonitions of failure pass like a cloud before the sunshine of my hopes.

When it comes time to leave, Samuel walks to the car, wan with pain and the loss of blood, smiling at his unsteadiness but refusing any help. His malaria attack has passed and he says he feels much better despite his wound. He even thinks he's going to drive until I make it clear he is to lie down in the back seat and stay there.

Nirina comes out from the house looking young and fresh in a flowered dress of Sarah's. For the first time, I see the innocence behind her toughness, the good heart behind its fortification of wariness. Something of what's passing through my mind must show in my face, for she gives me a dazzling, guileless smile that asks for nothing. When I smile back, hers disappears and I think of how hard a thing it must be to be a beautiful young woman.

When I offer to take her back to Antananarivo she tells me no. "I need to go back to my village."

I offer to take her, and she nods.

In the back seat, Samuel is already drifting off to sleep.

We say our goodbyes to the Barrows and drive down the dirt road toward the highway in a silence that grows like the monsoon thunderheads, waiting to break.

When I can't go any longer without speaking, I opt for the banal. "I see you decided to come back to your family. How's your father?"

"He's dying."

She says it simply and I understand that she has already done whatever she needs to do to prepare herself.

"So, you decided to come home."

We are both remembering how she stood outside the Continental that night, telling me she had no home.

"I cannot explain it to you," she says now. "But I have lost my place and haven't yet found a new one."

The words sound oddly formal, perhaps a phrase she has worked out in her mind long ago.

"How did that happen—losing your place?"

This, too, she answers quickly. She has thought about these things for a long time. "Everyone in my family lives in the way of the ancestors. My older brother is a fisherman. He and my younger brother will one day have our father's lands. But I—" She stops, fighting for the words now. "My father saw I was different and sent me to the convent school in Antananarivo. And there I learned too much to ever really go back, to ever again think that the world is entirely the one our ancestors have made for us. The nuns are mostly from France and Belgium and they taught us about their world, how superior it is to ours. For us, it is frightening, a world where anything could happen, where the ancestors are killed twice, once when they die and again when they are forgotten. One of the nuns was from America, Sister Deborah. She was forever telling us 'change is good.' Is that something Americans say?"

"We say a lot of things."

"Madagascar is not about change. Telling us change is good is like telling us death is life."

"But you're saying you changed."

"As frightening as it was, I was fascinated by this other world. I wanted to see it, wanted to go where everything can change every day. To others, I became like a *tromba* woman, except that I had not run away. It was they who cast me out. But I didn't want to just leave my village and go live in the woods like other ,. I wanted to leave Madagascar, to see that other world."

I keep my eyes on the road as I say, "So you meet Walt at the Continental or maybe some Marine party. He falls in love and tells you he'll take you home with him."

She doesn't deny it.

I want to tell her it isn't going to happen, that Walt is both married and broke. But I know that telling truths like that creates obligations, obligations I'm not ready to accept.

Nirina shakes her head. "Why am I telling you all this?"

"I thought you knew. I don't."

She frowns. "Why are you always the joker, Monsieur Knott? Maybe it is because you're even more frightened than I am."

How can a girl who hardly knows me read me like a book?

"Anyone can see it, Monsieur Knott. You're frightened all the time—except for the one thing you should be frightened of."

"Yeah? What's that?"

"The Colonel."

"Picard?"

"He is a dangerous man, Monsieur Knott."

"That's what he tells me."

"You are in his debt, yes? You had a look in your eyes that night when you left the Continental. I've seen that look before."

"You think you can tell from the look on someone's face that—"

"There was a boy from Tamatave who liked to gamble at the Colonel's tables. He soon owed the Colonel more than he could pay. The Colonel told him to get the money from his family. They owned a hotel in Tamatave. But he told the Colonel he wouldn't. His family had influence, and he was sure the Colonel wouldn't dare to do anything to him. We told him not to provoke the Colonel, not to make him look weak. But the boy only drank whiskey and laughed. A couple of us went to the Colonel to speak for him. He threw us out. I went back once more by myself to plead with him. But he wouldn't listen."

"You liked this boy?"

She says nothing. I glance at her, but she's looking out the window as if watching the scenery.

"So you know Picard."

"Yes. But I couldn't help this boy, and I can't help you."

"I'm not asking for help." I try to sound a lot tougher than I feel. "So what happened to this kid?"

"One weekend he came back home to Tamatave. He was driving along the coast road when a policeman stopped him and pointed him up a dirt track into some trees. Sometimes, when a policeman wants a bribe this is what he does. When the boy drove up there, the policeman shot him dead. Two men from our village were walking toward the rice paddies along a trail hidden in the trees and saw it happen. They came running back and told my father. He told them to say nothing to anyone."

"And you're going to tell me—"

"It was Captain Andriamana. The Colonel didn't want to do anything to the boy in Antananarivo, where someone would suspect him. So he paid Andriamana to kill him in Tamatave."

I want to tell her she can't know that Picard was behind it. But, for once, I think before I open my mouth and I start to make the connection. The Captain's sudden anger toward me, it wasn't about the Zebu Room but about its owner. Andriamana must have wondered if I knew something regarding Picard and the boy's death, had to be thinking maybe Picard told me about it, *vazaha* to *vazaha*.

Given the Captain's suspicions, I'm suddenly aware of how tempting it must have been for him to go ahead and shoot me in the village the previous night. My chest goes fluttery for a moment.

"You're sure about all this?"

Her silence is her vow.

"Well, thanks for the heads up," I say with unconvincing lightness.

"That's all?"

"What more do you want? What am I supposed to say?"

"After last night there is a bond between us, Monsieur Knott. The nearness of death has brought us closer than either of us wants."

"Hey, lighten up already." I take my eyes off the road to scowl at her. "Do you talk to Walt like this? I'm sure it does him wonders."

But she's right. There's an unsought intimacy between us. And, yeah, it scares me.

A couple of kilometers short of Tamatave, Nirina directs me onto a dirt road that runs a few hundred yards up to a clutch of wooden houses ranged irregularly around an open space with a large tree at its center. Neatly-kept rice paddies surround the village.

The arrival of an automobile jolts the village from its late morning slumber. Children come running, pointing at my bullet-riddled car and jabbering excitedly. When I look in their direction they laugh in ecstatic terror and run behind the houses. Adults stand in their doorways, looking at the *vazaha* who has brought home their prodigal daughter.

Samuel stirs in the back seat. I tell him we're only stopping for a moment.

No longer trusting what I might say to Nirina, I simply nod at her door handle.

She doesn't move. "You can't drop me here and leave without seeing my family. You might as well call me a whore in front of all my people."

I hesitate, but finally let Nirina lead me to one of the wooden houses built, like the others, on posts that raise it a few feet off the ground. She mounts the steps and I follow, ducking my head in the low doorway.

The interior is nearly bare, but clean and pleasant, with wooden shutters open to the sun. A woman, her hair salted with gray, bows as I enter before backing shyly into a corner of the main room.

Squatting against a wall sits a young man I recognize as Nirina's brother, the one I saw outside the bar of the Continental.

In the light spilling from one of the open windows I see a gray-haired man lying on a reed mat, his face deeply lined, his ribs pressing through his bony chest. His arms and legs are thin as sticks. Only his eyes are alive, bright as a hawk's. The fearsome authority of the dying fills the room.

He waves at his son to bring a stool for me, then says something to me in Malagasy, his voice surprisingly strong.

I find myself nodding, though I have no idea what he has said. In this unfamiliar house, in the presence of the dying man, I feel profoundly unsettled. I mutter something, I'm not quite sure what, maybe trying to tell him how much I respect him for letting his daughter find her own path.

Something in the room has shifted, and I realize that in this little exchange I've done what I needed to do, that my words, whatever they are, have carried the proper weight, set the right balance, and I can leave now.

Nirina follows me to the open door.

When I get to the bottom of the steps, I'm gripped by an impulse to tell her to come with me. I can take her back to the city, take her home with me, do anything but leave her here. But I'm beginning to understand that to her every place is foreign country now and that she'll do nothing that will put herself further in my debt.

Michelle Herr taps nervously at the arm of the sofa in her office and turns to Esmer, the security officer. "Paul?"

He takes a breath and raises his eyebrows, letting us see how much he's been through today. "I've spoken to Mathurin, over at Interior. They're madder'n hell that an embassy official was out spying on them, while—" He cuts me off with an upraised hand. "Yeah, okay, Robert, but that's the way it looks to them." He twitches his shoulders and speaks out of the corner of his mouth like he's auditioning for *Casablanca*. "But, I think they're willing to forget about it."

I roll my eyes. "Of course they're willing to forget about it. What I don't understand is why we're willing to forget about it. With all respect, Paul, every time one of us has a problem, you act like it's our own fault."

Esmer gives the Ambassador a sidelong glance, which is as close as he can politely get to pointing at his temple and making little circles with his finger.

"Robert, I told you to be discreet," Ambassador Herr says, playing the despairing mother.

"Ma'am, I wasn't the one who started shooting at people."

Lost in regret, she shakes her head. "Now it will be all over the papers. I can just see it, 'American Diplomat Runs Roadblock.'"

I throw my hands up in exasperation. "Or maybe, 'Police Wave Diplomat Through Roadblock, Then Shoot at Him From Ten Feet Away—And Miss.'"

"Miss?" Lynn breaks in. "The car has a dozen bullet holes in it, a missing fender, and Samuel's been shot."

"If he'd kept his head down …" I mutter, but I understand this isn't a tack that will gain me much sympathy. "Look, the papers are just a chronicle of who had lunch with the President. They're not going to say a word about this."

The rain-on-Knott party lasts a few more minutes, but there isn't much more to say. When Lynn and the Ambassador reach the limit of how many times they can shake their heads in sorrow and displeasure, and Esmer has sputtered himself into silence, I make a last attempt to recover my standing. "I'll get a cable off to Washington on the trip. I think it'll create a lot of interest back there."

But I know in my scalded heart that it'll be nothing more than another dispatch from the far side of the moon.

I make my way back to my office where my secretary, Cheryl is smiling, holding out two illegible phone messages.

"What are these?" I ask.

"That first is from a Mr. Picard. He wants you to see him this evening. I asked him what it was concerning and he just said in this real deep voice, 'He'll know.'" She laughs at her own mimicry. "He seems like a funny man."

I have to take a couple of breaths before I can manage to speak around the lump that fills my chest, "Yeah, barrel of laughs."

Trying to look normal, I wander toward my desk.

"Robert, you forgot to ask about the second one. That one should be really good news."

"Yeah?"

"Well," she says, "your career management officer left a message. He says he may have your next post for you." She cocks her head to one side. "Where's Ouagadougou?" she asks, though she pronounces it "Wog-a-doo-doo," which is actually pretty close.

"On the outskirts of hell."

I spend the rest of the day writing my cable.

11

"Well done, monsieur." Jacques Razafintsalama appears genuinely pleased that I've come out a winner tonight, if only by a few francs.

"Thanks, Jacques." I try to sidle past the Zebu Room's manager, who stands between me and the elevator. If I had any sense, of course, I'd stay away from this place, but I truly believe it's this or the bottle. Or is that only another of the thousand ways I try to kid myself?

Jacques' smile turns apologetic. "I'm sure you haven't forgotten your appointment with the Colonel."

Like a prisoner caught trying to escape, I fall in behind the Malagasy and once more walk down the long corridor toward Picard's office. We enter the private sanctum of the Zebu Room's owner to find him banging at his air conditioner. The Frenchman frowns at Jacques. "I told you to get this fixed."

Jacques bows slightly. "My apologies, Colonel."

"*Merde.*" Picard strikes the machine once more then forces a smile as Jacques backs out the door. "I hear you've had a good night, Robert. I'm so pleased."

I tweak my neck, trying to relieve a crick in my soul. "Now that I know how gracious you guys are about losing, I'll have to try winning more often."

Picard laughs a little too loudly before sitting down behind his desk. "What did you make tonight? Maybe ten thousand francs? At this rate you'll have me paid off in—what?—twenty years?" Like a stern uncle, he actually wags a finger at me. "Not good enough, Bobby. Can I call you Bobby?"

"No. What do you want, Picard? You want to write a letter to the embassy? Go ahead, write it. That won't get your money to you."

Picard throws out his hands in resignation. "You're right, Robert. Sometimes one has to be satisfied with taking one's payment in blood, so to speak." This time, when Picard sighs, it's not for effect. His normally ruddy face is pale and his look is inward. After a moment, he swivels his chair around and looks for a long time at the photo of his daughter. Over his shoulder, he says to me, "Your daughter …"

"Christine."

"How old did you say she was?"

"Sixteen."

"Sixteen." He is silent so long that I think of quietly sneaking out. But Jacques is probably outside the door, ready to shove me back in. "A daughter needs her father at that age," Picard says. "I never knew my daughter at sixteen. I saw her briefly when she was fifteen. A few minutes in an airport. She is twenty-four now." He leans back in his chair, addressing the photo. "And still unmarried. Still a maid."

A maid? I can't manage to laugh at the antiquated language or the sentiment behind it.

Picard swivels back and his eyes unhappily roam the confines of his office. Abruptly, he rises to his feet. "Let's get out of here."

The big Frenchman opens a door behind his desk. I can see the top steps of a circular staircase. Picard stands in the doorway and with a crooked finger beckons me to follow. He descends the steps, grunting at each tread. I hesitate. Who knows I'm here but Picard and Jacques? If I were to disappear....

I follow my host down.

A tall floor lamp is the only light in the large suite, a set of rooms decorated entirely in white—white walls, white furniture, white fixtures. The thick white carpet and heavy drapes deaden sound like a funeral parlor. The air feels dead, unbreathable.

"Make yourself comfortable, Robert." Picard waves toward a white armchair and drifts into the kitchen. "A drink?"

"No. Thanks."

"Ah, yes. Your problematic liver. A fruit juice perhaps. Please, let me play host."

I struggle against a sense of unwanted familiarity, as if I were watching him walking around in his underwear.

The former soldier of fortune comes back with a glass of wine for himself and hands me a tumbler of mango juice. He lifts his wineglass in casual salute and cocks his head at me. "So, Robert, you owe me a great deal of money, yes? I have shot men for less than this. Much less." Picard flips a dismissive hand. "No, I'm not going to shoot you. I've killed too many men. It is the great debit against my name." The Frenchman stares into his wineglass, his smile fading like a light winking out. "I can still see some of them. At night." His chuckle makes my blood run cold. "I sleep very poorly, thinking about these things—paying the interest on my outstanding balance, you might say. One day the principle will come due, I suppose." He shakes the thought away. "But now … Well that's not how I make my living anymore. Besides, as I say, I like you."

"I'm going all gooey inside, Maurice. I owe you money you don't think I'll ever pay back. And you've invited me down here because you want to do something about it."

Picard raises his eyebrows, lets them fall back. "Yes, Robert, this is a business meeting, isn't it?" Picard's smile reveals a picket of clenched teeth. He takes a deep draught of his wine and sets the glass on an end table. "Robert, I don't want to ruin you."

"It's gratifying to us sheep when the wolves claim they're pulling for us."

With a sudden, "*Bouf!*" Picard bangs his fist on the table, knocking his glass to the floor. The red wine spatters the carpet like blood.

"I have no use for your comedy. Tomorrow I could write a letter to your ambassador, telling her that you are in debt to me for thousands of dollars."

I decide to brazen it out. Is this a good strategy, or am I just tired of living? "They'd probably send me home in disgrace and an early retirement. That's swell, Maurice. But doing that wouldn't give you enough hard currency to pay taxi fare to the airport. If I'm thrown out, the money I owe you is lost."

"It's lost now."

"Well, as you say, you could have me shot." I decide to give him a glance at the card I'm holding in my hand. "Maybe your friend in Tamatave would do the job."

Behind his fixed smile, Picard's eyes go cold as death.

Sometimes you don't know you've gone too far until you've already crossed the line. I'd calculated that knowing

Picard's connection to Andriamana could be a bargaining chip. For the first time, I realize it could get me killed.

The two of us pass an immeasurable moment staring into the abyss. It's Picard who steps back first, blowing a long breath through his pursed lips. "Yes, the estimable Captain Andriamana."

Shaken by the glimpse into my own grave, I can barely whisper. "I'm told he's as ambitious as Beelzebub. You don't worry that what you think you have on him is in fact something he has on you?"

The Frenchman shakes his head almost imperceptibly. "I'm a *vazaha*. We once ruled this island. For the Malagasy, old ways of thinking don't die. He may despise me, but he won't touch me." Picard tries to regain his swagger. "Robert, you have a gift for self-destruction. For your sake—no, for mine—let me suggest a way out of your dilemma."

Not trusting my voice to remain steady, I only nod.

The owner of the Zebu Room tilts his head back and runs his fingers through his hair as he sits on the couch opposite me, tapping his fingers on its white upholstered arm. "You're going to get off easy. All you have to do is break the law."

"Lucky me."

Picard's jaw clenches. "Just be quiet a moment. Just ... be quiet. You mustn't get me excited. For a moment I felt my former self coming upon me. I was quite prepared to kill you."

"'Old ways are the best ways,'" I say, and consider Picard's claim that I have an urge toward self-destruction.

Picard actually chuckles. "So they say. However, it would gain me nothing—at least for now. Listen, we both have problems. You need out from under your debt, and I have mountains of Malagasy francs I cannot spend. Separately, our problems look insurmountable." He holds his hands a foot apart, measuring the predicament. "Yet, together we can solve them. In the future, when you come to my casino, I will have Jacques hand you a package. It will contain a stack of Malagasy francs—perhaps several hundred dollars worth at a time. You will exchange them at your embassy for dollars. If anyone asks, you can say you won them. I will back you up. The next time you come, you will hand the dollars to Jacques. Soon you will have discharged your debt to me and I will have enough dollars for my visa and my travels." He spreads his hands with a little wave at the end, demonstrating how the problem evaporates. "It's so simple."

"And, as you say, so illegal."

Picard throws his hands in the air. "Oh, everything is against the law. Are you saying you won't do it?"

"Why don't you just arrange for me to win, like Rabary?" I want to ask again exactly what Rabary has on him, but that's a topic for a different conversation.

"Pah! It's harder than it looks. Gamblers study the tables like mystics study the kabala. It is hard enough to arrange for one—but for two? People would notice. Very bad for business." He sounds like any harassed businessman trying to balance the competing needs of two valued clients. "Besides, there is another condition. You will no longer be welcome at the tables here. I can't be bailing out my boat while you come here every night and drill more holes in it. I know you like to take chances, but you'll have to do it somewhere else from now on."

Behind the hush of the apartment's deep silence, I can hear the murmur of voices from the gaming room above—the pleasant buzz of people indulging their vices.

"It's that important to you," I ask, "getting to France and seeing your daughter again?"

Picard scoffs at my naïveté. "France? I cannot go to France. They'll arrest me. Do you know what that's like? You have exiled yourself voluntarily. Me, I am a wanted man on two continents. I have nothing but this." He leans back on the couch and waves his arm, indicating the suite of rooms and the second-rate gaming room above them. "I will have to meet my daughter somewhere else. Perhaps Morocco. Maybe Malta. Meet her on the sly, as if I were some sort of criminal."

This isn't the moment to point out that, in fact, he is a criminal.

"And, tell me, if I go back, if I see her again, will I again be the man she knew so many years ago? The sort of man a father should be for his daughter, young and strong and energetic. And will she still be my little girl? Can I regain that time?" He flashes a smile that looks like a wound. "If I were to stay here, maybe I would come to feel as the Malagasy do, that those ancient times, when she was a young girl, are still there." His fingers trembling, he stretches out his open hand. "Just there, almost within my grasp. But if I stay here, I will never see her again." He closes his fist.

"Stuck," I mutter, more to myself than to Picard.

"Tell me, Robert, are you in or out?"

"How much do you need?"

He thinks for a moment. "Eight thousand should do it. That's quite a discount on what you owe me."

"Eight—" The sum startles me. "I'll have to think about it." I try to sound casual, but am talking around a lump in my throat as big as a tennis ball.

Picard slaps the coffee table with both hands and rises to his feet. "Fine. Think about it. But don't take too long, Robert. Don't take too long."

We both understand that I haven't said no.

12

"Why, Mr. Knott, I didn't think it was possible to win this much money all at once." Annie, the embassy cashier gives me a sly smile. "You know gambling's a vice."

"There are worse, believe me."

I told Picard I needed to think it over, but it didn't take me long to grasp the inescapable. Three days after my conversation with Picard I returned to the Zebu Room and received the first package from Jacques.

"You look like you were up half the night celebrating," Annie says with a laugh.

I don't want to tell her that I spent the night staring at the ceiling, contemplating the wreck I've made of my life.

"You want this in fifties, Mr. Knott?"

"Can you make it hundreds?"

"Certainly. I'll just have to get them from Miss Brandt. She keeps them in the—"

"No. That's okay. Make it fifties."

She counts out fifteen bills and change. "Sign here, Mr. Knott." She smiles again. "Congratulations, maybe this is the beginning of a big winning streak."

"Wouldn't that be lovely?"

Across the narrow street that runs in front of the embassy, a long flight of refuse-encrusted steps, cleaned only by the uncertain rains, leads up to the center of town. Every day a blind accordionist sits at the bottom of the steps playing jaunty little tunes.

Nearly every day for more than two years, I've walked by the man without giving him so much as a kind word. This time, as I pass, I drop the musician a thousand franc note, knowing it's less an act of charity than an attempt to slip a bribe to Fate.

Somehow the man senses the banknote settling on top of the few coins he has received that morning. He tips his head back with that disconcerting appearance of exaltation so characteristic of the blind and says, "*Merci*, M'sieur Knott."

"Jesus!" I skitter around the man like a startled terrier. How does he know my name? How could he have known who it was at all? What kind of place is this, where even blind men know the unknowable?

I run up the steps two at a time until I've left him far below.

Still shaken, I walk through the gardens in the Place de l'Independence and make my way past the Presidential palace before turning down a narrow street and descending the steps on the other side of the hill.

The sight of the American Cultural Center and the thought of being yoked to its director, Gloria, for the afternoon feels like a dash of salt on the snail of my soul.

I nod at the lone, unarmed guard outside the door—the extent of security at the center—and climb the stairs to the third floor, where I stick my head into Gloria's office. Without a word of greeting, I tell her, "Let's go."

She frowns, but grabs a chi-chi little blazer she wears to appointments and calls down the corridor, "Josephine!"

Josephine Andonaka, a short woman with a beehive hairdo, likes to say she's been the press assistant for us, "since the invention of the alphabet." She appears in Gloria's doorway, a cigarette hanging from her lip and a narrow look in her eye.

"Josephine," Gloria says, "we're off to Notre Madagascar to straighten out its owner about that baby parts article." Gloria invariably speaks to her staff in English. "While I'm gone, can you write up a press release on that book donation to the university?"

Josephine waggles her head. "Certainly, Miss Burris." She shoots me an indecipherable look and disappears back down the hallway, leaving a wraith of cigarette smoke uncoiling in the doorway.

"She's not coming with us?" I ask.

"I figured I should go on these visits without staff, establish myself."

"As someone who can't take advice from more experienced hands?" I want to ask, but settle for, "You could use a translator at these things."

She sighs for my benefit. "I can speak French."

"Yeah, you can hear what this guy says, but Josephine can tell you what he means." I lean against the doorway. "When I first got here, my predecessor in the political section, a guy named Schenk, told me, 'They all speak in code around here. When you begin to understand it, it's time to go.' Believe me, you're not there yet."

Gloria looks at me blankly for a moment, then laughs.

Though I'm accustomed to the hole-in-the-wall nature of all but the biggest Malagasy periodicals, I raise my eyebrows when Gabriel, the Center's driver, pulls up in front of the ramshackle house near the train station.

"This is it?" Gloria asks.

Gabriel, a pudgy man with a worried smile, nods. "Yes, Miss Burris, *Notre Madagascar.*"

I look at Gloria "You called, told them we were coming?"

Gloria nods. "Josephine made the appointment two days ago. They should be ready."

"Let's hope we are." I get out of the car and make my way up the dirt walkway. Gloria squeezes by me so she can knock on the door before I reach it.

A thin white-haired man in a raggedy sweater answers. "Yes?"

"Is Monsieur Randrianjana in?" Gloria asks in French.

The man's clear eyes widen and a smile lights his face. "Why, yes, I am he. You must be my visitors from the American Embassy. Please come in."

With a surprisingly youthful bounce in his step, Randrianjana tiptoes to the middle of the room and fiddles with the tea things he's laid out on a wooden table, nervously scooting the cups and saucers half an inch then moving them back again. On a large table against the wall a stack of cheap paper sits beside a grimy printing press of ancient make.

He beckons us to sit down. "I'm so glad you've come. Will you have some tea with me?"

The room smells of too much wood smoke and too few baths, an earthy mix of which, over the past couple of years,

I've almost grown fond. While we seat ourselves, the white-haired publisher circles around the table pouring tea into chipped cups, his lips moving in an internal dialogue that threatens at any moment to become external.

I thank him and sip at my tea, trying to remember the date of my hepatitis inoculation.

The old man's eyes glow with pleasure. "I have never before received the attention of the American Embassy. I can't tell you how pleased I am that you've come." He takes a swallow of tea, puts the cup down, then lifts it and sips again, like a hummingbird at a flower. Each time he lifts his cup he reveals ragged holes in the elbows of his sweater. "Perhaps you have read the article I published on the United States in my last issue."

I had anticipated several ways our conversation might begin. Randrianjana's frank reference to his article was not among them.

"Over to you, Miss Burris," I murmur in English.

Gloria sets her cup down and puts on her most professional manner. "Yes, Monsieur Randrianjana, that's exactly why we have come today." Our host's smile broadens. He waits for more. "Monsieur Randrianjana, the Embassy was very disturbed by the allegations contained in your article."

A glint of concern appears in Randrianjana's eyes. "Yes, I would think so."

Gloria appears knocked off-stride. "Yes, well. It's particularly disturbing because the story is entirely false." Gloria waits for a response. When the publisher continues to gaze at her, she adds, "I suspect the source of this story could hardly be called objective."

Randrianjana blinks but doesn't appear to believe that this requires a reply from him.

I step in. "Mademoiselle Burris is trying to say that the Russian government has been known to plant articles like this in local papers."

The publisher nods and smiles. "Yes, that is exactly where I got it."

Not much point asking if they paid him. Of course they paid him. "But you made no acknowledgment of the source in your story."

"Oh, I would never do that," the white-haired man says with a little laugh.

"Why not?"

"They asked me not to."

I look at Gloria. "There. I've beaten a confession out of him."

Gloria sweeps a stray bang from her forehead. The little publisher's happy admission has left us both at a loss. "Monsieur Randrianjana, do you ever check the facts on the articles you print?"

Randrianjana waves shyly at the modest room with its obsolescent printing press. "As you can see, I have no resources for anything like that. I wish I did. Sometimes my wife helps me compose the pages and print them, but other than that…" Still smiling, he says, to me "Besides, who am I to tell anyone what's true and what's not?"

I can't think of an answer that would make sense to the old fellow. So I ask, "I'm curious, Monsieur Randrianjana, how many copies of your publication do you sell each month?"

The publisher closes his eyes and takes a considerable time in making the calculation. "Oh, perhaps a hundred. A hundred and fifty if I have a picture. I don't have the means to print regularly." He raises his upturned palms, indicating a publisher's many cares. "I must tell you that if the Russians, and sometimes the French, did not pay for the articles they give me I couldn't afford to print anything." He brightens. "Perhaps you have something on this subject you would like me to print. Then we could let the readers decide which story they believe."

Gloria closes her eyes and sighs, "Monsieur—"

"I will give you a discount on your first article."

"I'm sorry Monsieur Randrianjana, but we can't pay you to run articles for us."

A look of confusion creases his brow. "But, Mademoiselle, yours is the richest country in the world."

I step in like a traffic cop trying to untie this snarl. "Mademoiselle Burris means to say that we don't work that way. We are not allowed to pay anyone to run articles."

"I see." Randrianjana frowns thoughtfully. "This is admirable, I think." He holds out his empty hands. "But it is very hard on a poor publisher like me."

I can't help but chuckle. I look to Gloria, expecting her most censorious slow burn. To my surprise, she's smiling, too.

The editor sits back in his chair, beaming in the pleasant regard of his newfound friends. "You must have some good stories you could tell me. Something I could print."

"All right," Gloria tells him, "We'll send a denial of your previous story that you can run. And we have a press release coming out tomorrow on a major book donation to the University of Antananarivo. I'll see that you are on the distribution list."

The man's smile fades. "But this release is something you will send to everyone. Don't you have something just for me?" He raises his hand. "I promise I will not charge you."

"Well, we're not in the habit of giving exclusives." Gloria leans across the table toward the old man. "But there's a funny story about things up at the prison."

"Gloria." I can see what's coming and try to put a note of warning in my voice.

She looks at me like the old fart I no doubt appear to be to her young eyes and goes ahead, relating the story I had told her about the prison guards allowing burglars to roam at night in exchange for a cut of their take. If she sees me squirming with uneasiness, she doesn't acknowledge it. At the end she only asks, "You won't mention your source for this?"

Randrianjana puts his hand over his heart and bows his head. "Oh, I would never do that."

Before Gloria can reply, I get up from my chair and, citing pressing business, tell him we need to go. Gloria's eyebrows rise in surprise, but she pushes back from the table and we make our goodbyes.

Randrianjana appears sorry to see us go. He accompanies us to the door, inviting us to return anytime he runs an article by the Russians.

"We just might," Gloria assures him.

"I would be so pleased. Goodbye for now." He stands in the doorway, smiling and waving, as we retreat down his walkway.

As we get to the car, I tell her, "You didn't have to do that." She can see I'm sore.

"Do what?"

"Ingratiate yourself. Tell him that story. If I'd known you were going to spread it around I wouldn't have told it to you."

"Is there something eating you, Robert? I mean, what's

the big deal? He'd been fair with us and I figured we could give him something in return."

"You're not the spokesman for the Malagasy government. It's not your job to tell him stuff like that."

"For crying out loud, Robert, you're not my daddy."

"I'm not your—? Well, thank God for small favors."

"I still don't see what the big deal is. I—"

"If I'd have let you go another minute, you'd have started talking about Walt Sackett, violating the regs on his privacy."

"Well, I didn't, okay? And I wasn't going to." Now she's hot. "Look, he said he wouldn't mention his source. We gave him a story. And now he owes us one."

"Well, just see that you don't start breaking all the regs at these things."

Gloria puts her hand over her heart and bows her head. "Oh, I would never do that."

13

I learned long ago that if you dread something sufficiently it usually turns out all right. I remind myself of this as I drive to yet another evening reception, this one at the French ambassador's residence to greet the French Embassy's newly arrived number two. Once again, I'll mingle with the usual circle of invitees and have the usual dull conversations regarding the customary range of superficial topics. Did I mention that the life of a diplomat is one of adventure and romance?

I greet Ambassador Herr, who actually enjoys these things, then go in search of Marc Forestier, my counterpart at the French embassy, an ambitious young diplomat at least a dozen years my junior. While we nibble at pâté and tiny pickles, I volunteer some hearsay on opposition party machinations, tidbits that carry value only because government restrictions on the press have raised gossip to the level of valuable intelligence. In return, I ask him about disturbances in the hinterlands, in part to see how much the French Embassy knows, in part fishing for any indication that the troubles have spread beyond the coast. Forestier plays it close, which is fair enough. I've given him little and can't expect much in return.

By eight-thirty the reception line has played out. A junior officer sticks his head out the door and tells the Ambassador that no further guests are in sight. Alain Jovert, a tall, graying Frenchman of youthful manner, gives the high sign to a couple of servants, who roll back the carpet in the large salon. With a playful skip, he crosses to the stereo and replaces the tasteful Debussy with some tropical dance music, then jumps into the middle of the room and beckons to his wife, a dark-eyed Parisenne, twenty years his junior, who takes his hand and begins to dance with the lambent grace of a candle flame.

For a moment, the assembled ministry officials, businessmen and diplomats cast uncertain looks at each other. Then, with a collective laugh, they follow their host onto the dance floor. The men loosen their ties and the women kick off their heels to dance in their stocking feet. The new French diplomat who is ostensibly the guest of honor—I've already forgotten his name—stands awkwardly to one side, a birthday boy who has found his party hijacked by guests more popular than himself.

The Minister of Health, a massive and amiable fellow, decorously asks a dance of Ambassador Herr, who blinks in surprise, then laughs and accompanies him onto the floor, where she breaks out a vintage but serviceable Twist.

Her husband, Max, a former car dealer a few years on the far side of seventy, takes a chair and a Vodka Collins. "Hey, Robert," he calls, "C'mon over here and talk to me. We embassy wives get ignored at these things."

I pour myself another fruit juice and walk over to chat.

"So, young fella," he says to me, "what are you diplomats up to this evening?"

"Just the usual, Max, sniffing each other's behinds and

taking our turn pissing on the corners of the walls. How about you?"

"I'm enjoying myself e-normously. Watching people go by, sizin' 'em up." He laughs. "We old guys take our pleasures quietly, eh?" He regards the crowded dance floor. "I look at 'em and think about what kind of car I'd try to sell 'em back home. See that big fella over there dancing with my wife? Cadillac, all the way. To close the deal, I'd tell him the one he's looking at is something we ordered for someone else, but I'd be willing to sell it to him instead. He'd love that." Max takes a sip of his drink and savors his imagined duplicity.

Glass in hand, I indicate a short, irritable-seeming man squeezing between dancing couples as he makes his way across the room. "How about this guy here?"

"Him? He'll kick the tires, won't accept your best price, accuse you of cheating him, and walk away mad." Max raises his eyebrows. "Hey, I'd better shut up, he's headed this way."

"Mr. Herr, good evening." Roland Rabary, gin and tonic in hand, smiles his homely smile. "Ah, Robert, I was at the Zebu Room last night. I didn't see you."

I squeeze the glass in my hand until I think it might break. "No, you didn't."

"Your losses there are making you a folk hero."

I turn to the Ambassador's husband, hoping rumors of his hearing difficulties are true. "Sorry, Max, but I gotta get to work."

I grip Rabary's skinny bicep and pull him toward a corner of the room. "You win again at Picard's last night?" I ask between clenched teeth. "A real shame they can't pay you in dollars."

The Malagasy arches a brow. "Ah, friend Picard has been indiscreet." He tries to straighten his tie, but I hold his arm tightly in place.

"What is it you have on him? This isn't some routine shakedown for a stamp on a piece of paper. What's up?"

"As usual, Robert, when you don't understand something you lumber around saying foolish things. You really must stop before you damage your reputation."

"What reputation?" I press my fingers deeper into the Malagasy official's arm. "But if you ever again mention the Zebu Room to me in front of another American, I'll throw my drink in your face. Believe me, you won't look good with papaya juice dripping off your chin."

Rabary cringes, but when I don't toss the drink at him he tries to regain his bland demeanor. "Brother Picard has been very indiscreet indeed."

"That's right. This is a small town in a lot of ways, and after a while the only thing we have to talk about is each other." I release Rabary's arm. "Smile, Roland, people are beginning to look over here. Just smile. Then walk away."

It's late by the time Monsieur Razafy opens the gate for me, offering a nod that looks even more ironic than usual. I tell myself that after my run-in with Rabary I'm simply reading my own folly in the faces of other people.

I go upstairs and have started to undress when I hear a noise near the bed. Real? Imagined? I freeze.

"Who's there?" I ask.

Then a voice, soft, low: "Don't turn on the light. It will hurt my eyes."

"Good God, you nearly gave me a heart attack." I catch a hint of familiar perfume in the dark room. "Nirina." Why do I want to say her name like that? I try to walk it back, sound tough. "How the hell did you get in here?"

"I flew over your wall. I am a witch."

That would explain a lot. For she is no longer the young thoughtful woman I talked to in the car near Tamatave. I can tell by her voice—by the fact that she has come at all— that she is playing the wanton girl of my dreams. I know I should be asking myself why, but right now I don't really care. And I know she's counting on that.

"You really know how to put the 'mad' in Madagascar, don't you?"

"I told you. I've become a *tromba* woman."

Now I understand the odd look I got from Razafy. She must have come to the gate and told him she was expected. He would have let her in without question. A woman's beauty is all the passport she needs.

I take one try at doing what I know I should do if I have any sense. "Great," I tell her. "Now get your *tromba* ass out of my bed and go home."

"You're not going to throw me out, are you?"

"Why not?"

"I haven't got any clothes on."

I allow a fatal pause before saying, "I don't care."

"I think you do."

I search her voice for the false smile, the feigned desire. I'm sure I've heard them, then sure I haven't, then absolutely certain I don't give a damn. Caught between what I feared and what I desire, anger is the easiest emotion.

"I'm getting tired of you stalking me, Nirina. Whatever it is you think you want from me—"

"Ah, but it is you who stalks me, isn't it? In your mind?" The sound of her voice gives me a shiver. "Tell me, how many times have you thought of touching me, of having me here, in your bed?"

I can't shake my head hard enough to get rid of the answer to that one. "What do you want?"

"The same thing you want—a life I can call my own in a place I am meant to be."

"That's fine with me. What's keeping you from it?"

"The same thing that is stopping you—the life I have here."

"You really are a witch aren't you?"

"No. It's that you are in a place so foreign to you that everything seems like dark magic."

I recall Adrianansoa, the Malagasy professor, telling me that Madagascar is the land where, the more fantastic the possibility, the more imperative that it come to pass.

I feel the sweat on my skin, and feel the distance between me and the bed shrinking, as if it's crawling across the room toward me. Nirina wants something from me and knows the world's oldest way to get it. Though I can see at least that much and understand the need to resist, the world's oldest impulse spurs me forward. I'm still telling myself not to give in as I slide into the sheets beside her. I feel the warmth of her bare thigh against me and her long silky hair brushing my arm.

I kiss her on the mouth and she slides over me, pushing my shoulders against the bed with both hands, her weight comfortable, fitting perfectly against me. "There," she says, "now you've caught me."

"What do you want?"

"Just. This."

"Ahh ..."

"You don't mind? Like this?" Her dim outline hovers over me.

"Not unless ... ah ...the neighborhood kids come in ... and start calling me a sissy."

Her laugh is like blossoms falling from a tree. Whatever it is she wants, I'd give it to her just to hear her laugh again. The world outside of my bedroom ceases to exist. She moves against me, rocking back and forth until I don't care about anything.

Afterwards, lying in the dark, feeling complete for the first time in months, I hear her say, "Monsieur Knott?"

"Mnmnh."

"I must find a way to get Walt out of prison."

There it is. The price. I suppose I should tell her she doesn't need to do this to get my help. I'd do it anyway. But I decide I can bring that up later.

She leans over me and her hair falls over my face. "There is someone I can talk to. A man who can get him out of prison, but I need dollars."

"What? Who can get him out?"

"I can't tell you who. He wants four thousand dollars."

"Four thousand dollars? Doesn't anyone believe in the franc anymore?"

"Can you get it for me? Can you do this for me? For Walt?"

Her hand slides between my legs and up my thigh, and I have a glimmer of how weak I am at that moment. I tell her, "I'll do whatever you want."

"That's good. So good. Lean back."

Swirling trails of cigarette smoke and cheap cologne burn my eyes as I look over the Zebu Room. Tonight the buzz of the gamblers' voices carries the sinister menace of bees confined in a too-small hive.

"Tonic water and ice," I tell the barman, who knew me as a scotch and soda man and has lost interest in me since I gave it up.

Turning my back on the now forbidden pleasures of both drinking and gambling, I drift toward the tall windows overlooking the city and find that I can no longer bear to look at my reflection. Unconsciously, I tap the stack of fifties in the breast pocket of my coat and wait for Jacques to find me.

"Hey, Robert, whacha doin' here?"

My head snaps around so fast I fear my eyes will get left behind. "Ah. Hello, Paul." I feel like a kid caught poised in front of a store window with a rock in his hand.

Outside the normal environment of the embassy, Esmer looks like an imposter, his polo shirt and khakis a feeble disguise over his security man's soul.

"Hey, you look like you're not feelin' so good," he says.

I force a smile. "I'm fine."

"So what are you doing here?"

"Slumming. How about you?" I'm glad to see Esmer's a little drunk, his focus slightly off.

He adopts an expression meant to convey steely vigilance, though it looks more like constipation. "Yeah, me too. Just keeping an eye on things." He looks at me, puzzled. "But, hey, you're not playing."

"Maybe later."

Esmer considers this. "Later. Yeah, me too. I've already lost six thousand francs. How much is that in real money? Eighty bucks?"

"Something like that." I add nothing more, hoping Esmer will go back to the tables. When he doesn't, I start to get nervous. I decide to leave and make the rendezvous with Jacques the following night.

I clap Esmer on the shoulder, a bit of overacting that he doesn't seem to notice. "Color me gone. See you tomorrow, Paul."

"What? You just came in here five minutes ago." The security man's eyes narrow. "You're up to something."

He doesn't look so drunk that he'll forget our conversation by morning. I grope for a way out. "It looks kind of dull in here tonight, that's all."

"Tonight? You come here a lot?"

"I've been here before. Who hasn't?"

"Hey, what I mean is, do you come here often?"

"All you security guys are suspicious by nature." Trying to act casual, I swirl the ice in my glass while a trickle of sweat crawls down my chest from where the dollars in my breast pocket sit like a cancer.

"Ah, Monsieur Knott isn't it?" Jacques Razafintsalama comes up to us, spreading his arms in greeting. "We see you so seldom."

I could kiss him.

We shake hands. "Yes, Robert Knott from the American embassy. And this is Paul Esmer, embassy security."

Jacques pops his eyes wide and withdraws his hand as if burned. "Ah, security. You're here to see if our dice are loaded?"

Esmer gives him the narrow-eyed look. "All us security guys are suspicious by nature."

Jacques beams. "We are so pleased you are here, Monsieur Knott. I know the Colonel will want to extend his greetings personally."

Esmer's face droops when he realizes the invitation doesn't include him. But he's accustomed to the fact that a security officer doesn't carry as much prestige as the head of the political office, even if it's only me, and doesn't protest as Jacques and I walk away. I resist the temptation to wave goodbye.

I ask Jacques, "Should I thank you for getting this guy off me or was that just coincidence?"

"As you wish."

"Sure. You knew who he was?"

"He was someone you didn't wish to speak to. Anyone could see that."

As we near the elevator Jacques stops and holds out his hand. "I think you have a little package for me."

I glance across the room and see that Esmer's still looking at us. "For God's sake, put your hand down." He doesn't budge, so I take his hand and shake it. At the same time I tell him, "I give this to Picard myself."

Jacques smiles his regrets. "The Colonel is not available at the moment."

"You mean he doesn't want to be seen with me."

The Zebu Room's manager shakes his head in a way that doesn't mean no.

"You just told Esmer he wants to see me. You're going to look funny trying to stop me."

I walk quickly along the hall leading to Picard's office with Jacques trailing behind. "No, Monsieur Knott. You mustn't."

But I already have.

I enter without knocking. The office is empty. "Where is he?"

Jacques is puffing with irritation and anxiety. "I told you. He is not available."

I cross to the private door behind the desk, throw it open and start down the spiral staircase.

Jacques' voice calls after me, "Monsieur Knott!" I hear his heavy tread thumping down the steps behind me.

I reach the bottom step just as the big Frenchman emerges from the door of his darkened bedroom. The whiteness of his bathrobe contrasts nicely with the black pistol in his hand. I freeze, one foot poised in the air at the bottom of the steps. The door of a bedroom stands ajar, and I glimpse a face caught for a moment in the spill of light from the main room. A young woman? A young man?

Picard closes the door behind him. "How are you, Robert?" he purrs.

Jacques has stopped halfway down the stairs. "I told him you were not available, Colonel, but—"

I break in. "But he also said you wanted to see me. So, I took my pick."

For a moment Picard keeps his pistol trained on my navel, then waves it away almost playfully. "I apologize for the drama, Robert. Sometimes a client loses more than he believes he can afford and goes a little crazy. I have to be ready." He sticks the hand with the pistol into the pocket of his robe. "You need to be careful, Robert. One of these days I may end up killing you. It would be a shame if it were an accident."

Weighing the ambiguity of Picard's remark, I unwind from the staircase and step into the middle of the room. I draw the envelope of fifties from the inside pocket of my coat. "Just making my first payment."

"You shouldn't come barging into a man's quarters like this. Ever." The big man's shoulders slump, the tension gone, and he raises his eyes toward the gamblers losing their money to him on the floor above. "War was much simpler than running a gambling den. Kill the enemy so that he doesn't kill you. What could be more clear? What could better trigger that exhilarating urge to survive?" He looks at the ceiling as if searching for an answer on its bone-white surface. "I've killed a lot of men, Robert. But it became a terrible bore." His eyes take on a faraway cast, then come back to me. Picard looks a little startled, as if he'd forgotten I was there. "The dead look so relaxed, so beyond caring, that one envies them." He executes a careless shrug. "I have tried to stop envying the dead. Now I simply steal from the living." He raises his chin toward the envelope in my hand. "Set it on the coffee table."

I toss the money down and take my first easy breath since I entered the room. But I don't take my eyes off Picard. "And you have something for me?"

"Jacques has it," Picard says. "You will make your exchanges with him in the future, not with me." He looks at Jacques, who descends into the room, takes a package of Malagasy francs from his coat pocket and holds it out to me, giving me a look that says he won't soon forget the embarrassment I've caused him.

Picard picks up the stack of dollars from the coffee table. His eyes darken with suspicion. "It feels a little thin, Robert."

"Yeah, the embassy is only giving us bank rates now, not the official rate, and they started charging a fee. Besides, I didn't want to exchange too much at once."

When I handed Nirina part of the stack of fifties the previous night, the lie had seemed perfectly plausible. Standing now in front of an impatient man with a gun in his pocket, I feel my confidence seeping out through my pores.

"All right, Robert." Picard flips his hand toward the staircase, letting me know it's time to go back to the Zebu Room. "I'm glad we had this little chat."

"Yes, it's been lovely."

Picard turns toward his bedroom, but stops and says to me over his shoulder. "And remember, don't ever again come in here unannounced."

14

I lean against the wall of the little cell and look at Walt
Sackett, see the dullness in his eyes and the waxy gleam
of his skin. Kneeling by the American's cot, Gloria hands
him a bottle of pills from Dr. André and tells him how
often to take them.

Speedy sits cross-legged on his bed, looking at Walt with
concern—and at Gloria with something else entirely.

"Mademoiselle Gloria?" he asks.

"Yes, Dokoby?" Over the last couple of visits, she has
softened toward the young Malagasy. She insists on using
his given name as a last line of resistance, but I can see that,
despite herself, she's giving in to his unceasing charm. Girls
are suspicious of charm. But Speedy sees something in her
that I don't—that nobody does—and she knows it.

"Monsieur Walt is going to get well?"

Walt's French isn't very good, but I'm sure he understands
the question. Gloria's answer seems directed at the aging
cowboy. "The medicines will make him better, and I've
brought some beef broth to make him feel stronger."

"Miss Nirina brings him food every day."

"Ah, yes, Miss Nirina. I must meet her someday."

"She's Monsieur Walt's girlfriend." Speedy chews this

over and decides it needs something more. "Everyone needs someone, Miss Gloria."

"All right, Dokoby, that's enough," she says gently. Is that a blush I see on her cheeks?

"Hey, I'm still here." Walt tries to make it a joke, but we all hear the tone in his voice and no one laughs. He looks away and says quietly, "I think I'm going to need to get out of here pretty soon if I'm going to get out at all."

"We're doing everything we can," Gloria says, though she has to understand how feeble that sounds. "The Ambassador will write to the Foreign Minister. The Ministry has said her letter will receive every consideration."

"Well, I guess that ought to do it."

Walt's gentle sarcasm knocks the props out from under Gloria and she slumps against his bed. Walt reaches over and touches her hair.

I've seen how much these visits take out of her. She needs increasingly more time to recover from each one, as if she takes home some measure of Walt Sackett's illness. She's one of those people who has known nothing but success, if only in a Rotary Club award kind of way, and her inability to get Walt out of prison is killing her.

Walt looks across the cell at me. "You're standing a long way off, Robert. Why don't you come over here and join the fun?"

I shuffle over to Speedy's cot and sit down.

"You act like you're at my funeral, Robert. Kinda tough on a fella's morale." Walt makes a try at his old laugh.

Speedy reaches under his bed and retrieves a fading chrysanthemum, a hint of the night's freshness still on it. "Miss Gloria, you didn't tell me what kind of flower you like, so I picked this one for you." He holds it out to her.

Like an overloaded circuit, Gloria's face goes blank.

"Be nice," I tell her in English, "Take the flower.".

The young thief adds in English, "Yes, Miss Gloria, be nice to Speedy. I picked it from in front of the Presidential Palace."

She takes the flower in the tips of her fingers. "Thank you, Dokoby," She breathes in its scent. "But be careful. Don't be caught picking flowers from the president's palace."

The young Malagasy makes a serious face. "Yes. They might throw me in prison."

Gloria is too moved to even smile.

Walt picks up the broken thread of the conversation. "So, Robert, have you talked to Nirina yet?"

I hope my face doesn't show the unease twisting my gut.

"Yeah, we finally had the chance." Does Walt know she's trying to find the money to get him out of prison? Maybe. Probably. And she knows that if she spends it to get him out of here, he can't pay her back, that there's no pot of gold waiting his return to America. Maybe she really thinks he'll marry her and she'll get the visa to go to the United States, finally see that other world.

Walt's eyes shine with his fondness for her. "She takes good care of me, Robert. Don't know quite why an old guy like me deserves it."

"She'll help you any way she can."

"She's a great little girl."

Surprised that my conscience can leave me too abashed to speak, I nod in agreement and tell myself that this stuff must be even tougher on decent people.

The two clergymen stand side by side in the embassy lobby, surrounded by the Malagasy and American staffs. The Protestant minister is the younger, dressed in the black suit and white collar of the local Methodist church. The Catholic priest, despite his white hair and stooped frame, makes an impressive sight in the full regalia of a bishop, a smoking censer in his hand.

Pale from overwork, her skin almost translucent, Ambassador Herr introduces the two clergymen, adding, "We are so pleased to have these reverend visitors with us this afternoon to bless the commencement of work on our remodeled entrance."

Though everyone knows the truth, the Ambassador doesn't mention the real reason for the clergymen's presence. Despite the pleadings of reason and faith, many within the Malagasy staff still refuse to risk bringing the former protocol secretary's curse upon their heads by entering the embassy through the space that was her office, and the two clergymen have come to perform a public exorcism.

The ministers smile gravely at each other before starting on a long, slow circuit through the lobby, offering their prayers and blessings, giving particular attention to the deserted protocol office, leaving behind them a haze of smoke and a whiff of incense.

Like all fine ceremonies, it ends with tea and cookies.

I wish my problems could be exorcised so easily. I grab a couple of cookies and head toward my office, but stop when Lynn steps in front of me, her eyes hard as agate as she reaches into the pocket of her slacks and pulls out a piece of torn cloth.

"What's this?"

"Um, percale?"

"Get serious. One of the mechanics found this shoved under the back seat of the car you took to Tamatave."

"I told you. We had a young woman with us when we drove away from the village after Samuel got shot. She tore pieces off her dress for bandages."

She looks at me with disbelief edging toward contempt.

"Oh, come on." It's been so long since I've been falsely accused of something that I feel righteous. "You think I'm tearing dresses off women in the back seats of embassy cars now?"

"No," she grunts. But the expression on her face says she would have enjoyed believing exactly that.

"This is a funny time to start getting jealous."

"Don't flatter yourself." The look in her eye only slowly changes from anger to suspicion. "And why are you suddenly exchanging so many francs for dollars? I'm not blind. I see you every few days at Annie's window, handing over a stack of francs."

"My luck changed. I'm on a roll down at the Zebu Room."

She scoffs. "You've turned your whole life into one long losing streak. The gods ain't smiling on you again in this lifetime. Robert, do you ever step back and take a look at yourself, ever ask yourself what you're really doing?"

"Self-awareness is a pretty heavy burden when you're a natural asshole."

"So, tell me about the money."

Caught off guard, I struggle to come up with a plausible lie. I'm beginning to fear I'll actually have to tell her the truth when, despite Lynn's assertion, the gods smile on me. Paul Esmer comes up to interrupt us.

"Lynn," the security officer says, "I need to talk to you and the Ambassador. We need Pete Salvatore, too."

Lynn gives me a last withering look before turning to Esmer. "What's up?"

"Our friend's report of trouble at the coast." He nods toward me. "It's old news now. Word is that there was some sort of riot down at Antsirabe in the last couple of days." Antsirabe is only a two-hour drive to the south.

"Anti-government stuff?" I ask.

"Anti-everything. Shops looted, a policeman shot, city hall stoned. Or so they say. I don't know how much of it is true, and there's nothing in the papers or on TV. The part that has me worried is talk of gangs mobbing foreigner's houses, overwhelming the guards and breaking in. Smash, grab, gone."

"You figure it's heading this way?" I ask.

"A contact over at Interior tells me there was trouble in Fort Dauphin a week ago. So, it seems to have been working its way north for a while."

"You want to meet right now?" Lynn asks.

"Yeah. I need to brief the Ambassador and DCM on this, and I need to talk to you about beefing up the guard force." Though the security office supervises the guards, it's admin that hires and pays them.

Esmer spots the Ambassador saying goodbye to the clergymen. He rolls his shoulders and says, "I'd better grab the old gal before she gets away." When things get tense, Esmer's Bogart shtick becomes more pronounced.

With Esmer gone, Lynn eyes me again. "We both know I should be talking to Paul about your sudden need for dollars, cashing in stacks of Malagasy francs."

"But you're not going to."

"Shut up, just for once." Her eyes flare with anger. "No, I'm not going to. You know why? Because I used to see something pretty decent in you. Idiot that I am, I still think it's there somewhere. But you'd better find it quick."

"Oh, Robert." The Ambassador's words cut through the spell. "Lynn and I have to meet with Paul in a moment, but I wanted to ask you if you've seen Gloria today."

Though I don't really want to attend the meeting with Esmer, I feel the wound of not being asked. And I wonder when the Ambassador started assuming it was my job to keep tabs on her Public Affairs Officer.

"No, ma'am, I haven't seen her."

Michelle Herr's worry lines deepen. "I needed to talk to her about something, but she wasn't in her office. Apparently she hasn't been in all day."

"Did anyone call her house?"

"The phones are dead in Ivandry, and we can't seem to raise her on the radio." She gives me the smile she uses when she's about to ask me for something she thinks I'm actually capable of doing. "I think you live closer to her than any of us. Why don't you stop by on your way home? You know how we all love her."

Whenever I want to resent her, she says something like this and means it.

"Sure."

"Thank you, Robert," she says and heads upstairs.

The PAO's house is at the bottom of a narrow lane above the rice paddies bordering Ivandry. The guard opens the gate as I pull up.

"Is Miss Gloria in?"

The old guy, a fellow named Masiso, had briefly been my

guard a year earlier but is still too shy to speak to me. He waggles his head and points toward the front door.

When no one answers my knock, I let myself in.

"Gloria?"

No response. No maid, no houseboy, no cook. I picture finding Gloria with a box of Kleenex, nursing a cold and watching TV in the living room. But the TV isn't on and the room's empty except for a lot of still-unopened packing boxes.

I know the modest single-story house from my evenings of bringing the former PAO home drunk. In every corner lurk the ghosts of those nights when Boswell could barely stumble through the door and his wife glared at me with undisguised loathing.

I head down the hall. To my surprise, the master bedroom is unused, empty but for a desk and a twin bed pushed against the wall. I go to the next room down the hall, wondering why she would take the smaller bedroom for herself, as if she were a guest in her own house. The picture of a Gloria different from the one I've known begins slowly to come into focus.

I tap on the door and go in. The dark bedroom smells of sickness and sweat—odors that pose unspoken duties on anyone without enough sense to back out of the room and go away.

"Gloria?"

A groan comes from the bed.

I pull back a curtain and open the sliding glass door. Daylight pours in and a wave of fresh air swirls through the room.

Gloria, looking small and gray, lies sunk in a pile of pillows. She groans again and squints against the sudden light, but she doesn't have the strength to put a hand over her eyes.

"What's with you?"

She tries to raise her head. "I'm sick."

"Yeah, I can see that."

A pot, half full of something I don't want to look at, sits on the floor next to her. Magazines lay scattered on the rumpled bedclothes alongside a plate with a bit of crusted food on it. Today's Monday. She must have been sick all weekend.

"What've you got?"

Like a bad phone connection, there's a lag before she replies. "I don't know. I've been sick to my stomach and have a fever." Her voice trails off.

There's no point pressing her for detailed symptoms. I'm not a doctor and Madagascar is full of unidentified fevers that come and go, occasionally taking the sufferer with them.

"Don't you have any staff?"

"No. I meant to hire some, but ..."

"You haven't even unpacked yet."

"I haven't had time."

I swear quietly to myself and pick up the pot by the bed. I empty it in the hall toilet, take it into the kitchen and fetch a new one. I set it on the floor beside her bed and put my hand on her forehead.

"When was the last time you took your temperature?"

"I don't have a thermometer," she croaks.

"You have any aspirin?"

She shakes her head as if it might break. "I threw them up."

I go back to the kitchen and fill a pan with water and ice.

I grab a bottle of water from the fridge and a towel from a rack by the stove. When I come back to her room I heft the bottled water. "Here, see if you can keep this down."

I unscrew the plastic cap and hold the bottle toward her. Instead of taking it, she puts her hand on mine and tilts the bottle toward her, sipping from it like a baby bird before falling back onto her pillow, panting.

Taking off my coat, I sit on the edge of the bed, soak the towel in the ice water and lay it sopping wet on her forehead. The cold water runs down her face and neck. She gasps and her hands jerk into the air.

"Okay, okay. Don't start flying around the room," I tell her. "Why didn't you call the embassy, get Dr. André out here?"

"The line is …" She nods vaguely toward the phone on the nightstand.

"How about using your radio?"

"I let the battery run down and was too sick to plug it back in."

"Why haven't you got any staff?"

"I can look after myself."

"Yeah, I can see that. Just like you're going to make yourself well without any help. And your boxes are going to unpack themselves. And you're going to supervise your office staff right into the ground. Oh, shit, you're not going to start crying, are you?"

She tries to say something, but I can't make it out.

"Look, you've probably got one of those things that you're just going to have to ride out." I don't tell her that I believe she has become sick for Walt's sake, trying to take some of it from him. "When I get to my place I'll radio Post One to send Dr. Andre out here."

"Don't go." She can barely croak the words out. "Stay."

"No way. If I hang around here, I'm going to get whatever it is you've got and ... Oh, for crying out loud." I hand her my handkerchief.

She dries her eyes and collects herself. "Please don't go," she says a little more firmly.

I pick up the phone. Still dead. "You got any Jell-O?"

"Jell-O? I might have some in the pantry. It's—"

"I know where the pantry is. I saw Boswell throwing up in there once."

In the kitchen, I mix the Jell-O with hot water, throw in a little salt and grab a couple of ice cubes from the freezer. "You make your ice with bottled water?" I ask, calling toward the back bedroom. When I get no response I throw the ice away.

Drinking the Jell-O seems to do her good. I take one of the magazines from the bed and start toward the living room.

"Don't go." Gloria looks at me with such pleading that I stop. I stand at the foot of her bed and flip through a few pages.

"Good gawd, what is this?" I look at the cover, "*Marie-Claire*. How old are you?"

"Twenty-four."

"You're young enough to be my—"

I realize later I shouldn't have stood there so long without finishing my sentence.

"What?"

"Nothing." I settle into a cane chair near the sliding glass door.

She looks at me, little lines of puzzlement furrowing her smooth young brow.

I flip a couple more pages without looking at her. "I'll bet you got in the foreign service straight out of college."

"Yes. Brown," she says with a hint of pride.

"Figures. Straight A's in high school, probably at Brown too. Debate club. Voted 'Most Likely to Succeed.' Degree in International Relations. Never dated."

"Engineering," she whispers. "The rest is pretty close."

"Engineering?" I snort. "I'll bet your dad was tough on you. Wanted a boy, expected the world of you."

"And I did it. Made myself do it all."

Despite her illness, something almost savage in her voice gives me an idea of the determination that drove her—and a glimpse of what it cost her.

"It's our survival skills that finally kill us," I say quietly. She says nothing. "And you cry too easily."

"How old is your daughter?"

"What's my daughter got to do with anything?"

She looks at me for a long time before saying, "Okay. I get it."

Only then do I get it too. I don't want to know what a shrink would make of it, but I see with frightening clarity that my problem with Gloria has something to do with my daughter. Could reconciling with Gloria put me on track to patching things up with Christine? Maybe. Probably not.

Out of the quiet lacuna that follows she says, "I'll bet you did well in school, too."

"Me? I got voted 'Most Likely to be Found Dead in a Motel Room'."

She looks at me. "Married."

"You or me?"

"You."

"Not anymore."

"How old is your—?"

"I thought we'd dropped that." I shrug and act like I don't care. "Sixteen."

She looks at me quietly. "You don't do well with women, do you?"

I grunt.

"It's because you're afraid."

Has she been talking to Nirina? "Just another foreign country to me." I lean back in the chair and pretend to read.

"And you don't understand because you don't want to."

"I think the fever's making you crazy."

Her eyes look so weary—physically, emotionally—that I think for a moment I might cry, too.

She lifts her chin and says quietly, "Pax?"

"If you bat your eyelashes at me, I swear I'm going to walk out that door and leave you here to die."

She's still pale and weak and the smile she gives me looks like one of those things a good mortician works onto a corpse. "Pax?"

"What do you want? Someone to draw up a peace treaty and have me sign it?"

"Pax?"

"Yeah, fine. Pax. Whatever." Her eyes stay on me until I have to look away. "What's that other mag you got there?"

She looks at it. "*Vogue*."

"You can have this one back. Slide me the *Vogue*."

We sit together for a long time, saying nothing, looking through our magazines. About five o'clock she falls asleep. When it gets dark, I turn on the light and find a book to read.

15

I see it first in *Midi*.

I arrive late in the morning, after Cheryl has already laid the morning papers on my desk. As I'm hanging up my coat, she calls to me from her desk. "That's funny about the burglars, isn't it?"

"What are you talking about?"

"That story you and Gloria gave them about the burglars."

A sickening dread lowers over the burned stump of my being. "Oh. That. Yeah."

With the self-conscious nonchalance of a condemned man carefully combing his hair before walking down that long corridor, I make myself a cup of coffee, sit down at my desk and pick up the morning's *Midi*.

The story is page one: "American Embassy Accuses Prison Guards of Abetting Burglaries." My eyes run quickly down the untidy columns. It's all there, the guards letting the burglars out at night, taking their cut, letting them back in. No quotes from government officials, guards, or burglary victims—much less the burglars—only a paragraph citing the American press attaché as the source. Even as my heart falls into my socks I wonder how in the hell they got the story. And in the same instant I know there's only one possibility.

"Cheryl," I call through the open door, "do we have *Notre Madagascar?*"

"It came in yesterday afternoon. Should be at the bottom of your pile."

Buried on page three, after a page one article on the prowess of the Russian national hockey team—did the Russians really think there were a lot of hockey fans in Madagascar?—and a page two piece regarding the wine industry in Burgundy, Randrianjana, that gray-haired loon, has run a brief story about the burglars, with an attribution to the American Embassy's press attaché.

"Well, bless his heart."

"Sorry?"

"Nothing." I'm sure that if I were to ask the old guy why he mentioned Gloria, he would tell me he wanted to demonstrate his professionalism by citing his sources. Never mind that he promised he wouldn't.

I hear Cheryl's phone ring. "Hi, Alice. He's right here, Alice. Right away, Alice." She hangs up and calls to me. "That was Alice."

"Really."

"The Ambassador would like to see you."

"When?"

"Now."

As overwork saps her health and erodes her defenses, Michelle Herr's Tennessee graciousness tends to either kick into antebellum overdrive or disappear under a layer of ice. When I walk into her office I see immediately which one I'm going to get. I've always known that, when crossed, she can throw a red velvet tomahawk with the best of them, but I've never seen her angry until now.

It looks like she's convened a court martial. Pete Salvatore, the DCM, gives me a look that says he doesn't need this kind of trouble right now. Lynn has come with her notepad. Esmer is reading the article in *Midi*, moving his lips as he translates the French to himself. Gloria is busy studying her feet.

I take the one seat remaining. At first the Ambassador expresses the hope that the story in *Notre Madagascar* is false. After all, Madagascar's best creative fiction is generally found on the front pages of the daily newspapers. When I shake my head, she suggests that the story's attribution to the American press attaché has come from the fevered imagination of *Notre Madagascar's* well-meaning but unbalanced publisher.

Gloria's downcast eyes and my awkward throat-clearing tell her all she needs to know.

"So you're saying to me you really gave him this story?" the Ambassador asks.

Lynn looks at me meaningfully but says nothing. I can hear her asking herself why she ever bothered with me. I haven't got an answer for her.

"Do you understand how this will look?" Michelle Herr asks me. I know better than to answer. "Due to your lack of success with your counterpart at the Foreign Ministry, the Malagasy government turned down our request for help on this UN resolution. Now they are going to think that, in retribution, we have decided to publicly embarrass them."

"I don't really think they'll see it that way, Ambassador."

"I disagree, Robert. I really do." A vein pulses through the layers of foundation on her forehead. "I sent you with

Gloria as the more experienced officer, precisely to see that this sort of thing didn't happen." She turns on her PAO. "And why would you tell them this story? Surely you knew the publisher couldn't be trusted."

Still pale and thin from her illness, Gloria blinks at the Ambassador, unable to speak. I know that if she starts crying Michelle Herr will give up on her as she's already given up on me.

Before Gloria can hang herself by blurting out either tears or the truth, I step in, "No, ma'am. I was the one who told him. He just got us mixed up."

The Ambassador's eyes shift back to me.

"It was right at the end of our visit. We were talking about this and that and I decided to tell him a funny story. That's all."

My confession makes her anger perfect, something she can indulge in with no risk of regret.

"I thought as much," she says with grim pleasure. Her fists clenched, she stands up and starts pacing the short distance between her desk and the couch, no doubt picturing her political friends back in Washington talking about how she made a mess of things in Madagascar. I want to tell her that no one cares what happens in Madagascar except us. But that would only make things worse.

"I expect a call from the Foreign Ministry any minute," she continues, "asking us to explain ourselves. Can I at least tell them that this story about the burglars is accurate? You weren't just making things up."

"That's right."

"And how are you so sure?"

"Walt Sackett mentioned it to me."

"He's the American you haven't yet managed to free from prison."

"Yes, ma'am."

Ambassador Herr's eyes narrow with displeasure. Gloria has returned to looking at her feet, though her eyes goggle in wonder as I weather Michelle Herr's wrath.

The Ambassador overreacts for a few more minutes, asking how this could have happened, etcetera, etcetera. Finally, when her anger has sucked all the air out of the room, leaving everyone unable to speak, the meeting breaks up.

I feel Lynn's eyes crawling all over me. She's seen me lie before and surely recognizes my phony confession for what it is. Still, I doubt that the look she's giving me is one of new-found regard.

As I reach the doorway, Ambassador Herr says to my back, "At least see if you can find out what's going on at the Foreign Ministry so I can be ready. Call your friend over there. What's his name?"

"Roland Rabary." I want to add, "And he's no friend," but it's too late to introduce new business to the agenda.

We walk down the hall together, me toward my office, Gloria toward the car waiting to take her back to the center. At the top of the stairs she stops and asks, "Why?"

"I'm screwed anyway. No point killing your career, too. Besides, it was a favor to her. It helps the old girl when she only has one person to focus on."

"Thanks. I mean …" She wants to say something more but can't find the words and finally turns and hurries down the steps toward the door.

As I continue down the hall, I can see Esmer standing all too casually outside the security office door, pretending to read *Midi*.

"Do they have 'Peanuts' in there?" I ask as I try to walk past. I can see he had wanted to get in the first word, to casually say, "Oh, Robert" as I go by, and it bugs him to have me step on his line.

"Oh, Robert." He tucks the paper under his arm, determined to recover the initiative. "A funny thing. I was talking to Annie down in admin the other day and happened to mention the casino. She tells me you've been coming in regularly with stacks of francs, saying something about a big winning streak."

I'm still in full defensive mode from the meeting and manage to absorb this new blow without blinking. "Yeah. What of it?"

"I thought you said you almost never went in there."

"No. I said I almost never see you there." Esmer's eyes narrow. I can see that his memory of our conversation that night isn't very sharp. "Sure, I go in now and then," I tell him, "and when you're hot you don't want to walk away." I switch subjects. "So, what's the news from Antsirabe?"

Esmer follows the bait. "It's gone quiet. The cops say they've arrested the ringleaders. And they're telling everyone it was the foreigners who stirred them up."

"And then the foreigners tried to deflect suspicion from themselves by ransacking their own houses?"

Esmer produces a lopsided grin. "The authorities hope no one wants to think about it too closely."

"What happens next?"

"That's what I'm asking my contacts over in the Interior Ministry. They're telling me it's all over."

"You believe that?"

"Nah. These Interior guys are like some half-assed fire department, beating out embers on the lawn while the house burns down in front of them. This ain't over yet. You got a gun?"

"You know I don't."

"Some of the gangs have been wearing a kind of magic vest they think can stop bullets. They go off to rob some house. The owner comes out with a gun. But he doesn't really want to kill anyone, so he fires over their heads. And these guys figure the vests work. Now they're not afraid of anything."

I raise my eyebrows to show I'm impressed.

Esmer continues, "Anyway, I've got a couple of extra pistols. Glocks. Military issue. Enough stopping power to knock Godzilla back six feet."

"Even if he had one of those magic vests on?"

Esmer smiles. He loves this kind of talk and adopts his Bogart twitch. "Look, Bob, if trouble starts heading this way, come over to the house and I'll lend you some heat. You'll thank me later."

"I'll keep this in mind." I walk away, happy to have ended the conversation on something other than the Zebu Room.

It takes half the morning to get through to Rabary.

"Don't pretend you don't know what this is about," I tell him by way of greeting. The line is silent so long I think it's gone dead.

"All right, I won't," Rabary finally replies. Clearly, he doesn't want to talk with me any more than I want to talk with him.

"How's this story going over with the Ministry?"

"Like the lead balloon."

I can see Rabary smiling to himself for coming up with the idiomatic expression.

"Is the Foreign Minister going to call the Ambassador on the carpet?"

Another long pause. I love overloading Rabary's circuits with a direct question.

"Look, Robert, we know you weren't the source on this story. Clearly, the Russians have this Randrianjana fellow in their pocket and they've given him something to embarrass the United States so that—What was that, Robert?"

"Nothing."

"If you think this is funny…"

"No, no, just clearing my throat." It should have occurred to me that no one at the ministry would think to take the article at face value.

Rabary continues. "We're only trying to figure out if the real target was you or us. Who are they trying to embarrass?"

A pot this juicy has to be stirred. I lean back in my chair, enjoying myself in spite of everything. "Hey, maybe it was aimed at both of us. They figured your government and mine might be getting too cozy. Planted this story to wedge us apart."

"Yes," Rabary says, "Exactly the thought here. But who? Everyone here believes it's the Russians. But, frankly, I think it might be the French."

"Yeah, sounds just like 'em, the bastards. What happens next?"

"From us?" Rabary asks. "Nothing."

"That's generally the wisest course."

"The President is very angry. Every burglary victim in the city is demanding compensation from the government."

"Hey, maybe he could reimburse them from his Swiss bank account."

Rabary sighs and hangs up.

I'm seeing Jacques at the Zebu Club so often I'm afraid people will think we're dating. In fact, though, the meetings are so quick I can't imagine anyone notices. At least that's my hope. Our handoffs would be even quicker but Jacques must relay increasingly impatient messages from Picard. Shorn of their anger, puzzlement, and implied threats, they boil down to the question of why I'm I bringing him so few dollars for so many francs.

I tell him the rates have changed, fees have increased, the embassy is low on dollars, the transit of Venus has left Mars in the house of Sagittarius. I tell him I have to hold some francs back to keep from looking suspicious. I tell him anything but the truth, which is that I'm giving a big hunk of every transaction to Nirina so she can free Walt Sackett.

My litany of excuses and pleading grows thinner with every meeting. Whatever friendly relationship I might once have enjoyed with Jacques I destroyed when I stiff-armed past him to run down the stairs to Picard's apartment that night. Now he adds his own bit of menace to Picard's importunings. "The Colonel's patience with you is at an end."

"What patience? He's been nagging me about this since day one. Tell him to back off or the well runs dry."

Who am I kidding? Certainly not Jacques. He sees my bluff for what it is, an act of defiance about as empty as a chicken flipping off the fox as it comes in for the kill. His glower turns a shade heavier. "The Colonel reads the papers. He knows the official rate. You have a week to pay him in full for all the cash he's given you."

"Hey, if he's going to believe everything he reads in the papers...."

I swear I can hear myself sweat.

Just in case I wasn't listening, he repeats, "A week."

I see the set of Jacques' face and don't have to ask "Or what?" Maurice may claim he's out of practice but, as he said himself, he's killed men for a lot less than not paying their dues.

I'm shaking by the time I get to my car.

16

I wake from a dream about Walt Sackett so vivid in detail and so obscure in meaning that I feel disoriented. The dark forms around me became gradually clear. Yes, I'm lying in my own bed. Beside me, Nirina breathes slowly in her sleep.

I never know when she will come. When she does, she comes alone and always at night. She seldom stays more than a few minutes, only long enough to take from me the dollars I'm stealing from Picard so she can buy Walt Sackett's freedom.

Whatever her intent, the nature of our brief transactions feels like an unholy middle ground between extortion and the harlot's trade, though in fact, after that first visit, she has kept me not only figuratively but literally at arm's length. I tell myself that she's only bruised my male pride by hammering home how utterly resistible I am. Truthfully, it's more than that. I can live without the girl I found in my bed that night, the one who walked away from me the next morning. But I long for the vulnerable young woman who spoke to me with such honesty in the car near Tamatave, the one who could make me desire the thing I always avoid, a real connection.

Not that I have much to worry about on that score. She understands that I want Walt out of jail as much as she does. She doesn't really need to offer me anything else. Ours is a strictly business relationship—or was, until this evening.

She hardly said a word when she arrived last night. When she spoke she avoided my eyes. When she finally looked at me, I saw such pain, such need that, in a staggering failure of imagination, I held out my hand and led her upstairs.

We struggled in bed like animals, panting and groaning and crying out. The moment we found our release we separated, dazed and unhappy.

Afterward, I hand her the money. At first she tells me to put it in the pocket of her dress, then asks to count it first. "A hundred and sixty dollars? That's it?"

"Admin's watching me. I can't cash big bundles anymore."

"And Monsieur Picard is happy with this?"

"No, he's not happy with this. I keep telling him this is all I can do, but he thinks I'm holding back on him."

"You are."

"You think I don't know it?" I'm shouting. "How about the guy you say you're bribing? Can't you delay him? What's the hurry?"

"He has his own needs. He tells me he needs it now."

"Who's it for? Who do you have on the hook? You've never told me."

"You don't need to know."

I've short-changed Picard nearly four thousand dollars, telling myself that I'll have plenty of time later to think of how I'll deal with the Frenchman. "Later" has come, and I haven't got a clue.

Well, what's he going to do about it, kill me?

Yes.

I look at the clock. It's only ten. I'd thought it was the middle of the night. Without waking Nirina, I slip from the coil of twisted sheets, put on my robe and go downstairs. I dial the phone in the dark and wait out the long pause while the signal travels halfway around the world. If I had any sense, I'd just call Christine on her cell phone and avoid the risk of my ex or her new husband picking up. Of course, if I had any sense I wouldn't be in my present fix.

Over the static in the line, I hear the ring, imagine it reverberating off the cold tile of the kitchen thousands of miles away, ringing from the small table near the front door, disturbing the peace of the upstairs bedroom, where my former wife lies every night with another man. I realize it's late morning back there and Christine is at school, the adults at work. My call rings in an empty house.

I let it ring a little longer, loopily imagining that I'm putting down layers of sound that might still be pulsing when Christine comes home and she'll know I called, that I was thinking about her before I was murdered.

I hang up, go upstairs, and climb back into bed.

"Where have you been?" Nirina asks, lying on her side, her back to me.

"Downstairs."

"You were trying to call your daughter."

"When did I ever tell you about her?"

"I knew."

"You've added clairvoyance to your witching skills?"

"Is that what you tell yourself? That I am holding you through sorcery?"

"You're going to tell me it's love?"

She won't face me. "There is no gain in loving you, only

loss. If I had thought I could love you that way, I would never have done this."

"You just jump into bed with me now and then to keep me under control."

"Monsieur Knott——" She says it like a school teacher bringing a miscreant boy to attention.

"I think you can go ahead and call me Robert by now."

"Monsieur Knott, I do this for love—as you do."

"Me? Are you kidding? I love no one." I hear the note of self-pity in my voice and despise myself for it.

"I almost wish it were true, but you are full of love. For your daughter. For Walt. For Samuel the driver. For Miss Gloria. For the woman from the embassy you speak of, the one who slept here before me. But you stay at a distance from all of them because you are afraid."

I think about telling her to shut up.

With a graveyard laugh, she adds, "You think you're wicked, but you are only frightened and cynical. And cynicism is only another way of being naive."

"You're too damn smart for someone your age."

"I'm Malagasy. I am thousands of years old."

"And I'm just lucky enough to get you when you're only—" I thought for a moment I wanted to guess her age, but suddenly realize I don't.

"You and I have each swallowed a stone." She says it so quietly I can barely hear her.

"Sorry?"

"A Malagasy proverb. We have each taken on problems too big for us."

The clarity of her judgment irritates me. "I can take care of my own problems. What about you? What happens if you manage to leave Madagascar with Walt and get to the

U.S.? Do you really think everything will be just fine after that?"

"I don't know. I'm only sure that I need to go. Perhaps I'll be more alive. Perhaps I'll begin to die." She hugs her pillow like a life jacket. "Do you believe in fairy tales?"

"Of course not."

"You should. They show the world we believe in, deep down. In your Western fairy tales there is always a young man leaving home to seek his fortune. He slays the monster, finds the hidden treasure, marries the beautiful princess. In ours, a young man leaves home and is eaten by a magic tree, or his brothers die because he is not there to protect them, or he marries a woman, brings her back home to his village, and she is murdered by his parents."

"You're saying nothing good comes of leaving home."

"Of changing anything."

"But you're going to do it anyway."

"Yes. And I'll have to make this journey without my family. Or maybe I will find that they're always with me, no matter where I go—my brothers, my mother."

Do I love her? I honestly don't know. But I admire the hell out of her. She's got more courage than I've ever dreamed of having. "Your father too? He'll be with you?"

She lets go of her pillow and turns onto her back, staring at the ceiling.

The soft parting of her lips before she speaks stirs a nerve deep inside me. "My father is dead. It was a week ago."

All the usual words of condolence demand to be said, but I can't bring myself to say them. I've been such a phony she wouldn't believe me.

"So it will be that much easier to leave now," I tell her.

Did she laugh, or sob?

"Walt thinks you're in love with him." She says nothing. "What will you do when you get him out of prison? He'll stay with you here in Antananarivo?" I can barely discern the shake of her head. "All right. When you spring him— if you spring him—he can stay here with me a few days. The embassy will lend him the money to get a plane ticket home." She stares at the ceiling. I bore in. "And I'll bet you think you're going with him when he leaves for America. You're going to live with him there."

It takes her a long time, but finally she speaks. "I know he has no money. At one point, yes, I thought he was wealthy and would help me. I was going to go to America with him. And when I got there I was going to leave him and find Bud."

"Bud!?" The image of the red-headed Marine pops into my mind like the clown from a jack-in-the-box. She has got to be shitting me. That jarhead? "Bud!"

"He's the most kind and gentle man I have ever met. He would let me be who I need to be."

"Bud?" Somehow I can live with the idea of her being let down by Walt, or me, but not with the notion of her being happy with Bud. "Look, tell me—now—who's the money going to? My guess is that you're being fleeced by some low-grade flunky who'll just pocket the money and take off to Paris with it. I don't even want to think about how dumb—" Paris. It hits me like a hammer which is what I apparently need in order to see the obvious. "It's Roland Rabary, isn't it?" It's all coming clear. "But he doesn't know it's coming from me. Doesn't know that we're stealing from Picard to pay him." I try to laugh, but I'm too shocked to pull it off. "How in the hell do you know Rabary? Of course, you seem to know any man who might come in handy when you need—"

"He's from Tamatave."

"He's what?"

"From Tamatave. He was a provincial official there."

"Just tell me if I've got this straight—yes or no. You want to spring Walt, even if he can't take you to America. And Rabary needs dollars to bribe himself into that posting in Paris. Otherwise, you could have just fucked him to get Walt out of prison instead of fucking me."

I finally get what I've been looking for all along. Her slap catches me hard enough to make my ears ring. And hard enough to drive from my mind a thought, just forming, about Rabary and Tamatave.

I grab her arms as she tries to hit me again.

Panting with rage and fear, she works loose, grabs her dress from the end of the bed, takes the money from the pocket and throws it in my face.

We crouch on opposite sides of the bed, breathing hard, like two prizefighters resting in their corners, waiting out the bell for the next round. But neither of us moves, and after a while I feel the tension evaporate. I understand the futility of trying to be something to her that I'm not, and the cruelty of punishing her for my own failure. "It's okay, Nirina. Really it is," I tell her. "We all use whatever we've got to do whatever it is we have to do."

I fumble around the bedclothes until I've gathered the money into a neat stack. I push it to her across the bed, but she won't take it.

For a long time the only sound I hear is her breath trembling on the edge of sobbing. When I can't bear it any longer, I tell her, "Say something. Anything."

What she tells me is this: "The money's gone."

The words are so unexpected I can't take them in. "What?"

"The money's gone. Everything but what's lying on the bed."

"What do you mean, the money's—?"

"I spent it."

"You spent it," I repeat, unable to comprehend.

"On my father."

"Your father's dead."

It's a long time before she says anything because she needs to put it in words I'll understand. "In our village my father was a great man. When we buried him we had to show him all the honor we wished him to continue to have. If we held back anything we would lose our place in the village and among our ancestors—and in our own hearts. We needed the finest cloth for his shroud, rice and beer for everyone in the village, and a great feast, as if our money had no other purpose. My family hasn't got much money. But everyone in the village thought I did. I live in the city and they think everyone in the city has lots of money. The funny thing is that, right then, I did. So I paid for all of it. You won't understand me when I say I had to."

I fall back onto the bed. "Gawdalmighty. I risk my life to get you the money to have Walt freed, and you spend it on a funeral."

"I'm not truly free." Her head drops. "No one is. Freedom's too frightening."

"No," I whisper, "no one is."

I want to ask if she had held any money back for Walt's funeral too, because if he doesn't get out of prison soon he's going to need one. Not to mention the funeral I'll need for myself once Picard realizes I've stolen nearly four thousand dollars from him.

"What did you think you were going to do?" I ask, surprised at how calm I feel about it all. My wiring must be fried.

"I don't know. I found the money once. Maybe I can find it again." She doesn't say it as if she believes it.

"So Walt stays in prison until you find it. And you stay in Madagascar."

"Yes. Do you think Monsieur Rabary would still—"

We both jump at the sound of the telephone. I fumble for the receiver. "Yeah?"

"Mr. Knott, this is Sergeant Alcala at the embassy."

"What's up, Jess?"

"Sir, I just received a call from Ambassador Herr. She wants you and Mr. Esmer and Mr. Salvatore to meet at her residence in forty-five minutes."

"You're kidding."

"No sir."

"What time is it?"

"Twenty-two-thirty."

"What's this about?"

"I'm not sure, sir. Some kind of trouble in the city."

I hang up and turn to Nirina. "I've got to go. I may be a couple of hours." I turn on the light. Nirina sits on the bed, arms crossed over her breasts.

"Take me home."

"You don't … You don't have to go."

She doesn't bother to reply.

We drive the dark streets in silence, Nirina saying no more than, "Turn here," or "The next left," then finally, "Stop here."

We're in one of the shanty towns on the edge of the city. The tin and tar-paper shacks lie scattered along a slope above a stinking stream that glows a ghastly gray in the moonlight. The orange glow of kerosene lamps leaks between the gaps in the walls. I've seen places like this and know enough to stay away from them. The air is full of mosquitoes, the shacks full of sick children and parasite-ridden adults. Living here, Nirina won't stay young very long.

She gets out of the car and leans in through the open door.

"Now leave."

It's past eleven by the time I arrive at the Ambassador's residence. Esmer and Pete Salvatore are sitting in the living room in their shirt sleeves. Michelle Herr, in her dressing gown, has her feet propped on the coffee table.

Torn from my bed, still reeling with the hangover of Nirina's confessions, I barely feel present. I pull up an armchair.

Esmer lays out what he knows. It isn't much. Security maintains a roving patrol at night, two Malagasy guards in an old Land Rover, ostensibly to maintain coordination with the residence guards, but in truth to see that they stay awake. At about nine o'clock the patrol is taking a shortcut between Ivandry and the embassy when they see two trucks filled with soldiers heading toward the university. Very strange. They decide to follow. When they get to the university the trucks stop long enough to drop off a few of soldiers who throw up a roadblock across the entrance to the university. The rest of them continue onto the campus. The soldiers at the roadblock tell the embassy guards to drive on. They do, but not before they see fires among the dormitories, hear the crash of breaking glass and the stutter of gunfire.

Pete Salvatore sags in his chair, rubbing sleep from his eyes. "Do we know what's going on?"

"Can't be sure yet," Esmer says, "but when buildings catch fire you usually send for the fire department, not the army. It looks like the troubles have reached the capital."

"The campus is isolated. Maybe this won't spread," Ambassador Herr suggests.

Esmer nods. "Who knows? The government will do everything they can to keep it from snowballing."

Only a lengthening silence tips me off that someone has directed a question at me. "What do I think? I think the government will figure they can't keep the trouble on campus. So they'll make it spread—and quickly."

Esmer snorts in derision and mutters something to Salvatore, who looks at the Ambassador.

Something in me snaps. "Look, you asked me what I think, so you get it!" I hear my voice rising with each word. "If you think the folks in power here are like you guys, you'll never understand what's going on here. They didn't go to fancy schools or spend their summers in Maine. There's not going to be anything in the papers or on TV, but word's going to get around that buildings are burning and people are getting shot. These guys want to blame it on the *vazaha*, but they can't do that if it stays on campus. So if they can't snuff it out immediately—and they probably can't—they'll want it to spread, even if they have to help it along. They need a sense of crisis. They need people to be frightened. And they need a scapegoat.

That's us. And the Indians. If you guys don't understand that, you don't understand anything."

Like a man having an out-of-body experience, I look down and see that I've risen to my feet and am standing over Esmer with my fists clenched. "Oh, god." I run a hand over my face. My fingers are trembling. "Sorry … I have a lot on my mind these days." I try to smile, as if my behavior is just a misfired joke. But I know it's too late.

"Why don't you sit down, Robert?" Michelle Herr says, with the same tone of voice a cop uses to talk a man off a ledge. She looks at Esmer and says oh-so-reasonably, "Perhaps we should look into increasing the guard force at the residences."

Esmer glances at me before replying. "I'll get on it."

She turns to her deputy. "We'd better call a country team meeting for tomorrow morning. Pete, can you make the calls tonight?"

She looks at me, and I can see in her eyes that I'm through. I won't be a factor in discussions from here on, won't be assigned anything but the most routine duties. If it's important, I won't be a part of it. I can probably stay on until the end of my tour—the Ambassador's too kind a soul to have me sent home. But from this night on, I'll be only one more ghost on an island already crowded with them.

The meeting breaks up a few minutes later. Everyone makes a point of wishing me a good night.

Outside, the air is cool and clear. I sit in my car and wait until first Salvatore's then Esmer's tail lights have gone down the hill and turned toward Ivandry.

I start my car and head downtown.

At the Zebu Room, the usual walls of chatter, chinked with groans and the occasional cry of joy, sound more than ever like a sado-masochists convention.

I walk up to the cashier's grill. "Two hundred thousand in chips."

The cashier's eyes widen as she looks up from her cash drawer. "Monsieur Knott," she whispers, "I've been told not to give you any more chips."

"I've got cash—dollars."

She licks her lips nervously, retrieves her lost smile. "Let me call Monsieur Jacques."

"No. It'll be fine. Just give me the chips." I shove under the grill the hundred and sixty bucks Nirina threw in my face earlier that evening.

The cashier looks at the eight twenty dollar bills, but doesn't pick them up.

"Don't worry. They're real," I tell her.

After a moment's hesitation—she's probably never said no to a *vazaha*, doesn't know how—she counts the bills and hands me a stack of chips.

A charge goes through me at the sight of the chips. I feel like an artist on the high-wire, the crowd gazing up at me in wonder. I look out over the gaming tables and am suddenly unsure what to do next. The place closes at one. I don't have much time to win back the four thousand dollars I need to keep from getting killed.

Then I see what I hadn't known until that moment I'd been looking for.

Quietly elegant in an expensive suit of European cut, Roland Rabary stands at the roulette wheel, his homely face lighted by the fantasy he is allowed to indulge—the gentleman gambler blessed by Fate. Surely it's a short step from there to becoming a real Frenchman. Only Pinocchio could understand the yearning Rabary feels.

Shouldering my way through the kibitzers, I find a spot at the roulette table across from Rabary. "How's your luck running tonight, Roland?" I speak rapidly and in English to keep the others around the table from understanding. "Tell me, do they let you win every bet, or do they make you lose a few just to make it look better?"

With the self-control of a Zen master, Rabary barely looks up. "I think you need to leave, Robert." The Malagasy hesitates, holding a small stack of chips over the betting field. The rest he keeps back, avoiding, I suppose, the drama of making big wagers. Finally, he places his bet and waits for the wheel to spin.

The croupier senses the tension at our end of the table. The Malagasy diplomat gives him the barest nod, indicating he should continue play. The croupier poises the ball over the wheel. "*Faites vos jeux.*" Place your bets.

Rabary puts his chips on black and loses. He puts them on Even and loses again. He follows this with a big bet on the first twelve, and wins.

Only because I know there's a fix do I see the pattern— losing on the low-risk bets often enough that no one pays much attention when he wins at longer odds. Over the course of the evening, conspiring wordlessly with the croupier, he quietly makes a bundle.

Knowing now what to do, I follow Rabary's bets. Within a few minutes I've doubled my money. I look at my watch, make a calculation. Yes, I may just have enough time to make up what I still owe Picard.

Rabary never looks up. I might think he's forgotten me but for the fact that after every wager he draws out his handkerchief to wipe the sweat from his hands. He knows that with every bet he wins Picard is getting screwed twice—once by himself and once by me—and he can't be sure the Frenchman won't think we're conspiring against him. That's rich, but can Rabary really be sure he'll be able to convince Picard we're not in cahoots?

By midnight, being careful not to follow Rabary's bets every time or put down so much money that people are bound to see what's going on, I've got nine hundred bucks. Will that be enough to at least buy me more time from Picard? I doubt it.

Wringing the handkerchief in his hands, Rabary catches the croupier's eye and inclines his head almost imperceptibly toward me. Then, with a rueful smile, he gathers in his chips.

"What's wrong, Roland, afraid your luck is wearing thin?" I ask. When he doesn't respond, I tell him, "If you walk away now, I swear to you I'll start shouting the game is fixed."

"No, you won't," Rabary replies. But he's no longer walking away and his voice betrays a trace of unease.

"Tell me what I have to lose."

Rabary raises his chin and says, "You are too intelligent to indulge in such folly."

"Like hell I am."

The Malagasy's smile is as false as the wheel. "Why this sudden need to win, Robert? I would have thought—"

"You won't be getting any money from the girl. It's gone."

Rabary tilts his head to one side, nothing more.

He's really good, I have to hand it to him.

Out of the corner of my eye I see the croupier motion a waiter over and whisper something in his ear. Sensing the tension, the other gamblers around the table look curiously at Rabary and me. The croupier holds the ball in his hand but makes no move toward the wheel.

Rabary strokes his ill-favored nose and, with a sudden exhalation of breath, turns back to the table and sets his chips down. Black. I recognize it as the sort of bet he loses. When it's too late for him to change his mind, I put mine on red.

Confused, a layer of anxious sweat on his lip, the croupier spins the wheel. Twenty-seven. Red.

"Monsieur Knott, how nice to have you with us this evening." Jacques Razafintsalama grasps my arm in what probably looks to others as a friendly gesture. "Please, won't you join me for a drink?"

"No thanks. Don't want to leave the table. My luck's in tonight."

"Perhaps not as much as you think." Jacques' voice carries a steeliness I've never heard in him.

I look at my pile of chips. Not enough. Not nearly enough.

Smiling faintly, Rabary puts his chips in his pocket and backs away from the table.

I feel the urge to start shouting but twist it into a laugh as I call out to Rabary. "The girl spent the money. That door's closed. You want to get to Paris? You're on your own now, baby."

Rabary appears unconcerned. With a little wave of his hand, he smiles and drifts away.

For a moment I think of following through on my threat to denounce the game, cry foul, but Rabary has sized me up well. I'll say nothing.

I jerk my arm from Jacques's grip. "Tell the man to spin the wheel." But I know the evening is a bet I've already lost.

A stir among the gamblers makes me look across the room.

Maurice Picard is striding across the floor toward us. He's surprisingly quick for a big guy. Without breaking stride, he grabs the front of my shirt in one meaty hand, his face twisted with anger. "You want trouble? Yes? Good. I can give you plenty of it." He pushes me into the table.

The other gamblers dart away like a school of fish in the presence of a shark.

"You're a fool, Robert. I never fully saw it until now. We worked a way out for you. But you're not smart enough to take it." He thrusts out his jaw as he speaks, the spittle from his rage hitting me in the face. "Where's my money? Where are my dollars, Bobby?"

I knock his hand from my chest. "You lost it, Maurice. You took a gamble on me. You should have known better. It's gone."

"You're lying, Robert. Where's my money?"

I want to laugh, but I'm afraid that if I start I won't be able to stop. "Believe whatever you want, Maurice." I nod toward the windows and the darkness between us and the university. "It's too late anyway. This place is finally starting to burn. Why? Because you live in a country where half the people haven't got enough to eat, where kids are rotting with leprosy or walk on their hands and knees because they're born with broken backs. You live in a country where the ones in charge buy gold-rimmed china with the money they steal from hungry people. That includes you, you murderous son of a bitch. And all you're going to get with all that money is a fancy funeral, 'cause you're going to be buried here." I heft my chips—it all feels so righteous—and fling them into Picard's face. Then I walk toward the door, praying with every step that Picard hasn't brought his gun with him. With all the men the Frenchman claims to have killed, he must have shot a few of them in the back.

17

Halfway up the winding road to the national prison, I roll down my window and stick my head out like a dog, gasping for my sanity, trying to exhale from deep in my lungs the knee-buckling sense of doom I've brought on myself with the previous night's folly at the Zebu room. I'll be lucky if word doesn't get back to the embassy about my confrontation with Picard. I'll be even luckier if he doesn't kill me before the day's out. He already had enough reason to have me killed in cold blood, but now his blood is hot and I'm thinking my life isn't worth a dime.

The Country Team meeting we held earlier this morning went nowhere. I knew they would decide nothing. The interminable weighing of possibilities and the rehashing of events over which the embassy has no control radiated nausea into every corner of my body until I thought I'd puke out every bit of bile built up by two decades of professional civility, uncounted years of reasonableness, numberless seasons of balanced views, and endless days of well-considered judgments—everything that isn't passion and madness, the only values I trust anymore.

Inevitably, they eventually opted for the habitual dodge of "awaiting events" because it sounds so much better, more action-forward, than "let's do nothing." In fact, there's nothing for them to do. Just like me, everything is slipping out of their control.

Toward the end of the meeting we discussed, for entertainment value, President Ramananjara's sacking of the prison superintendent for allowing the burglars to roam free at night and his order that prison guards were henceforth to live on their salaries, which is a laugh. The fact that they make next to nothing is what caused this problem in the first place.

The President's statement led to the only action to come out of the meeting, the Ambassador's request that Gloria and I go up to the prison to make sure Walt Sackett's all right. The guards have probably guessed he's the original source of the story about the burglars. They might take things out on him.

Now I'm hanging out the window with my ears flapping in the wind.

"Robert, what are you doing?" Gloria reaches across the car seat and pulls me back in. After blowing my top at the Ambassador's residence last night, I suppose I should be grateful to be doing anything that smacks of official business.

I take a couple of deep breaths and try to ignore the look in Gloria's eye. "I'm fine," I mutter, by which I mean I haven't started frothing at the mouth yet. In the rearview mirror I catch Samuel's eyes darting away from me. It's the first time I've drawn him as my driver since that night near Tamatave. His face betrayed nothing that morning when he opened the car door for me in the embassy parking lot, but once behind the wheel, he turned around and said, "This time I think it's better if I drive, and you ride in the back."

You can't say he's lost his sense of humor.

We're topping the last rise on the winding road outside the city when Gloria grabs my arm. "Ohmigod, look!"

Below us, the massive prison is sprouting flames from a dozen places. The French built the prison's outer walls of stone, but constructed the inner structures out of wood. And that wood is burning fiercely in the morning sun.

As we draw closer we can see that the guards have thrown open the gates and are busily waving out the collection of scarecrows that make up the prison's population. The liberated prisoners are scattering across the bare hills in every direction, putting as much distance as possible between themselves and the prison before the guards can change their minds.

I tell Samuel to get us as close to the gates as he can.

The driver sighs, "Monsieur Knott ..."

"It's going to be fine. Go."

Like a salmon swimming upstream, the embassy car crawls through the swarm of fleeing prisoners. The healthier ones are running as if chased by demons. Others, gaunt with hunger and illness, are barely able to walk.

While we're still twenty yards short of the gate, a guard spots the embassy car and, like a traffic cop at any busy intersection, puts up a hand to stop us while he continues to wave the prisoners through.

I open the car door into the mass of escaping criminals. "Samuel, turn the car around and point it back toward town. Keep the engine running." I've started toward the prison gates before I think to add, "I mean it this time."

Over the hubbub of the escaping convicts, I hear a car door slam. I look back to find Gloria running up beside me.

"Get back in the car," I tell her.

Her chin set at a determined angle, she says, "I want to get him out of here myself." It occurs to me we aren't talking about the same man, but it doesn't matter. There'll be no stopping her.

Together we plunge into the crowd, scanning the faces of the escapees streaming past us. Ignoring a guard's shouted warning, we shove our way through the gates.

Inside, we find a few feeble prisoners bringing up the rear of the exodus. I look in every direction, but see only the burning buildings and the empty prison yard. In a couple of minutes the fierce heat will do what the guards couldn't and force us to run. I tell Gloria, "They must have got past us. Maybe we can find them along the road."

I've started back toward the gate when I hear Gloria shout, "There he is!"

Like a mirage, two men appear through the shimmering heat of the burning buildings. The shorter of the two has thrown an arm across the back of the larger, struggling to hold him up. Raising my arm to shield myself from the heat, I run across the courtyard and get a shoulder under Walt's other arm.

Exhausted, his eyes unfocused, Walt lets himself be dragged across the open ground. Gloria has a different idea of how to help. She tucks herself under Speedy's shoulder and puts an arm around him. Caught between Walt and the diminutive Gloria, the young Malagasy lurches back and forth like a teeter-totter, laughing as we struggle toward the gate.

While Gloria and Speedy pile into the car, I throw Walt into the back seat, slam the door after him and jump into the front. "Okay, Samuel, let's get out of here." I look back over the seat at Walt. "Well, cowboy, it took burning down the prison to do it, but you're a free man."

The embassy maintenance crew removes the desk and file cabinets from an unused office and bring in a cot for Walt, who is pale and exhausted. Bill Tuttle from our economic development office brings him a sandwich he'd brought for lunch. Doctor André frowns when he listens to his heart, palpates his stomach, and regards his dehydrated frame, but eventually declares him in decent shape, everything considered.

It seems that half the embassy wants to squeeze into the room to visit the redeemed captive. Pete Salvatore brings bottled water and magazines. Lynn brings a few candy bars from the commissary. One of the Marines has scrounged up a set of clothes that fit him well, and Walt can throw out the rags he's been wearing. Ambassador Herr has him raise his head so she can fluff his pillow for him.

When Walt has taken all the kindness he can bear for the moment, the Ambassador clasps her hands in front of her and smiles. "We'll get you to someplace a little more comfortable this afternoon, where you can rest up for a few days. Then we can get you on a plane home. In the meantime, you have to tell us what caused this fortuitous fire."

"The fire?" Walt makes a rueful smile. "It was set, ma'am."

Pete Salvatore raises his eyebrows. "That's a pretty desperate escape plan."

Walt looks up in surprise. "It wasn't the prisoners who set it."

"Then who—"

"It was them guards."

The DCM looks as if he must have heard wrong. "The guards set fire to their own prison?"

"Yessir. They come 'round this morning, opened up the cell doors and told us to start runnin' 'cause they were going to burn down the prison. Hardly gave us time to follow 'em through the door." The old cowboy chuckles. "Speedy—he's my cellmate, or was, anyway—he told me it was all because of that story that got into the papers. When President Whatsisname told the guards they had to stop lettin' prisoners out, well, they—the guards, I mean—got pretty unhappy and decided to burn the place down." Walt looks at the unbelieving faces around him and adds, "I think they were pretty drunk when they figured all this out."

Michelle Herr says, "I guess we owe a real debt of gratitude to the guards."

Walt nods to Gloria and me. "The way I see it, I got free because Robert and Gloria told that story to the newspapers. If it weren't for that, I'd still be rotting in jail."

The smiles on Michelle Herr's and Pete Salvatore's faces curdle like a quart of bad milk.

I don't need to remind myself that in Madagascar the implausible isn't just possible, it's mandatory.

The same Malagasy maintenance crew that set Walt up in comfort gives Speedy a metal chair in the hallway and tell him to sit. No one brings him food or a pillow or asks the doctor to look at him. Three of the local employees have been burgled in the past year and for all they know it's Speedy who did it.

Am I the only one who notices that Gloria doesn't go straight back to the Cultural Center once Walt's settled in? She wanders the halls, finding little errands that bring her along the corridor where Speedy sits. She stops with him a little longer each time she passes, refusing the offer of his chair, finally sitting on the floor beside him, her arms wrapped around her legs.

After passing by the two of them for the third time that morning, the Ambassador asks Pete Salvatore, "Hasn't that young man got someplace he should be going?"

Salvatore is about to order a Marine to escort Speedy out when his secretary tracks him down in the hall and tells him someone from the Interior Ministry is waiting in his office. He's hardly through the door before the official launches into an ill-tempered harangue that ends with a demand that the embassy return Walt to Malagasy custody.

The DCM leans back in his chair. "If the Malagasy government can't keep its prisoners behind bars, it's not the business of the American Embassy to hand them back."

Stuttering with rage, the ministry official adds that prison guards saw a Malagasy prisoner leaving with Walt and insists on his return as well.

Increasingly offended by the official's manner, the DCM tells him that he will "consider the Malagasy government's request regarding its citizen and respond in an appropriate manner."

The ministry guy recognizes diplo-speak for "go screw yourself" when he hears it and storms out.

A few minutes later, Pete describes the scene to the Ambassador, who tells him to arrange for a car to run Walt Sackett up to her residence, where he can stay in a spare bedroom until he's well enough to go home. Within minutes Lynn and one of the Malagasy security guards are hustling Walt toward the motor pool.

It's too late. A loose cordon of half a dozen Malagasy police stands outside the embassy, spoiling to arrest either Walt or Speedy if they come out.

Walt is hustled back to his converted bedroom office. As punishment for getting him out of jail, I'm tasked with telling him that at least for now he isn't going anywhere. For the first time since his escape the cattleman's good spirits desert him. "Robert, just get me into that car and get me out of here. This is an embassy. They can't stop an embassy car."

"Actually, Walt, they can. And while they can't arrest a diplomat and make it stick, they can arrest you. The embassy will jump up and down and lodge a protest, but in the meantime they'd have you locked up again."

Walt stands at the window of the small room and for a long time looks out at the blue skies and lush trees on the other side of the embassy wall. "This sort of shit never happens in Oregon."

"No, I don't suppose it does."

Walt leans his head against the glass. "It looks to me like I just got myself out of one prison and into another."

"At least the food's better here."

The mention of food makes a connection in Walt's mind. "Nirina. Nirina said she was gettin' ready to get me out of that shithole. Get her over here. If you guys can't figure a way to spring me out of here, I'll bet she can. And Speedy. Where's Speedy? You gonna set him up here with me?" He looks around the office. "Hell, I think our cell was smaller than this place."

"We can't do that, Walt. He's Malagasy. We can't shelter him. He's going to have to take his chances."

"What chances? They'll arrest him soon as he sticks his head out—"

Before Walt can finish his thought, Gloria appears at the door, grasping each side of its frame as if she might fall down. "Robert, they're going to push Dokoby out the door." There's real fear in her eyes.

"What is it you think I can do about it?"

"I don't know," she says, her voice rising to a righteous pitch, "but you've spent months telling me how you're one of the old bulls in this organization. Now show me what it's good for."

Gloria sinks into the back seat of the embassy car and wrinkles her nose. "I feel ridiculous," she says. But the smile touching the corners of her mouth makes clear that other emotions are also in play.

"Just sit up straight and act like everything's normal," I tell her. I lay a hand on the blanket-covered bundle lying beside her on the floor. "And, Speedy, don't you even move until Gloria tells you it's all right."

Curled up on the floor, Speedy grunts affirmatively.

Gloria frowns. "Shouldn't you tell Security what we're doing?"

"I'll write Esmer a memo and send it to him through Washington. He should get it by Easter."

I lean through the window and say to the driver, "Gabriel, the young man will give you directions to his home. Then take Miss Burris back to the Center."

Looking like a man strapped into the electric chair, Gabriel gulps and nods.

With Speedy under wraps, Gloria allows herself to gaze at him with unguarded fondness. Then she remembers I'm watching and covers it with a decisive nod of the head. "All right. Let's go."

As the gate rattles closed behind them, I see the embassy car slipping past the policemen, who barely look up from their game of "cops and robbers."

By the time I visit Walt in the afternoon, his cot is made up into a proper bed with sheets and blankets, and admin has found an old armchair, in which he is reclining, a cold beer in his hand and a smile on his face.

"Hey, Robert, do you think if they brought a TV in here, I could catch the Trailblazers game?"

"You can read the score online."

Walt chuckles and says, "I guess that'll have to do." But his smile fades and the toll of his months in prison show in his pallid face. "I'm not going anywhere for a while, am I?"

I sit on the edge of the cot and say as gently as possible, "Doesn't look like it, cowboy."

"Speedy still around?"

"I snuck him out in a car with Gloria."

A glimmer of hope lights Walt's face. "Why don't you do the same with me? I could at least get up to the Ambassador's place."

"Speedy couldn't stay here. We had to do something. And, frankly, I was willing to risk his skin to sneak him out. So was he. If they stop you, you go back to jail."

"If they stop him, so will he."

I don't need to tell him that, of the two of them, Speedy

is the one who would probably live long enough to finish his sentence.

Walt leans back and stares at the ceiling for a long time. A glint of light appears in his eyes. "Robert, you think there's something going on with those two—Gloria and Speedy?"

"Yeah, I do."

We take a moment to remember the roller coaster of young love.

In an offhand tone Walt asks, "Any chance Nirina's going to come by tonight?"

I shake my head. "I'll send a driver for her in the morning."

"The driver knows where she lives?"

"I do."

Walt reads my face and everything goes quiet for a moment.

"Y'know, I think she figures I'm going to take her back to the U.S. with me." He gives me a look. "I never told her anything like that. Not exactly." He lays his head back and gives a long sigh. "My God, she's a beautiful woman. Why she should be interested in an old—" But he knows the answer to that one and doesn't finish the question. "I gotta tell her, don't I? That I can't ..." His eyes redden, and I look the other way.

Outside, the afternoon clouds are piling up like mountains. In a few minutes they'll let go, but for the moment everything is poised in a tense equilibrium.

Walt leans forward in his chair and stares down at his clasped hands. "I was always a ranch hand, a cowboy. Worked other people's cattle. I never promised Kathy anything, 'cept that I'd make a livin' for her. It's not an easy life. And maybe I didn't do everything I could to make it any easier." He seems to have a hard time getting the next part out. "It's … it's a lot more dangerous a life than most people understand. There's always the risk …" His voice thickens with emotion, and he starts over. "Kathy was always tellin' me that I never tried hard enough to get ahead. I got to be top hand on a couple of ranches, but it never seemed to last. And I was happy just herdin' cattle, ridin' fences. Well, with one thing and another— and a couple of things happened that … Well, I guess she finally had enough. Left me. After thirty-two years." He looks like he still can't believe it. "You'd think you'd be safe after that long. I figured maybe she'd think twice about it, take me back—we're still not divorced yet, not legally—if I showed her I could still make something of myself after all these years. Anyway … We had some money. Not enough to stake me to a ranch in Oregon, but I'd read an article about Madagascar in *National Geographic*, and I thought … Well, I'm not sure now what I was thinkin', except that it seemed like a bold idea. So I took what I had and I borrowed some more from my brother, thinkin' …" He runs a hand through his thinning hair. "This was a crazy idea." He coughs as if his soul has stuck in his throat. "We had a boy. Kathy and me. A cowboy, too. He's dead now."

I wait, thinking there's more. But this is it. The cowboy has told his story, explained everything, his whole life, if I'll only understand how to hear it. And if I don't understand, there's no point saying more.

Walt takes a deep breath, lets it out. "We met at a bar, Nirina and me. And, I guess I didn't want to think about why she was willin' to spend time with an old fella like me, but things were going well and maybe I just figured I deserved it." He raises a crooked finger to make his point. "I didn't mean to lead her on, Robert. But I knew how she was countin' on me. Well, the longer it went on, the more I wondered how I could take her back to some dusty old ranch in Eastern Oregon. And how to tell her I was still married."

The old cattleman's head drops, his thoughts too heavy to bear. It's hard, watching the pain in his weathered face.

"Don't beat yourself up too much," I say. "I think in her heart she knew, once she got to the States, it wouldn't work out. Not for long. She's very fond of you, and she's feeling maybe she was deceiving you, too." I try to say the next as gently as I can. "Walt, she's a good woman, has the best heart I've ever known. She's just doing what she can with what she has—which isn't much."

Walt Sackett lets out a long sigh, tilts his head back and closes his eyes. "Robert, it's been kind of a long day. Maybe I'll rest my eyes for a while."

"Somebody from Admin'll bring you some dinner soon."

"Thanks for listening to me. Probably you should forget all that stuff I've been sayin' and I just ..." He wipes at his eyes, looking very old.

"Don't worry about it. Get some sleep."

I've started to shut the door to give him some peace when he gives an odd little cry, like someone having a nightmare.

"I want a cheeseburger," he says with odd vehemence. "Tell them I want a cheeseburger. And I want some French fries. With ketchup." He slaps at the arm of his chair. "That's all. I just want a cheeseburger and some French fries."

Walt has never tried to describe to anyone the horrors of his months in a Malagasy prison, but he's somehow managed to squeeze it all into an order for a cheeseburger and fries.

"I'll see that you get it, Walt," I tell him, but the old guy has already fallen asleep.

Dusk is coming on by the time I work through my in-box and decide to go home. As I head for the stairway I see a light under the DCM's door. I can tell Pete has shrugged off my tirade up at the Ambassador's residence, at least more than Esmer or the Ambassador have. He's been in the service a long time, mostly in Africa, and knows that sometimes you just snap.

I tap on his door and let myself in.

The DCM's working by the light of his desk lamp, its shadows making him look nearly as played out as Walt Sackett. He nods me into a chair. "How's our desperado doing?"

I give him a readout on Walt's health and disposition. "How long do you think it'll be before the Malagasy throw in the towel and let him go?"

Pete leans back in his chair, taps a pen against his palm. "They're madder than hell about this whole thing. The government's blaming all their troubles on us. The story in *Notre Madagascar*—yeah, they finally realized the story came from us—then the prison burning down and all. Like you said the other evening, they need a scapegoat and it's us."

It's Pete's way of saying my blow-up at the Ambassador's place is behind us. I'm grateful.

"Along those lines …" I offer, seeing he wants to go somewhere with this.

"Along those lines, I got another call from that guy with the Interior Ministry. He wasn't real direct about it—he wouldn't be—but he wanted me to know they're pushing the Foreign Ministry to declare one of us *persona non grata*—PNG—over this thing. Boot one of us out of here." He gives me a look that slowly reveals its meaning.

I let out a little "ah" of surprise. "And you figure it's me."

"They'd want someone fairly high-ranking. They know you're the one that drove Sackett away from the prison. And there's the ... Is there something funny about this?"

There is. But I can't tell Pete that if the Malagasy government chooses to PNG me over Walt Sackett, I get to go back to Washington as a sacrifice on the altar of diplomacy, trailing the aura of a hero, second-class. With a little bit of luck I could break my assignment to Ouagadougou and be on my way to—why not?—Canada. Most of all, Picard doesn't get to kill me. This could literally be a life saver.

"Funny?" I repeat. "No. Not really. Should I start packing my bags?"

"Things move slowly here. It'll be a while. Besides, you never know, they could decide to boot Trapp, or even me." He flashes a tired smile. "But I'd put my money on you."

18

I wander from room to room of the place that for almost two years I've called my house but never considered my home. Packing will go easily. Most of the stuff belongs to the government anyway. If I get booted, Lynn and Jeanne will see that the packers do a good job with my personal effects.

Once it makes up its collective mind, the Malagasy government will likely give me forty-eight hours notice. I'll leave Jeanne with three month's salary and a letter urging my successor to hire her. I'll leave something for Monsieur Razafy, though, as a guard, he's paid by the embassy, so will still have a job. Other than that, there's not much I need to do. Someone in the embassy will take over my section until a successor can get out here. I won't leave much mark that I've been here.

The emptiness of the house comes on me with a little spasm of panic. There will be no visit from Nirina tonight, nor, certainly, from Lynn. I think for a moment of calling Steve Trapp, asking him if he wants to go out for a drink. Just one. No. Given my track record, my call would be about as welcome as an invitation for a midnight stroll with Dracula. Would Picard have enough nerve to send over someone to make a short, violent visit on me? I tell myself no, but the thought rattles me further.

I pick up the phone and dial from memory. She picks up on the third ring.

"Hello?" The long hiss in the lines tells her who it is. "Daddy?"

"Yeah, sweetheart."

"It's really early here, Daddy." Again, that long pause.

"I wanted to catch you before you went off to school."

"You woke everyone up."

I take a deep breath. "I'm sorry, honey. Look, I called because I think I'm going to be moving again."

"Where?"

"Coming back home."

"You're moving in here?" Her voice wavers with a tremolo of teenage horror.

"No, Christine, I didn't mean …" I chuckle to let her know it's all right. "I wanted to tell you we'll be getting to see each other more often. And your mom, too."

"We have a new life now, Daddy."

"I know you do, sweetheart. I don't mean to say—"

"Why are you suddenly so big on seeing us? You never had time for us when we all lived together."

"You know that's not true." I hear my voice rising.

Her voice becomes muffled, talking with her hand over the receiver.

"What are you saying, Christine?"

"That was Howard. He's asking me who's on the phone. I told him it was you."

It sounds like an accusation.

"Look, there's no need—I only called to say—Shit, Christine, it's not like I'm—"

"Daddy? Have you been drinking?"

"Not yet."

"If you're going to yell—"

"I'm not yelling!"

"I'm putting Howard on the phone."

I slam the receiver back into its cradle hard enough to bring down the entire Malagasy phone system. I stumble out of the living room and reel toward the kitchen, my body already anticipating the effects of the alcohol it craves. I need a drink. No, I need to get drunk, and self-loathing will make the booze go down better than any handful of peanuts.

Later, I vaguely remember crashing through the plates and glass in the kitchen, looking for the bottle of scotch I've so carefully hidden from myself. Did Jeanne at some point come into the kitchen, and did I shout her back to her room? Maybe. Certainly.

Then the alcohol, blessed relief, like oxygen, blood, sex, drugs, every balm a man ever longed for.

After the months without so much as a sip I'm out of training. No endurance. No capacity. The sickness later is memorable, vomiting in the study and the hallway, finally collapsing around the toilet like a frat boy, vomiting great gouts of bile and goo until it all comes out, everything in me, every bit of the poison of being a bad husband, a rotten father, an indifferent officer, and a lousy gambler, of being a mediocrity in almost every aspect of the one life given to me, leaving me hollow and empty.

It's light outside by the time I pull my face off the filth of the bathroom tiles and prop myself against the wall. My legs twitch, kicking over the scotch bottle, which spins across the puke-stained floor. Empty. Jeanne must have come in and poured the last of it into the toilet. I couldn't have drunk the whole bottle—not unless I was trying to kill myself, a possibility not easily dismissed. If that was my unspoken intent, I've screwed up even that.

I survey the wrack I've left in my wake, the empty bottle, a broken drinking glass, twisted clothing lying on the floor. The bathroom looks like a crime scene, an existential slaughterhouse. With a start, I see I'm naked as a newborn.

Short of killing myself, I've done about the worst I can do. And I'm sick of it, sick of the life I've made, sick of myself.

Yet, from somewhere inside, leaning hard against the headwinds of my endless capacity for self-destructiveness, I feel the stirring of something else. At first I just think I'm going to be sick again. But through the layers of residual nausea, the incipient headache, the feeling that my vitals have been dropped from a great height and landed splat on the sidewalk, I feel something new coming over me, the hint of an odd, detached sort of euphoria. Nothing more than a glowing coal, but I can feel its heat.

I've lived through this night, and I'm all cleaned out now. Is my life going to get better? Unlikely. Am I going to get thrown out of Madagascar? I suddenly doubt it. It would be too neat, too fortunate. Am I going to die? Yes, and maybe soon. But I don't feel stuck anymore. My life has been grooved into an endless loop of folly and despair. No more. From here on I'm going to act, not simply get acted on.

It's a big responsibility, and a part of me wonders if I'm up to it.

Groaning with dread, I pull myself up the wall and lurch into the shower.

Cheryl doesn't try to hide her shock when I stumble into the office. "Robert, you look like shit."

"Yeah. Something I ate."

She gapes like a passerby at a fatal car crash.

"Look, is Walt still in his— Hell, of course he is. Where else would he be?" I know I'm raving. Somewhere I read that Trotsky, after receiving his fatal blow, tried to chase down his assassin with an icepick sticking out of his head. I feel much the same.

Ignoring Cheryl's horrified gaze, I go back down the hall.

Walt's just finishing breakfast, already looking healthier than I've seen him in weeks. He must have got that cheeseburger and fries. "Look, Robert," he starts to say, then stops. "Whoa! You look like shit."

"Yeah. Something I ate." I sit heavily in a straight-backed chair and feel my brain clunk against the inside of my skull. "How you doing?" I ask. The sense of resolution I felt back at the house is leaking out of me like the air from a bad tire.

"I feel a heckuva lot better. Slept in a real bed last night. First time in months. Seems like years." Without looking up from his plate, he says, "Look, about all that stuff I said yesterday—"

"It's all right. What happens in a converted office-bedroom on the backside of hell stays in a converted—"

Gloria stalks into the room trailing smoke. She nods toward Walt before turning on me like a rabid squirrel. "Robert, I need to talk to you *now* about—Gosh, you look like—"

"Shit. Yeah, I know." The morning is starting too fast, too many people. I wasn't counting on this. I had a plan, bold and clear. But I've already forgotten what it was. "How'd it go with Speedy yesterday?"

Gloria's gaze slips to the floor.

"You got him home, yes?"

She thrusts out her hands, overacting badly. "We got to his place and the police were already there. They nearly saw him before he could duck back behind the seat."

"Gloria, what have you done with Speedy?"

"I couldn't just leave him there."

"Where's Speedy?"

She waggles her head. "I decided he'd better stay at my place."

Walt and I both burst out laughing, though I suppose Walt's laugh doesn't make his head feel as if it were about to crack open.

"He slept on the couch," Gloria protests against our laughter. "Nothing really happened."

"Nothing really happened?" I ask.

A series of conflicting emotions blow across Gloria's face. "I didn't— We didn't—"

"Gloria, it's okay." I regard her with new eyes. In the days since the blow-up over the story in *Notre Madagascar*, she has seemed somehow more comfortable with herself, her work more professional. Relations with her staff have improved. And now love. In her few weeks in Madagascar she's learned more of what she needed to know than I have in two years.

I look at Walt, wondering if he sees the same thing I do. But Walt isn't looking at me or Gloria. His eyes are fixed on Cheryl standing in the doorway.

My secretary looks at the three of us. "Sorry to interrupt, but I got a call from Post One asking me to bring up a visitor."

That's when I realize that Walt isn't looking at Cheryl either, but at someone just over her shoulder, a woman who walks slowly into the room, her head down, uncertain of her welcome.

Gloria looks at her, puzzled. Then her expression clears. She holds out her hand and says in French, "You must be Nirina."

She takes Gloria's hand. "And you are Gloria."

The two women look at each other, one dark where the other is light, one privileged where the other is poor, their attributes wholly opposite and wholly balanced. They see it too and a smile of recognition passes between them.

"I've wanted to meet you. You've done so much for Mr. Sackett." Before Nirina can reply, Gloria snaps to, standing ramrod straight, "But I've got to get back to my office. I'll leave you with these two." Where before she might have looked at us, or at least at me, with resigned exasperation, this time she smiles crookedly at us both, and we can't help but smile back.

My God, is she learning to flirt? This is like handing her the atom bomb.

With a last glance over her shoulder, she disappears down the hallway with Cheryl.

Nirina looks toward the doorway as if thinking of following them out. While her attention is elsewhere, Walt looks at me. He knows what he has to do.

The old cowboy struggles out of his recliner and stands, swaying slightly, in the middle of the room, his arms held away from his body, as if inviting a blow, or maybe an embrace. "How you doin', darlin'?" Unable to look her in the eye, he lowers his head. "Uh, look, Nirina, before you say anything, there's somethin' I gotta tell you."

Nirina shakes her head. "No," she says, "There is nothing you need to tell me."

"Yes, there is. Now let me say it." He sounds like a grandfather chiding a favorite granddaughter. "You've made me feel like a young man again. And you kept me from dyin' in that prison. I don't deserve half of what you did for me. And all along I knew I didn't have any real way of payin' you back. So maybe I tried to do it with a bunch of promises, things I knew I would do for you if I could. I said I'd take you back home with me. And I told you I loved you." Walt took a deep breath and squared his shoulders. "The truth is I can't, not like you deserve. Not like I made out and—"

But Nirina has already crossed the room, put her arms around the old cowboy and laid her head on his chest. "Oh, Wolt, I don't love you, too."

Walt Sackett slowly places his big crooked hands on her back and holds her tight, free from the need for more words.

I work late that night. By the time I drive home, the streets of Ivandry are empty, and the walled residences look more than ever like fortresses in hostile territory. Normally, my headlights would have picked up a few souls walking along the road, rice farmers and charcoal makers from the hamlets that surround my upscale neighborhood, or a guard squatting by a smoky fire, waiting out the long spirit-filled hours of the night. Tonight there's no one.

The first clear sign of trouble is nothing more than a slight disturbance in the order of things—the gate ajar, too much light coming from the house. The air vibrates with quiet menace.

Razafy does not come to open the gate and greet me with his usual ironic nod. I turn off the ignition and get out of the car. In the silence, my footsteps scrape loudly on the concrete drive. With one hand, I slowly push open the gate, like opening a dead man's mouth.

All the lights in the house are on, their yellow glow spilling out onto the lawn. The front door stands wide open.

Slowly, I walk up the drive, cold shivers running up and down my back. Light spills onto the carport through the broken pane of the kitchen door. Holding my breath, I push it open and walk in. Broken glass crunches under my feet.

From its place next to the stove, I pick up the long metal rod used to turn off the water main. Holding it in both hands, like a baseball bat, I go into the living room.

Signs of the intruders are everywhere—overturned chairs, smashed crockery, the sofa slashed.

Holding the iron rod at the ready, I creep upstairs, eyes and ears straining for any sign of someone lurking in the shadows or behind a door.

The covers have been pulled off the bed and lay twisted on the floor. In the study, the TV lies tipped over on its side. Books litter the floor.

Whoever broke in has gone through each room, smashing, overturning, scattering its contents. The disorder is oddly haphazard. My radio—a valuable item in Madagascar—is still on the nightstand. The easily stolen DVD player remains on its shelf.

I head back for the living room.

I'm halfway down the stairs when I hear a faint scraping on the kitchen floor. With my blood rushing into my face and uttering an animal growl I didn't know I had in me, I raise the iron rod, ready to swing.

"Don't hit me!" a voice cries.

Hiding behind the kitchen door is Jeanne, a single wide eye visible around the door frame.

"Oh, Monsieur Knott!"

"What happened, Jeanne?"

"O-h-h-h," she moans.

"Jeanne, tell me, what happened."

"Men came." She blinks slowly, frozen with fear.

"How many?"

"I don't know. I got under my bed when I heard them. I was sure they would find me and kill me." She begins to whimper, the pitch rising toward hysteria.

"Jeanne."

She swallows hard, breathes a little more slowly.

"When did they come?"

"I don't know. A while ago."

"How long have they been gone?"

"They were here and then they were gone." She looks at me, her eyes wide. "They called your name, Monsieur Knott."

"They what?"

"They called for you."

I pick up the phone and call the Marine on Post One. The last person I want to talk to is Esmer, but if I don't report the burglary it'll raise all kinds of questions I don't want to answer. And once I report it, I know Esmer will come running.

After I receive the Marine's assurance that he'll send Esmer, Jeanne seems to be a little better.

"Where's Monsieur Razafy?" I ask her.

She gulps and shakes her head. She doesn't know.

I go back outside and find Razafy crumpled in the grass near the gate. A groan comes up from deep inside him as I kneel and turn him gently onto his back.

"Razafy."

Like a sleeper, he mumbles, "Monsieur."

"Razafy, can you tell me what happened?"

As he recognizes my voice, the guard's eyes widen and he tries to get to his feet.

"No," I tell him, "Just lie still. Do you know what happened?"

Razafy blinks vacantly. "Men came. I opened the gate and they hit me."

"A gang?"

The guard's eyes glaze over as he begins drifting back into unconsciousness.

"Razafy, was it a gang?"

Razafy shudders into wakefulness. "No. Two men. They came in a car. I asked them what they wanted and they hit me in the head."

"Just the two men?"

"No. There was another man. In the car. I didn't see him well. A big man."

I feel vaguely flattered that Picard would give me such personal attention. On the other hand, despite my fears, part of me thought he wouldn't really try to kill me. That part of me knows better now. It's not a happy thought.

A pair of headlights come up the driveway. Behind their glare I can make out security's Land Rover.

I bend over Razafy and speak quickly. "Listen, Razafy, not a word about the car or the big man. Do you understand?

Tell security it was a gang, all on foot, young men, but you didn't see anything else before they knocked you out."

"But Monsieur Knott …"

"Nothing about the car. It was a gang."

He sighs. "As you say, Monsieur Knott."

Though I know the intruders have fled, I ask the two security men to look for them in the house. I don't want them talking to Razafy yet. I won't have time to talk to Jeanne and tell her the story I want her to give to security. I can only hope she won't repeat the fact that the intruders were calling for me by name.

By the time Esmer comes a few minutes later, I have my story straight.

"A gang of kids overpowered Razafy and ransacked the house," I tell him. "Must have been just before I got home from work."

Esmer purses his lips. "I called the police. They told me there've been a couple other break-ins tonight, about two kilometers up the road." He looks out at the dark street. "Odd they would skip everyone else along the way and end up here."

I need to break his chain of thought. "It doesn't look like they took much. Just smashed the place up."

Esmer looks at me, puzzled. "Funny. At the other places they took everything but the paint off the walls."

"Something must have scared them off," I suggest. "You figure the police will come by?"

Esmer shakes his head. "They've got enough problems tonight. Riots downtown," he says with perverse satisfaction. The world has descended into the security man's domain. Guys like him are in charge tonight. He tells his driver to radio the embassy to send for Doctor Andre, then nods toward Razafy, sitting up now, his head between his curled-up knees. "Can he talk?"

"Yeah." Just to cover my bets, I add, "I'm not sure he's making much sense."

But Razafy sticks to the story I gave him and Jeanne doesn't mention that the intruders had been looking for me.

Esmer leaves one of the men from the Land Rover to replace Razafy and tells me he'll send over a replacement in the morning.

Telling myself that Picard isn't likely to come back, I pick the bedclothes from the bedroom floor, wrap myself up and try to sleep, knowing who I'll have to talk to in the morning.

19

The ruins of the Queen's Palace sit atop a hill with a commanding view of Antananarivo. It was built in the nineteenth century by Queen Ravanalona, the Lady Macbeth of Madagascar, who wanted to impress the Europeans bent on undermining her rule. Her efforts eventually failed and the ruined walls now serve as a monument to—some say a tomb for—her defiant nationalism. Neglect and that most mutable of Madagascar's commodities, time, ate away at the building. A few years ago a fire hurried things along.

My solitary footsteps scrape along the paved walk as I look at the burned-out shell and think about how hard the old queen tried to keep out people like myself.

When I turn away, I find Roland Rabary gazing at me with his perpetual frown.

I don't offer to shake his hand. "I'm surprised you came."

"No more so than I." Rabary turns his back to me and looks out over the city. I amble over to stand beside him. Without looking at me, he says, "Did you know, Robert, that from this cliff Queen Ravanalona threw to their deaths thousands of Malagasy who had adopted European ways? She did the same with a few French and British missionaries, trying to eradicate the menace they posed to our culture."

"Didn't work out, did it?"

The Malagasy shrugged. "Who knows? Maybe there is a moment, still waiting, in which we Malagasy rid ourselves of all of you and our culture can flow on uninterrupted."

"And maybe there's one where the ancestors are happy. From what I've seen, they could use some cheering up."

Rabary looks over his shoulder at the ruined building. "In her heart, Ravanalona must have known that if she had to build a European palace in order to impress Europeans, she had already lost."

"Funny you should say that. I was coming out of my driveway this morning and saw something making its way up the road, pulled by three or four guys on foot with a couple more pushing from behind. With the heat shimmering off the pavement, I couldn't make it out at first. I thought maybe they were pulling a cart loaded down with an altar of some sort, some kind of religious procession. But as they got closer I could see what it was—a bunch of guys standing in the shafts of a zebu cart that had no zebu, pulling a cart loaded down with an old car that had no wheels. It struck me as a metaphor for the whole country."

Rabary raises his eyebrows as he tries on the idea. "Yes, the very picture of the Malagasy people impoverished by their thralldom to foreign ways." With a casual flick of his hand he indicates the palace behind us. "I know what you're thinking, Robert. And you're right. I am exactly what she detested most. I am like this house, claiming to be Malagasy, but, finally, made along European lines. And just as empty."

"Cut the philosophy, Rabary. I just want to make a deal. Something the old queen would love. I'm thinking your ministry would like nothing better than to nail a Western diplomat's hide to the wall. The Queen would love it. So let's make it me. I'll tell you all you need to know about my gambling debts and how I'm not paying them off. You can tell your bosses I'm thumbing my nose at Malagasy law. Abusing diplomatic privilege. I've also been under-tipping at local restaurants. That should be enough to get me PNG'd, and you can lay it all on the desk of your bosses tomorrow."

"Like a cat laying a dead mouse at the feet of its owners."

My stomach tightens with the effort to remain civil. "However you want to look at it. Then you can have me thrown out of here. You win your government's undying gratitude. They give you that post in Paris. You end up sipping Pernod at the Café de la Paix, while I go back to a cheap apartment in the burbs of Washington."

"It sounds inviting. But I don't understand why."

"One condition. I need it done in a hurry."

Rabary says nothing as we stroll along the bluff overlooking the city. I can hear his mind clicking over, wondering what this is all about.

"Robert, you made a very ugly scene the last time we met. And you deceived me about the provenance of that story in *Notre Madagascar*."

"Here's your chance to get even."

"Why are you so anxious to embrace disaster? You've never wanted to be expelled before now."

"No one wanted to kill me before now."

Rabary raises his eyebrows. "Who would—?" The Malagasy stops in mid-sentence as the last tumbler falls into place. "Ah. Yes. Our friend Picard is even more displeased with you than I am," Rabary says, adding with a sniff, "But surely you exaggerate his anger."

"I don't think so. Not only did I humiliate him in front of a casino full of his clients, but he seems to think I'm lying to him about the money being gone, that I have it hidden somewhere. He can't believe I'm as big a fool as I claim to be. But I am. Two guys came by my house last night. They beat up my guard and broke in, looking for me and the money. When they didn't find either of us, they tore the place apart to make it look like a street gang had ransacked it. Picard was with them. If I'd been home we probably wouldn't be here having this pleasant chat. I'd simply be another victim of the unrest in your country."

The Malagasy looks narrowly at me and senses I'm telling him the truth. He throws back his head and laughs, the sound echoing off the old stone walls. It makes me want to throttle the little potato-nosed bastard.

"So," Rabary says, still chuckling, "as always, it is we Malagasy who are at fault. We don't go to your country and tell you to be more like us. But you cross oceans and continents to come to this distant island and tell us we should live like you. And when that approach brings you to grief, it is we who are to blame. Pah!" Rabary's face turns hard. "So now you want to leave and you think I will help you." His laughter dies with a bitter snort. "You don't understand. We are both, um…" He searches for the idiom. "… screwed. Even if gambling debts were enough to get you PNG'd—and I don't think they are—I believe my superiors are already considering throwing you out of the country over this Sackett affair. If so, your expulsion will have nothing to do with my efforts. And I will receive none of the credit."

"So you haven't got much time left to take up my offer." I sound like one of those guys pushing exercise equipment on late night TV. Maybe if I agree to throw in a set of steak knives. "Look, I can give you everything you need to throw me out before they decide to do it themselves. Rile 'em up good and they'll PNG me this week, maybe in the next day or two. I'm only asking that you get them to do it before Picard catches up with me."

Rabary smirks. "You're really frightened, aren't you?"

"Damn right I am."

We walk silently along the edge of the bluff. "Yes, perhaps you're right about Picard," Rabary says finally. "Most people want revenge served cold. Picard would prefer it hot."

"And Picard isn't afraid of committing murder. After all, he got away with it once before, didn't he?"

Rabary stops, stony faced. "I have no idea what you're talking about."

"You're really good, y'know? The hell you don't understand. That's how you have your hooks into him, isn't it? He paid Andriamana to kill a kid from Tamatave who wouldn't pay his gambling debts. You were an administrator down there and somehow you found out. Or, after you moved to the capital, maybe Picard told you in a careless moment. I'd say it might have been Andriamana who told you, but he's never had a careless moment in his life. In any case, you know Picard's murderous little secret. And you've kept it to yourself until you could make it pay off."

Rabary looks at me, the hint of a smile on his lips. "You never know when you've gone too far, do you? You have to blurt out everything you know. Play out every impulse." Rabary speaks calmly, like a doctor informing a patient of an incurable disease. "You have in the past dismissed my warnings that you were steering yourself toward destruction. Let me try just once more, then my conscience will be entirely clear." He looks at me, making sure I'm taking in what he's saying. "Do not underestimate Andriamana as much as Picard does. Picard caught him at a vulnerable moment. Andriamana was just another police officer when this happened, and he needed money quickly to gain a promotion. So he murdered this boy for Picard—and has lived with this sword over his head ever since. A charge of murder against him, even an old one, would be a boon to his many enemies and an impediment to his advancement. But Andriamana did one intelligent thing. After he got his promotion and became the man we know him to be, he came to me. Yes, we'd known each other when I toiled down there as Customs chief. He knew that I could find a way of making Picard keep quiet about it. And so I did. Picard needs an exit visa if he is to ever leave Madagascar, and I can make sure he gets it only on the terms I offer. So, on behalf of the Captain, I demanded his silence."

"And on behalf of yourself you demand a bribe for the visa."

Rabary bows his head as if acknowledging a compliment and says, "Despite all this, Picard still thinks this secret gives him power over Andriamana. He doesn't understand. If Picard remains silent about their little transaction—a wise course—the captain is content. If not, if Picard somehow decides to make a fuss, or demands one favor too many ... Well, the captain would decide he must rid himself of this embarrassment."

"You're right. Picard doesn't see it that way. He thinks Andriamana wouldn't dare do anything to a wealthy *vazaha*. He thinks he's in the clear over this."

Rabary clasps his hands together. "Well, as you say, that's fine." He looks over the bluff we walk along. "Picard underestimates us Malagasy. He forgets that we are known to throw foreigners off cliffs." He shakes his head and laughs. "But you, you make it too easy. You throw yourself off." He essays that Gallic shrug. "I can't help you. For my own interests, I wish it were otherwise. But what you are offering up is not enough to get you expelled and, in any case, you come to me too late." He holds up his hand, two fingers extended downwards and wiggles them, mimicking a running man. "So it is time for you to run away. Any way you can." He holds up his hand as if about to take an oath, but waves it dismissively. "I have no more time for you."

He turns his back on me and walks off, still looking over the edge of the cliff.

Pushed by a tailwind of fear and self-disgust, I drive back to the embassy just in time to find I'm being called to another emergency Country Team meeting regarding the deteriorating security situation.

Everyone in the conference room makes a show of good cheer, demonstrating how well they deal with pressure. Steve Trapp is full of jokes and the gunny wants to start an office pool, placing bets on when President Ramananjara will flee to Switzerland.

For now, though, the President's party still holds the reins of power, and the news media remain firmly under his control. Even with riots spreading across the country, with the Malagasy franc falling like a shotgunned pigeon, and the government teetering on the brink of collapse, news reports focus on the visit of a North Korean diplomatic delegation.

Rumor fills the vacuum. *Radio trottoire*—sidewalk radio—

speaks of foreign agitators, but also of several deaths near the main market and of university buildings burned to the ground. Reports are incomplete, contradictory, and sensational to the point of fantastic, yet reflect something real about the chaos and confusion spreading across the country.

In the surest sign that the government has decided the disturbances have spread far enough and it's time to put the hammer down, roadblocks have popped up on every road leading out of the city.

Esmer says he can neither confirm nor deny any of the rumors, though police officials have told him gangs are roaming Ivandry, breaking into foreigners' houses and beating up anyone they find at home. "Including, last night, the residence of our political officer." He looks down the table at me. "Fortunately, he was not at home at the time." He makes it sound like a character flaw.

Pete Salvatore starts laying out possible evacuation routes in case the balloon should truly go up—to the airport if it's open, or, if it's closed, by a caravan of automobiles down to Tamatave and a rendezvous with an American naval ship.

I brighten at the possibility that all my problems might be solved by such a taxpayer-funded *deus ex machina*. Then I remind myself of how many evacuation plans I've worked on over the years, and not one of them ever came to pass.

"On the other hand, the government may be in luck," the DCM concludes, "There's a storm brewing. I mean that literally. High winds, rain. It should hit the coast late this afternoon and be here by evening. That'll keep people inside tonight and maybe for a couple of days after. No one's going to demonstrate in the middle of a hurricane."

I wonder how this storm stacks up against the low pressure system building in my gut. I remind myself that I've vowed to take my fate in my own hands, to act, but my resolution is slipping. What was it Don Quixote said? "Fear has a thousand eyes and can see things underground." Could I be more afraid of doing something, of acting, than of getting killed?

It's nearly dusk when the meeting breaks up. As I walk back to my office, I run into Cheryl heading for the door. She says goodnight over her shoulder then stops and asks me, "Should I take that girl back down to Post One with me?"

I start to ask, "What girl?" But I already know. "No, I'll see she gets out."

All three of the room's occupants look up as I appear in the doorway. Nirina has pulled a chair over to Walt's recliner and sits with her hands resting on the old cowboy's arm.

Cheryl hadn't mentioned Speedy. The young thief sits on the floor, leaning against the wall. He smiles and tips a straw hat he has picked up since I saw him last.

Whatever they've been talking about, they stop when I come in.

I ask, "Does Miss Gloria know you're here, Speedy?"

The young Malagasy's eyes shift away. He says nothing.

"You're lucky you didn't get arrested walking down the street to the embassy." I hear the edge in my voice and wonder if they can tell how taut my nerves are.

"Speedy knows how to get past the cat," he says with a wink at Walt.

I look around the room, not knowing what I'm searching for until I find it. Poking out from behind Walt's chair is a heavy cloth strap. I cross the room and look over the back of his recliner. On the floor are two large satchels.

"Going somewhere?" I ask.

"Caught," Walt said, affecting lightheartedness.

Nirina rises to her feet. "We're leaving. Tonight."

Walt throws his hands up. "Robert, I can't be sittin' around for months, wonderin' when this government's going to let me go. I gotta get outta here."

How many times has Walt said the same thing? And how many assurances have I given him that the embassy was doing everything it could? None of them have come to anything.

"What if we could sneak you up to the Ambassador's residence?" I suggest. "It wouldn't be half as risky as just breaking out of here. The cops are still out there, but the fact that Speedy got in tells me they're not paying much attention anymore."

Walt shakes his head. "No, dammit. I 'preciate everything you done for me, Robert. But all you've managed to do is get me into a prison that's a little higher class than the one I just left. I want out. I wanna be free."

I turn to Nirina. "Do you even have a plan?"

"We are heading for the coast tonight," she says, "My brother is a fisherman. He will have his boat waiting for us near Tamatave and take us to Mauritius."

"You didn't get the weather report? A big storm is working its way here. If you try to drive to the coast you'll be blown off the road."

Nirina's eyes widen but her voice is firm. "Still, we are leaving."

"Okay. Let's assume you live long enough to make it to Tamatave and somehow don't drown on your way to Mauritius. Then what?"

Walt and Nirina look at each other.

"Wait, don't tell me. You haven't thought that far ahead."

Walt tries to smile. "We'll think of something."

I look at Speedy, sitting on the floor. "You're getting out of here too?"

Speedy shakes his head and smiles. "I am just the driver, Monsieur Robert."

"You have a car?"

Speedy squints up at me. "Not yet."

"You're going to steal one."

"No, Monsieur Robert." He *tsks* at the thought. "A friend is going to steal one for us."

"Why would someone steal a car just so you can get some American out of here?"

"After what you and Walt did to get us out of prison, all the criminals love the USA."

"Another key demographic swings our way," I say. "It'll never work. The police have set up roadblocks all around the city to keep the riots from spreading any further than convenient." I turn to Walt. "If you drive into one of them they'll throw you back in jail, even if they have to build a new one to hold you. And, Speedy, I don't know how you snuck in here, but they'll probably nab you when you go out to get the car." I see that none of this makes any impact with them. "You're all nuts."

No one argues the point.

Looking at their determined faces, I remember my pledge to get my life unstuck. The moment has arrived to slam on the brakes or keep going.

"Look, I'll be back in a couple of hours. Don't go anywhere until then."

A rising wind rattles my Peugeot as I drive out through the embassy's main gate. Heavy clouds riding over the city give off an odd yellow-gray tinge, like a deep bruise. Lightning lights the sky and rain begins to fall in sheets.

The windshield wipers can't keep up as I drive along the city's deserted streets and turn onto the Avenue de l'Independence. And I suddenly see how wrong Pete can be.

Long lines of policemen have formed up in the wide grassy strip in the middle of the avenue, their thin blue uniforms turning dark in the pouring rain. On the other side of the avenue large knots of sullen young men stand under the porticoes of the old colonial buildings, trying to gather the collective will to do something, milling around like extras in a movie to which no one has yet written the next scene.

Things are spinning out of control in my own life and in this unhappy country. I'm about to break out of the norms that have constrained me for more than twenty years. I might end up dead. At the very least, taking off now, leaving the country without authorization, I'll likely end up dismissed from the service. The old Knott quakes at the possibility. The new Knott says "so what?" If I stick around for Picard's ax to drop on my neck, getting fired is the least that might happen to me. Besides, I can always try to claim that by taking off in a storm-tossed boat with Walt Sackett I'm demonstrating admirable zeal in assuring that a persecuted American escapes to freedom. It might even work. Over the years, I've noticed that the steady water torture of small mistakes dripping onto the forehead of the Department will get you fired, while total jaw-dropping fuck-ups often go unpunished, as if they somehow imply vision or have short-circuited the crabbed imagination of the bureaucracy, leaving it helpless to act.

These thoughts instill a strange sense of exhilaration as I speed out of town. I can't suppress a wide smile that speaks even to me of irretrievable madness. But I have one more errand to run before heading home.

Rather than turning up route Hydrocarbure, I head toward Ambodivona, the part of town where Paul Esmer lives.

Esmer answers the door holding his son in his arms. He's a cute kid, about three. I can never remember his name, but Esmer's a different guy around him, you can see the love in his eyes. He's a good dad, a loving husband. I try to remember that when he's driving me crazy.

If his eyes brighten at the presence of his son, they dim again on seeing me. He puts his boy down. "Go to the kitchen and see if you can help Mommy." Then he says to me, "What brings you out on this dark and stormy night, Robert?"

I squint ruefully at him. "Y'know, Paul, I was thinking maybe you were right. Last night kind of spooked me. If the offer's still open, I'd like to borrow that gun you mentioned."

Esmer looks at me like he's thinking of telling me, "I told you so," but I've sunk so far in the embassy hierarchy that it's not worth the effort.

"Sure," he says.

Leaving me standing in the doorway, he goes down a hallway and comes back a moment later carrying a nine millimeter automatic. He holds it in his open hand. "You pull back this slide to put a round in the chamber. See? I didn't actually pull it back just now because it's loaded. If you go around with this tucked in your waistband and a live round in the chamber you'll end up blowing your dick off." He hefts the gun. "After you've pulled the slide back you just squeeze the trigger for each shot. Fifteen round clip." After demonstrating once more, he hands me the gun with the air of a dad handing the car keys to a teenage son. "You want an extra clip?"

"No. I just want a little protection. I'm not storming the Winter Palace."

"Whatever. Just bring it back when you're through."

Through with what, I wonder. I make a little wave with the gun by way of thanks, stuff it into my coat pocket and get back in the car.

I arrive home to find Jeanne has cleared out the broken chairs and lamps and thrown blankets over the slashed furniture, doing her best to tidy up the previous night's wreckage.

I dash up the steps to the bedroom and start throwing things into a bag.

"What are you doing, Monsieur Knott?" Jeanne stands in the doorway. "You're not going to leave me in this house alone, are you?"

"I've got to make a trip. I'm not sure if I'll be back." I take a wad of francs from my wallet and open a cabinet in the bathroom, missed by last night's intruders, where I keep a little more. I shove it all into her hands. "Here, take this. It should be at least three month's pay. It's yours." Trying not to look at her frightened eyes, I kiss her on the forehead and run downstairs, calling over my shoulder, "If anyone calls, you didn't see me."

A pounding on the front door. I freeze. I look at Jeanne and cock my head toward the door. "See who it is."

Deep worry lines form on Jeanne's brow, but she goes to the door and opens it. "It is Miss Gloria," she calls to me.

Gloria brushes past Jeanne, her hair a mess, her raincoat buttoned all wrong. "Where's Speedy?"

I hesitate, but decide I'd better tell her at least part of the truth. "He's at the embassy."

"What's he doing there?"

"You don't want to know."

"I do so! When I came home he was gone. He's risking arrest just by going out the door. And I'd bet anything you're encouraging him."

I should have known that if she ever fell in love it would be with everything in her overachieving soul. And there would be no lying to her. "He's going to drive Walt and Nirina to the coast. They've got a boat waiting to take them to Mauritius."

"In this storm?"

"Walt wants to take his chances. Speedy is just doing the driving. If everything goes right, he'll be back tomorrow."

She eyes my bag on the floor. "You're not going too are you?"

"Maybe. Listen, I've got to get out of here. I don't want to explain."

She stares at me as if I've gone crazy. She's probably right.

I cock my chin in the direction of the distant embassy. "Don't tell Mom, okay?"

"Oh, I'm supposed to just go home and keep quiet and wait and see if you and Speedy get yourselves killed?"

"That's about it."

"So I didn't come here tonight. I didn't talk to you. I don't say a word to anyone."

"Pretty simple, isn't it?"

She sees the finality in my face and can only whisper, "Get Speedy back to me."

"I'll do my best. I really will, Gloria."

Her fists clenched, she leans in toward me. I brace myself for a scene. To my surprise, she kisses me on the cheek. Less to my surprise, she then punches me in the chest hard enough to hurt, and walks back out into night.

A few minutes later, bag packed, I'm heading for the door.

Jeanne takes a deep breath. "Goodbye, Monsieur Knott."

"Goodbye, Jeanne."

"I'm afraid you're going to die, Mr. Knott."

"So am I, Jeanne." I wonder at the logic of getting myself drowned or driving off a cliff in a hurricane to avoid getting shot. I try to forge a smile for Jeanne. "Well, small loss."

I head for the car, but instead of getting in, I walk toward the back yard. I have two guards since the break-in, both new, standing under the cover of the carport. They watch me as I peer through the pouring rain toward the Seuss-like tree on the knoll.

I've been told that the Malagasy believe certain trees lead directly down into the spirit world. Could there be a separate tree for each spirit? Maybe this is the one that could have brought me to an understanding of this alien land, the Island of Ghosts, if I'd only walked up to it, touched it, breathed in its unknown scent. But I never tried.

It's too late. The night is dark, it's raining, and I can't see it.

Time to go. Like ice breaking on a frozen river, I've begun to move and can't stop now.

I wave for the guards to open the gate. As I get into the car I shout to them over the pounding rain, "There's a chameleon who lives here. If you see him, tell him the place is his now."

Then I pull out onto the street and drive away.

20

The wind blows the rain in horizontal sheets, rocking the car as I head for town in the dark. A few hundred yards from the house, the road takes a downhill turn toward the Route Hydrocarbure, which leads to the city. I try to persuade myself it's only my frayed nerves that makes the Citroen sitting by the side of the road look as if it's lying in wait for someone. On the other hand, if my mounting paranoia is slipping me some truth this time, I've caught them by surprise, coming in a direction they hadn't expected after detouring by Esmer's place.

I turn onto the Route Hydrocarbure and the distinctive headlights of the Citroen blink on and turn onto the road behind me. It takes a lot of crust for Picard to have another crack at me the day after his first attempt failed. But Picard has never lacked for crust.

Would it do any good to tell his two thugs that I hadn't been joking when I told Picard the money was gone, that I'm not just holding back? Probably not. After ransacking the house, they'd only think I was keeping it somewhere else. And besides, at this point Picard probably doesn't care. He's been double-crossed and publicly humiliated, both capital offenses in his personal code of jurisprudence.

Yet my mind still harbors hopes that I'm wrong. I decide to test my hopes against my fears. I step on the gas, the car fishtailing a little in the rain. My Peugeot gradually creeps up to more than a hundred kilometers an hour on a road that doesn't encourage speed on the best of days. Jarring potholes, hidden by the rain, threaten to break the suspension or destroy a tire. If these guys are intent on murder, that would be the end of me. But so would slowing down.

Slowly, the yellow headlights—one of them must be broken, as it gives off a narrow beam of white—grow larger in the mirror as the more powerful Citroen speeds up. All doubts evaporate. They're after me.

For the first time, I'm grateful for the cordon of policemen in front of the embassy. Even if Picard's men might try something in the middle of the city, they aren't crazy enough to grab me or shoot me, or whatever it was they were told to do with me, in front of half a dozen cops. I need to get there before they catch me.

I thread the Peugeot through the roundabout near the railway station at the edge of town. The Citroen has backed off a little as if uncertain what to do now that we're in the town. That, more than anything, tells me Picard isn't with them. Not far now to the embassy. I think I've got this race won.

I turn up the Avenue de l'Independence—and immediately stand on the brakes, fighting my car to a slithering stop.

In the time it took me to stop by Esmer's, run home for a moment, and get back into town, the milling students have found the nerve to turn into a mob, spilling out onto the boulevard. The police, batons held chest high, have turned to meet them and the two lines, police and students, face off at a distance of maybe a hundred feet, trembling across all four lanes, blocking the road.

I grind the gears throwing my car into reverse. The engine whines as I back down the avenue.

With nightmare suddenness, the pursuing Citroen fills my back window. He's going to hit me. Still in reverse, I slew to the right. The Citroen, its horn blaring, slews left, straight over the curb and onto the grass median.

The front-wheeled Citroen shudders sideways in the wet grass, its wheels spinning, throwing up spouts of mud. I jam my car into first and turn up the nearest side street. Nothing looks familiar. This is a hell of a time to realize I should have gotten to know the city better. I imagine twisting aimlessly on these tiny streets until Picard's thugs catch me. Blindly, I turn up one street and down another.

Totally lost now, I fish for the grip of Esmer's pistol in my pocket, ready to go down in a blaze of ignominy. Through the darkness and the pouring rain, I see the brightly painted sign of a Chinese restaurant I've been to several times. Suddenly, I know where I am.

Like waking from a nightmare, I turn down a familiar street toward the embassy. A moment later the Malagasy guard is opening the gate for me. I bring the car into the parking lot just as the Citroen appears at the end of the street.

Picard's men stop, maybe a hundred yards from the embassy. For a moment the Citroen's lights glow like the eyes of cat, then blink out. They'll wait.

It takes me a moment to find the strength to get out of the car and dash through the rain into the embassy. Still trying to breathe normally, I walk up to Post One, the Marine Security post at the embassy's main entrance.

"Good evening, sir." Rudy Saenz, the Marine on duty, looks at me from his glassed enclosure. "You gotta be a little crazy to drive in this weather," he says with a smile.

"You don't know the half of it."

He frowns momentarily. "Sir, I thought you were still upstairs with those visitors. I was told they were your responsibility."

I apologize for the misunderstanding and run up the steps to the second floor, still shaken from the Citroen's pursuit, knowing that its waiting presence complicates my plan.

It looks as if no one has moved since I left. Nirina is resting her head on the arm of the recliner while Walt blinks as if he's been dozing. Speedy, sitting on his heels, leans against a wall.

I turn to the young thief. "Tell me how you're supposed to get this stolen car."

"It will be in front of a restaurant a few blocks away."

"You don't think the cops will arrest you the moment you walk out the door?"

Speedy waggles his head uneasily. "They didn't arrest me when I came in. I think they're only interested in Mr. Walt."

Nirina sees the bag in my hand. "You're coming with us?"

I avoid the question by saying to her, "Tell me what happens next."

Walt shifts in his chair. "When Speedy pulls up in front with this car, I guess we'll just get in and drive away. Pretty simple," he says, as if trying to convince me—or himself.

"It won't work. You'll never get through the roadblocks between here and the coast." I turn to Speedy. "Go down and ask the Marine to buzz you out the front door so you can fetch the car."

Walt looks puzzled. "Didn't you just say—"

"Trust me." Speedy's on his feet now. "When you go past the Marine on Post One," I tell him, "just say, 'Goodnight, Corporal.' In English. He's new. He'll think you're one of the local employees going home."

Speedy experiments with the phrase. "Goodnight, Corporal." He tries it again with a different tone. "Goodnight, Corporal. Corporal, good night."

"You're not after an Oscar. Just say the words. Once. When he lets you out, get this car of yours and bring it up to the gate of the embassy parking lot. I'll tell the guard to let you in."

Speedy gets to his feet, a faraway look on his face.

"What?" I ask.

"I wish Miss Gloria could see me now."

Young love. "She'd have you arrested for posing as an embassy employee."

He laughs. "Yes, she's a very serious woman." He pulls his straw hat low over his face. "I'll see you in a few minutes."

My God, I think, he's having fun.

"Wait." Speedy stops and looks at me. "I need to make a change in your plan. After you bring your car inside, I want all of you to get into mine. That's the one you'll drive out."

"You figure we're better off in an embassy car?" Walt asked.

"That's only part of it. There are two guys in a Citroen waiting for me out there." I can feel Nirina's eyes on me. "They work for Picard," I tell her. "I think they mean to do me harm. When they see my car leaving, they're going to follow—especially if you pull out quickly. Speedy, I'm asking you to draw them away, stay ahead of them until you get to the Hotel Colbert. Pull up to the curb there and stop. I'm pretty sure they're going to come up to the car. You have to let them. When they see it's you, they're going to ask where I am. You tell them you have no idea, that I asked you to take my car and you don't know anything more. They'll head back here as fast as they can, but it'll be too late. I'll be gone by then."

Walt looks at me, skeptical. "So, you're using us as bait?"

"Yeah, I am. And I won't pretend there's no danger in it for you."

He thinks it over, glances at Nirina, then Speedy, then back at me. "Okay. You've done a lot for all of us. I guess we can afford to give some back."

"Thanks, cowboy."

"And where are you going to be, while we're doing all this?" he asks.

"I'll leave a couple minutes after you and go the other way. We'll meet up after they've let you go."

"If they let us go," Walt says.

I know he's speaking the thoughts of the others. I have to be straight with them.

"That's right—if."

"Okay, where do we meet you?"

I haven't thought it through very well. A hot flush of anxiety runs through me. If I can't think even a few minutes ahead, how will we ever get away with this?

Nirina rises from her chair. "We will meet at my place." She tells Speedy, "I'll direct you," and then turns to me. "You know where it is."

I avoid looking at Walt. "All right. We'll meet at Nirina's."

Speedy says, "I'll have to drive fast."

He's looking forward to it. I smile and shake my head. "Speedy, you're o-kay."

Ten minutes later, I'm standing under the awning at the edge of the parking lot with Walt and Nirina when Speedy drives up in an ancient Renault. Even in the pouring rain, the Malagasy guard takes his time, looking in the trunk, running a mirror around the underside of the car, but the police on the street barely look up.

Finally, the guard lets him in and shuts the gate. Nirina and Walt bundle into my car. Speedy jumps behind the wheel. The engine rumbles to life. Opening the gate once more, the guard gives me a look that says he doesn't much care for my making him run around in the rain while people drive in and out for no good reason.

I motion for Speedy to roll down the window. "Remember, drive quickly and draw them away. Good luck. I'll see you at Nirina's."

Speedy pops the clutch. The car jumps through the open gate and squeals on the wet pavement and into the street.

Like a cat jumping after a mouse, the Citroen with the broken headlight speeds down the street after them.

The guard frowns. "There go three men in a hurry, sir."

"In the Peugeot? They're just—"

"No, Monsieur Knott. In the Citroen."

"Three? I thought there were only two."

"No, Monsieur. Another car dropped off a large man a few minutes ago and he got in with the other two. It was very strange, sir, the way they seemed to be waiting there. I was going to speak to the Marine. But now they're gone."

I try to sound casual. "This third guy, was he Malagasy?"

"No, sir. A *vazaha*."

I grunt like I've been hit in the stomach. Nothing to be done about it now. But I feel a wave of real fear for Walt and Nirina and Speedy.

A few minutes later I get into the stolen Renault and drive out through the gate into the empty street.

Shantytowns surround Antananarivo like the rings around Saturn. Coming from the direction of the embassy, I have trouble finding the particular area Nirina had directed me to the night I drove her home. After to-ing and fro-ing for a quarter of an hour I finally stumble upon it. My car is nowhere in sight.

There are plenty of reasons why I might arrive before they did, none of them good. I've been improvising every step I take, dragging the others with me. Any misstep, any failure to anticipate what might happen next, can get them all killed. Me, too. But I'd only be getting what I had coming.

The intensity of the storm continues to grow. I wonder if the demonstrators and cops on the avenue have been blown away in the wind, taken into the sky like those nannies in *Mary Poppins*.

The car is rocked by the wind and pounded by the rain while I wait out the longest minutes of my life. I'm raked by worry and the sense of my own culpability if anything should happen to the three of them while they carry out my plan—a plan that looks increasingly harebrained.

I'm about to turn around and head back for the embassy, thinking that for some reason they might have returned there, when a pair of headlights appear in the mirror. Speedy? Picard? I feel for the pistol in my pocket before I notice that the headlights are clear, not yellow, and show no sign of a broken lens. The car pulls up behind me and I can make out the lines of my Peugeot. I let out a long sigh of relief.

Struggling against the rain and the gusting wind, I get out of the stolen car, walk back to my own and jump into the front passenger seat.

"It worked just as you said, Monsieur Knott," Speedy tells me. "The car followed us to the Colbert. When we stopped, the other car stopped beside us and two men jumped out with their hands under their coats." As my eyes adjust to the dark, I can see that Speedy appears shaken, his eyes wide. "I thought they were going to shoot us. But they were looking for you." He shouts to be heard over the wind. "I told them you were still at the embassy. They talked to someone waiting in their car, then left again."

I look at Nirina, sitting next to Walt in the back seat. "You'd know Picard. Was it him?"

She nods. I can see she's frightened. I want to tell her the worst is over, but a drive over dissolving highways followed by an ocean crossing in a small boat during the middle of the monsoon lay ahead. There are still plenty of ways this could end badly.

"You did great," I tell Speedy and lean over the back seat to look at Walt. "How ya doing, pardner? "

The old cowboy is leaning against Nirina, breathing shallowly, his face slack with fatigue. A couple of days in the embassy had done him good, but his reserves are low.

"A little winded, s'all. Not used to all this runnin' around."

I motion to Speedy, "Let's switch places. I'll drive for a while. We'll leave the Renault here."

I get behind the wheel. The wind buffets the car, whistling through gaps around the windows. The rain pounds against the roof. I can't bring myself to start the car.

"What's wrong?" Nirina asks.

"I'm fighting twenty years of caring what other people write in my annual evaluation."

"You don't have to do this," she says. "We can take the other car, try to make it to the coast ourselves."

I shake my head. "Once the police know Walt's gone—and Picard will likely tell them—they'll be looking for him everywhere. I don't think you'd get through the roadblocks in that car. Besides, I need to get out of here, too. My old life is over. I've made up my mind."

The exhilaration I had felt earlier in the evening has evaporated, leaving me with an emotional hangover. I turn the key, put the car in gear, and head out of town.

21

Only the pounding rain and the gusting wind break the silence of our escape. As we drive away from Antananarivo and rise into the dark hills east of the city, the old Chinese-built road narrows and we're forced to dodge small mud slides and fallen trees.

We've been underway perhaps an hour when I brake to a stop.

"What's the matter?" Walt asks from the back seat.

I point at two orange flames flickering in the rain a hundred yards ahead of us. "Roadblock."

We've already breezed through a checkpoint at the edge of town. The diplomatic plates and my assurance that I was heading home with friends were enough. My presence here, in the middle of a hurricane, will be harder to explain.

Flashlight beams point in our direction, but we're too far away for anyone to clearly make us out.

Walt props himself up on one elbow. "Any chance they're looking for us already?"

"Maybe. If the phones are working. Or if they're in contact by radio." The weight of the gun in my pocket feels like an anvil. I put the car in gear and the Peugeot crawls forward.

The roadblock consists of a couple of oil drums topped with hurricane lamps, and a metal gate set between them. Three policemen stand out of the rain on the covered porch of a darkened shop.

"Let me do the talking," I tell the others. I stop the car and am about to get out when something in the mirror catches my eye. A flash of light? Something moving in the darkness? I turn around and look through the back window. Nothing. I'm jumpy as hell, seeing things in the dark now.

"What's up?" Walt asks.

"Nothing. I thought maybe …" Through the curtain of rain and the swirling wind the light appears once more, far below and perhaps a kilometer away—maybe twice that distance along the twisting road. Once more, the light disappears then returns—yeah, just like a car on a twisty road. After a few seconds the image resolves itself into the beams of a car's headlights flickering yellow through the gaps in the trees. Did one of the lights throw a white beam as well, like the broken headlamp on the Citroen?

"Nirina, you saw Picard when his goons stopped you by the Colbert. Do you think he got a look at you too?"

She turns in her seat and looks into the darkness behind us. "I don't know," she says in a hushed voice. "Perhaps."

"He knows you, yes? From that time you talked to him about your friend who owed him the money. The one Andriamana shot."

She blinks uncertainly. "I'm not sure he would remember me." Her voice has gone quiet as she understands what lies behind the question.

"Let's say he does." This is no time to mention that there's hardly a man in the world who wouldn't remember seeing her. "So, Picard chases after you this evening, finally catches up and finds I'm not with you. He goes back to the embassy, has one of his men talk to the cops waiting outside and figures out I'm gone. Maybe it takes him a few minutes to put it all together, but he finally understands he's been suckered." I tap my fingers nervously against the steering wheel. "My bet is he's going to remember you're from the coast, like the kid he had killed. And he's going to guess that's where we're headed."

I jump when a gray-haired policeman taps at the window. I show him my diplomatic ID and explain that I'm traveling with staff members to give a speech in Tamatave the next day. The man doesn't ask why I would drive through a storm like this simply to give a speech. *Vazaha* are alien beings and their ways unknowable.

The cop motions for the other two policemen to move the barricade aside.

If that's Picard behind me—and everything in me says that it is—I hope the police take more time with him than they have with me.

Driving the twisting highway isn't easy at the best of times, but in the dark, with gale winds and heavy rain, it's a slow and dangerous business. A landslide chokes the road nearly shut at one point. A couple miles further on, part of the pavement has fallen away, narrowing the road to a single lane for a hundred yards.

Nirina leans over the seat, her mouth close to my ear. "Do you think the Colonel would phone Andriamana and have him arrest us?"

I can hear in her voice the residual fear from the night the police captain had eyed her in the village, the night we came close to dying in each others' arms. Could Picard be so unaware of his own peril with Andriamana that he might call on his help again? "I don't know. With any luck the phones are out."

She nods, but I can sense her fear.

For the next hour we make slow, steady progress along the narrow highway. I look in the mirror, searching for yellow headlights in the distance, but find only darkness. Still, I can't afford to doubt that Picard and his men are back there, hidden by the storm and the twisting road.

An hour later, as we come up on the town of Moramanga, I'm beginning to feel better about things. There's no sign of Picard, and the rain and wind are starting to let up. Maybe I'm feeling a little smug as I round a corner on the narrow roadway.

"Sonofabitch!" I shout and slam on the brakes. The car slews sideways on the wet pavement and I fight for control before it lurches to a stop.

Walt, who has been asleep, wakes with a start in the back seat. "What the hell's goin' on?"

"I think we just ran out of luck," I tell him.

A fallen tree blocks the road in front of us. I glance in the mirror. I haven't seen the headlights of the Citroen in fifteen minutes and have been telling myself that something must have happened to Picard, a breakdown, an accident. But I don't believe it.

I squeeze the steering wheel until my knuckles hurt, my mind running in circles. I can't go forward, don't dare go back.

It's Speedy who figures a way out.

"Monsieur Knott, I saw a road just in back of us. Maybe we can reach Moramanga that way and find another road from there down to the highway."

It's better than any idea I have. I back down the road and turn up a dirt lane that soon becomes a river of mud.

I shove the gearshift into low, flutter the throttle. The car shudders, threatening to whir to a halt in the clinging mud. I tell myself not to panic. With any luck, Picard will miss this road and end his night stuck in front of the fallen tree.

No. Too easy.

Toward the top of the long slope, the road becomes firmer. The little Peugeot tops the rise heading into town. Relaxing my death grip on the wheel, I look in the mirror at Walt leaning against the car door, gray and unwell. I think of the miles ahead and the long sea voyage to Mauritius in stormy weather. Could Speedy and Nirina be so determined to liberate the old guy that they kill him in the process?

I take my eyes off the road for an instant and glance at the car's gauges. "Damn!" After hours of slow driving and wheel-spinning, the gas gauge twitches just above empty.

I drive slowly into town, barely touching the accelerator, searching the gloom around us for a gas station.

"There," Nirina points to a ramshackle building with a fuel pump in front, shuttered for the night.

A wisp of smoke rises from a vent in the roof. We're in luck. The owner lives in his station.

Standing in the rain with Nirina beside me, I bang on the door hard enough to shake the walls. From somewhere inside a voice grumbles at us. It doesn't sound like, "Come in." I pound harder. Finally, Nirina calls to the attendant in Malagasy. After much shuffling and griping, the door opens a few inches and a lone eye peers through the crack. Its owner gives a shout and shrinks back at the sight of a tall, bedraggled *vazaha* looming out of the storm. He tries to close the door, but I've put my foot inside the doorframe. I say to Nirina. "Tell this guy we're in a hurry."

Nirina lights into him like a banshee, shrieking orders and

pointing to his pumps. More afraid of her wrath than my presence, the man finally comes out, growling uncertainly, and fills the tank from his ancient gravity-fed pump. Nirina points to a road leading through the darkened village. Trembling, the attendant nods. Nirina says to me, "He tells me we can follow this road back to the highway." I can see her white teeth as she smiles in the dark. "You see? It's useful traveling with a *tromba* woman."

"I never doubted it. But we'd better get out of here. I'm surprised Picard isn't on us already."

"I am driving now, Monsieur Knott. You're tired." Speedy stands by the driver's door, holding out his hand for the keys.

He's right. After my adventures of the last day and a half, I'm nearly as beat as Walt. "Okay."

Soon we're back on the road, and discover that on the eastern side of the hills the storm has done its worst and moved on. The reach of the Peugeot's headlights increases in the gentler rain and Speedy leans back in his seat.

"So, Monsieur Knott," he says, "do you think the phones are working?"

"No idea, Speedy. I hope not. If they are, I think Picard will have called the local police."

"Or maybe the police radios are working."

"The radios only reach so far. They'd have to go through a couple of relays to get to Tamatave. By the time it got there, the message might be so garbled they'd think they're supposed to hold a parade for us."

"Maybe." Speedy thinks it over. "On the other hand, if Monsieur Picard was able to call, or managed to have the police radio Tamatave before he left Antananarivo, I may get a chance to meet the formidable Captain Andriamana tonight." His eyes light up as if talking about meeting a movie star. "With the Captain in front of us and the Colonel in back of us, we'll have to hurry or we will get caught between them." He takes his hands off the wheel and squeezes them together in a gruesome gesture.

I slump in my seat. "This hasn't been much of a plan, has it?"

His eyes on the road, Speedy seems game enough for a regiment. "We're almost there. Besides, we're not doing it for ourselves. We're doing it for Mister Walt," he says with a glance at the back seat. "But we all get something from it, don't we?"

"Yeah?"

"Nirina will go with Mister Walt and start a new life. You will get Mr. Walt out of Madagascar, like you promised. And that will make you free."

"Free." Could it be so easy? "What about you? What do you get from all this?"

"I'll help my friend go home. That's better than giving him Peter Stuyvesants in prison. And when I return to Miss Gloria, she'll think I'm a hero."

"Y'know, Speedy, you may be right."

"Of course I am."

For the first time Speedy's smile strikes me as not so much a reflection of his unquenchable optimism, but as a way of hiding depths he normally wished to conceal from a *vazaha*. I think back on what Rabary told me the night of the dinner at my house, that my mere presence, my inability to speak the same language as the Malagasy, makes it impossible for me to truly understand them. I see only the façade they adopt when around me. I look at Speedy and realize I'm traveling with a stranger—but one I trust.

"Well, then, speed on, brother."

We reach the coast highway, the rain forest giving way to rice paddies and long stretches of flooded road. In the deepest spots water laps at the car doors and Speedy slows to a crawl. I imagine potholes big enough to sink a bus hiding under the placid surface of the water. But the engine runs strong and we drive steadily north with the metronome of the windshield wipers marking time.

It's still dark, but dawn can't be far away. The rain is easing up. We pass a road sign saying we're thirty klicks from Tamatave. I lean over the back seat and gently shake Nirina's leg to wake her.

"I think we're getting close. You'll have to tell us where to turn off."

Nirina blinks awake and looks around, her eyes half-closed—the same face she wore when she woke next to me in bed. As if she reads my thoughts, she looks frankly into my eyes. I turn away, reminding myself that it's all over.

Walt sits up, his face slack with fatigue, and I give him a smile that I hope looks more confident than I feel.

He stares blankly at me, wide-eyed as a child. "Where are we?"

"On the coast, nearly to the boat."

He grunts weakly. I wonder if he's up to the voyage that still lies ahead. Too late to worry about that now. "Okay, where do we turn off?" I ask Nirina.

She peers into the darkness and soon points to a clump of trees near a fisherman's hut, apparently a landmark. "There's a gravel road to our right, one or two kilometers ahead. It will lead us down to the beach."

Not believing in our luck, I again look in back of us for the Citroen and see only darkness.

Before I can turn around, I hear Nirina catch her breath and whisper, "Oh, no."

The roadblock in front of us is much like the one we went through earlier that night, two oil barrels and a metal gate between them. But these policemen—four of them—are out in the open with no shelter from the storm. They're soaked, weary, ill-tempered—and better armed.

As Speedy rolls up to the barricade two of the policemen aim Kalashnikovs at our Peugeot. A third, wearing sergeant's stripes, holds up his hand, ordering us to stop. He waves at the fourth policeman to put down a two-way radio and train his flashlight on Speedy. His hand on his holster, the sergeant motions for Speedy to roll down his window.

The sergeante pokes his head inside, his eyes dark and humorless. Water drips from the visor of his cap. He grunts something at Speedy in Malagasy.

Speedy says something back, then turns to me. "I told him we work for the embassy. He wants to see your identification," he tells me.

The policeman frowns at my diplomatic ID and waves at the cop with the flashlight to shine its beam on the front of the car. The sergeant steps back, regards the diplomatic plates and frowns again. He has the man with the radio send some message. Like cops in the U.S., they make a show of not being in a hurry. After several minutes he hands my ID back and again speaks to Speedy in Malagasy.

Speedy says to me, "He wants to know why you are out on the road at this hour."

Behind the policeman a tinny voice crackles over the two-way radio.

I ask Speedy, "Does he know who we are? Is he looking for us?"

"I don't know."

I repeat the story I gave to the policemen near Moramanga, that I'm delivering a speech in Tamatave. While Speedy translates, I glance nervously in the mirror.

"Listen," I say to Speedy, "tell him that the mayor of Tamatave is waiting for me. I don't want to have to tell him I'm late because his police force held me up."

The policeman glares at me and drops the pretense that he doesn't speak French. "No, you listen, Monsieur. I do not answer to the mayor, but to my superior, Captain Andriamana. You are in Madagascar and will obey the orders of Malagasy authorities. I have been told to look for a car with diplomatic plates. I am going to ask you to pull to the side of the road. Captain Andriamana is on his way here. You will wait for him."

Something in the sergeant's eyes, or maybe the fact that he doesn't know what he's supposed to do until Andriamana arrives, speaks of a small wormhole of uncertainty.

Walt stirs in the back seat. "Robert, what the hell's going on here?"

"They've pulled us over. We're supposed to wait for some captain to show up." I don't tell him that we may be waiting for our own deaths. I try to think of a way out of this. If I tell Speedy to make a run for it, they'll shoot us to pieces. If we stay, maybe we get shot anyway. I feel for the pistol in my pocket, but know it would do me no good. I might get one poor son of a bitch of a Malagasy policeman. Then they would get us.

Walt grumbles unintelligibly for a moment, then bursts out, "Robert, you tell them to let us through."

"Take it easy, Walt. They've all got guns."

"Hell, where I come from everybody's got guns. I ain't impressed."

The sergeant frowns at Walt. "Who is he?"

Speedy speaks rapidly in Malagasy, smiling and nodding toward Walt in the back seat. The officer looks at Walt, then at Speedy again. He tries to maintain a sneer of disbelief, but I see doubt creeping into his eyes.

"What are you telling him?" I ask.

Over his shoulder, Speedy says to Walt in his pidgin English, "Sit up, Monsieur Walt. I am telling him you are the Ambassador of America and you don't want any delays."

"Speedy—" I start, but Walt growls over me.

"Good. You tell those sonsabitches that the Ambassador—"

I'm about to tell Walt to take it easy when I catch a distant glimpse of approaching headlights in the side mirror. Whatever hand Walt thinks he's holding, I figure it's time to let him play it. I lean over the seat and say, "Ride 'em, cowboy."

Walt jumps into his role with both feet. "Tell this pissant cop and these other peckerwoods that I'll have their badges for this. Hell, I'll tell 'em myself." He opens the car door and steps out. I can't hear him clearly, but the words don't matter now because he's got the tune exactly right.

All the frustration of six months under the thumb of Malagasy prison guards has broken through Walt's depleted store of patience. His finger shakes as he points to the policemen at each end of the barricade, the ones with rifles, and chews them out like a drill sergeant.

Speedy doesn't bother to translate.

Trying to regain control of the situation, the sergeant barks something at Walt but backs up a step while he does it, then another. The two policemen with the Kalashnikovs lower their weapons. The sergeant waves at them to raise them again. But Walt's in charge now, kicking at the pavement and shouting orders. With a sweep of his arm he tells them to "open that goddamn barricade, and do it now!"

The two policemen need no translation. Caught between their sergeant and a rampaging *vazaha*, they waver a moment, then pull the barricade aside even as the sergeant rages at them to close it again.

Barking a few last words over his shoulder, Walt gets back in the car. "Okay, Speedy, get us out of here."

By now, the beams of the Citroen's lights are only a few hundred yards away, coming steadily along the half-flooded road.

I get an idea. "Speedy, tell the sergeant it's the car behind us they want to stop."

Now Speedy sees the Citroen too. He leans out the window and calls to the sergeant. As I hoped, this message erodes what little confidence remains to the policeman. Buffeted by doubt, and with his authority crumbling, he turns his anger on the other policemen, motioning them to let us pass.

I tell Walt, "Great job, Mr. Ambassador."

"Buncha peckerwoods," Walt mumbles, slicking back his rain-soaked hair. He slumps in the back seat, exhausted by his efforts.

Behind us, I see the police closing the barricade. The sergeant, trembling with fury, orders the Citroen to halt. I almost wish I could stick around to watch.

We've traveled only a few hundred yards when Nirina points to a graveled track leading off to the right. "There's the road."

I look back as the big Citroen pulls up to the roadblock. They can see us turning. They'll know exactly where to chase us down.

Jouncing in his seat as he turns down the roughly cut road, Speedy says, "Maybe they will call for the Captain and maybe Monsieur Picard and wait for him before doing anything."

"Picard figures Andriamana's on his side, and he's not going to wait if he thinks he can get me now." I remember what Rabary said at the Queen's Palace and wonder if Picard understands how dangerous an ally Andriamana might prove. I finger Esmer's gun in my coat pocket like a man working his prayer beads.

Within a hundred yards, the gravel disappears and the road turns into a pair of muddy ruts. The Peugeot's tires began to slip. Through the rain and the woods around us, I catch a glimmer of yellow light in the mirror. The cops must have let Picard straight through.

"Damn! Can't you make this log go any faster?"

A note of impatience creeps into Speedy's voice. "I can't even go this fast, Monsieur Knott." As if to prove his point, the car suddenly toboggans from one side of the narrow track to the other. Speedy fights the wheel, working to keep the slithering Peugeot pointed forward.

I'm beginning to think Speedy could drive through anything when the young Malagasy shouts, "Merde!"

Rounding a curve, the road drops into a swale and the Peugeot's headlights catch an expanse of muddy water that spans the road. The car hits it hard, sending a wall of water over the windshield. Tires whirring in the mud, the car slithers across the road like a snake.

Over the roar of the engine, I hear a whoop and a crazy laugh and realize it's coming from me. The perverse ecstasy of danger infects Walt too. He sits up in the back seat, a wild look in his eye and yells, "Go, Speedy, go!"

Speedy downshifts and laughs maniacally. The rev counter soars over the red line. "She's swimming!" he shouts.

A violent bump shakes the car and its nose cants up as the tires find some purchase and we leap out of the water, throwing mud in every direction. The Peugeot scrambles up the slope, our headlights pointing into the sky.

Speedy fights the car through another twisty stretch of mud. Even Nirina cheers.

"What a driver!" I laugh.

A huge grin on his face, Speedy starts to say something as he wrestles the car around a sharp corner. Before he can get a word out, the headlights pick up a tree that has fallen across the path. Speedy stands on the brakes, but it's too late. The car barely slows before smashing into the fallen tree.

22

All four of us snap forward then bounce back into our seats as we hit the tree and the engine dies. Over our shocked silence, a light rain patters on the roof of the car.

I throw open the door and stagger out. Aside from a crumpled fender and a shattered headlight, there's little damage, but there's no way around the fallen tree.

A loud splash from the pool of water behind us cuts my inspection short. Picard is only seconds away.

I lean through the open door. "Everyone out, fast! We'll have to go on foot." I say to Nirina, "We can't stay on the road. They'll find us. How well do you know this area? Can you find your way through the woods?"

Nirina climbs out of the car and twirls in a slow circle, struggling for her bearings. "I'm afraid …" she starts, her voice hardly a whisper. "I'm afraid that if we go into the woods we'll be lost."

The sound of pounding surf comes from somewhere in front of us. From close behind comes the rumble of the Citroen thrashing through the water, roaring like a beast. Yellow beams jump crazily among the branches of the trees as the car rises up the short incline and levels out.

"Quick!" I shout. "Into the woods."

Nirina and Speedy skip quickly into the cover of the trees. I start to follow when I notice Walt, exhausted and disoriented, still standing in the road. I call to Speedy for help. We grab Walt under the arms, and drag him into the trees. As we lumber toward the woods, I feel my coat flapping loosely. The gun has dropped out of my pocket.

"Take Walt," I tell Speedy and run back to the car.

For an eternity that probably lasts all of five seconds I fumble around the floor of the Peugeot trying to find the pistol. After knocking aside a paper cup and an old comb, my hand closes on the barrel of the pistol. At the same instant the Citroen roars around the corner like a charging lion.

Clutching the gun against my stomach, I run for the woods, crashing through the treeline in the dark. Within seconds, I'm lost. Fighting panic, I stumble over roots and run into limbs until I can just make out Nirina standing in a clearing, looking into the darkness.

"Okay," I whisper as I run up to her in the dark, "which way?"

Behind me I hear three car doors slam shut. The sound of men's voices comes faintly over the last traces of the storm.

"Be quiet," Nirina says. She turns slowly, searching in the darkness. "There's a small village somewhere in these woods. We will find it and hide there."

"Isn't that the first place they'd look for us?" I ask.

Nirina turns and I feel her eyes go straight through me. The hair on the back of my neck prickles as if I were looking at a ghost. Her rain-soaked dress clings to her, and I feel the stirrings of desire, but can't escape the impression that she has become someone far different from the young woman I know so well—and so little.

"Look." Speedy points. "I think I see some huts. It must be the village." He runs across the clearing and out of sight, thrashing through the trees on the other side.

Behind us, the voices of the three men grow louder. Flashlight beams create jagged lines through the trees. Two of them head away at opposite angles, the third comes directly toward us.

"They've split up to find us," I tell Nirina and Walt. We head toward the woods on the other side of the clearing.

We catch up to Speedy, who has waited at the edge of the woods. We've made it only a few yards into the trees when the old cowboy stops. He's panting hard and holding a hand to his chest.

"Walt, you're not having a heart attack, are you?" I put an arm around his shoulders and at the same time cast an anxious glance behind us. One of the flashlights is already probing the corners of the clearing.

Walt tries to dismiss my concerns with a wave of his hand. "I'm just—" He shakes his head, says nothing more.

I look at "Nirina, which way?"

Walt points into the distance and says, "There. I can see it. There." He thrashes forward into the undergrowth.

Nirina and Speedy quickly overtake him and run ahead just as I hear a whirring over my head, followed by a loud crack.

He's shooting at us. I run to catch up with the others.

Walt shakes his arm free of Speedy's grip. "I ain't afraid of nobody who thinks he can hit us in the dark with a pistol."

With the wind moaning overhead, we stumble blindly through the woods. The rain has stopped. A silver light shines through the palms overhead as a half-moon emerges through the racing clouds.

A few feet ahead, Nirina and Speedy stand among the trees, looking in opposite directions.

"Do you see anything?" I ask.

Speedy shakes his head.

"I was sure I saw it." Walt's voice has turned peevish and old.

"This is nuts," I grumble. "Everybody sees this village and we still can't find it."

A loud crack tops the sighing wind. A flashlight beam veers across the darkness only a few yards behind us.

"Robert!" a wind-whipped voice calls.

It's Picard. I heft the pistol and wonder if I have the nerve to use it. How much of a chance would I have against a professional killer, anyway? I put it back in my pocket.

"Which way?" I ask no one in particular.

Then I see it through a break in the trees, the faint glow of lamplight from a clutch of huts. "Come on!" I push the others toward the light. A limb whips me in the face, and I taste blood in my mouth. I hear Picard crashing through the woods, coming to kill us.

I stumble over a tree root and fall onto my hands and knees. When I look up I can't see the lamplight anymore. All the tensions and exertions of the endless night catch up to me at once. Time has ceased to exist, or at least to signify. It doesn't matter if five minutes have passed since we ran into the woods or two hours. Only finding the village matters.

Nirina's voice breaks through my funk. "There it is," she says, a strange huskiness in her voice.

I scramble to my feet. "I don't see anything."

"It's there."

Nirina walks into the darkness. We follow.

Behind us, Picard is gaining.

Walt stumbles. I grab him by the arm to keep him from falling.

"I can do this," Walt mumbles to himself, "Gotta get out of here. Gotta …" His voice trails off.

I have no idea how much time has passed when Nirina stops. With eerie detachment, she announces, "We're there."

We've come to the edge of a large clearing. I squint in the moonlight. With a shiver of dread, I see there is no village.

Waves pound against the beach somewhere in the distance.

We've walked maybe ten paces into the clearing when I see a group of dark figures loom out of the darkness in front of us. I fumble for the pistol.

"No," Nirina says sharply. "Look closely."

At her words, the figures become clearer. Macabre totems rise out of the ground—horned creatures and carved figures, vibrant with obscure and atavistic power.

"What the hell kind of a village is this?" I ask. Then I see it clearly. It's a cemetery.

After hours of disorienting flight through the storm, the twisting mountain roads, the roadblocks, the killers behind us, it has come down to this: a *tromba* woman leading us through the darkness to the only village we will find, the abode of the ancestors, the realm of the ghosts.

I think back to the dinner at my house, of the Fulbright student who spoke of spirit-possessed women, of the mysterious village that vanishes from sight only to reappear again, still just beyond reach, and of the sacred reburial of the ancestors, from which I learn that even death represents only a punctuation mark in the continuum of their lives. Now, despite—or perhaps because of—my efforts to ignore this world, to refuse the spell of Madagascar, it has come to find me. It won't let go until I surrender what's left of my pride and my faith in logic and accept the world in which I have come to live.

In the moonlight the undefined shapes began to resolve themselves into tall wooden posts marking closely packed graves, most adorned with zebu horns, many topped with a wooden carving—a boat crowded with oarsmen, two women pounding rice with wooden poles, a man with a spear. Scattered among these are modest stone shafts, curiously like miniatures of the Washington monument. All of it glows in the moonlight, like images from a too-vivid dream.

Yes, as Nirina says, it is, after all, a village—a village of ghosts.

I fall in behind Nirina, the one protective spirit who might guard me from the phantoms roaming this macabre site.

The beautiful young Malagasy walks purposefully across the clearing, advancing on the cemetery's unsettling images.

Speedy's voice cuts through the darkness. "Monsieur Knott. Quick."

I find Walt lying on the ground at Speedy's feet, breathing heavily, eyes closed. Nirina turns back and kneels beside him, putting his head in her lap. "He has to rest," she says.

I look across the clearing and see Picard's flashlight bobbing ever closer.

Nirina's voice is clear and calm. "Pull Walt in among the graves. We will hide him there."

I look at her, then at the cemetery. I can't begin to explain how much I don't want to go in there.

Half-dragging, half-carrying Walt across the open ground, we make it to the middle of the graveyard and lay him on the ground. He begins to mumble incoherently. Nirina kneels beside him and holds a finger to his lips.

A beam of light probes the darkness, casting grotesque shadows among the carved images.

"Robert!" Picard's voice sounds clear and determined.

As we wait silently from behind the grave markers, we hear the crack of a gunshot and the whine of a bullet ricocheting off one of the stone shafts. Picard fires again, blasting to pieces a carving of a man herding zebu.

"Robert, I know you are in there," Picard calls in English. "Come out. I'm not interested in the others. I only want you."

A silence falls over the cemetery, measured by the distant surf and the faint sound of the other two pursuers, still some distance away, making their way through the woods toward the clearing.

"Robert, my men will be here in a few moments. They will not be as discriminating as I am. And they are loath to leave witnesses."

I look at Speedy, Nirina, Walt. If I walk out to meet Picard now, the others still have a chance. Walt can start the long trip back to Oregon. Nirina can resume her search for herself, resolve her *tromba* spirit. Speedy can satisfy his self-appointed duty to help Walt, and go back to Gloria head high, a hero, not a thief.

I put my hand in my coat pocket to reassure myself that I still have the gun. Maybe this is the easiest course. With the pull of a trigger I might resolve a world full of demons—either mine or Picard's.

I rise to my feet.

"Robert," Nirina whispers, "Get down."

I look down and think how lucky I am that my last sight might be of her. "I have to do this," I say.

The beam of Picard's flashlight strikes me full in the face. I put up a hand to shield my eyes.

"No, Robert. Put your hands out to your sides," Picard calls to me. "Come out here where I can see you." Picard's voice is flat, professional, a voice that carries the weight of being the last one many men ever heard.

Led by the beam of the flashlight, I step out of the graveyard and walk into the middle of the clearing, my arms held out.

Picard extinguishes his flashlight. His moonlit form slowly emerges from the darkness.

"Hel-lo, Bobby."

"Hello, Maurice."

My hands are sweating. Picard won't wait long. His men won't hesitate at all.

"They're not far off, are they?" I say and cock my chin at the two men struggling through the last stretch of woods before the clearing.

As I hoped, Picard, relaxed and in command, allows himself a glance over his shoulder. "No, they're—"

I go for the gun, grabbing the butt of the pistol. But as I try to pull it clear, it catches in the lining of my pocket. Frantically, I yank at it, ripping the pocket away, the weapon coming out muzzle first. Slippery with fear-sweat, I try to find the grips. The pistol slips from my hands and thuds to the ground. Cursing, I drop to my knees and try to find the gun on the dark ground.

"It's no good, Robert."

A wave of calm comes over me as I look up into the muzzle of Picard's gun and wait for the moment that will end my life. Good riddance, I think.

Picard laughs quietly. Still, the Frenchman doesn't fire.

As if weighted by my flickering will to survive, the muzzle of Picard's gun slowly drops.

"Ah, Robert," the Frenchman sighs, "I thought I could kill you. I really did. It used to be so easy. I should have seen the truth when I needed Andriamana to kill that boy for me, rather than doing it myself. My gift, such as it is, has deserted me."

"Well, that's fine with me. I can't seem to shoot you either."

"Yes, but in your case, it's largely a matter of incompetence." Picard expels a breath. "It's not so simple, is it, taking someone's life?"

The crashing of the two men breaking through the treeline and into the clearing reminds us both that Picard's momentary failure is of only passing importance. My only fear is that they won't stop with killing me. My chin sinks to my chest as I'm overwhelmed with the banality of my failure.

Picard grunts. "I marvel that they got around to this part of the woods so quickly. It really pays to hire the best."

Later, I realize Picard would have been smart to have kept his flashlight on. Or perhaps he should have called out to the two men. Or maybe it wouldn't have mattered; it would have worked out the same way, whatever he did.

What Picard does is turn toward them in the faint light of the moon with a gun in his hand.

Three bright flashes light up the darkness, covered by the crack of three gunshots. With an audible thump, one of the bullets hits Picard full in the chest.

He doesn't go down like the bad guy in the movies, clutching his chest and clawing at the air, or reeling backwards as if taking an uppercut from Fate. He simply collapses like a puppet with its strings cut.

Across the clearing, a voice shouts in French, "Don't move!"

With a flash of almost biblical revelation, I suddenly understand that the two men thrashing through the brush are not Picard's henchmen. No, poor Picard was up against someone who wouldn't hesitate when the moment came to kill. And he won't stop with killing Picard.

I see my gun glinting on the ground. I drop to my knees and find its grips at the same instant the beams of the distant flashlights converge on me. I aim toward the lights and pull the trigger. Nothing happens.

A quick arrhythmic *crack-crack-crack*, jolly as fire-crackers, accompanies the sound of bullets whizzing over my head.

Veering toward panic, I try to recall Esmer's instructions for firing the automatic. Tugging at the slide with my left hand, I put a round in the chamber and let the slide go, my hand recoiling into the air as the heavily-sprung slide jumps into place.

A blow hits my hand as if from a baseball bat, nearly knocking me over. For a moment I think it has something to do with the force of the slide's retraction, but as the numbing impact spreads along my arm I realize I've been shot.

My surge of fear comes with a chaser of anger. I fire wildly from my knees, pulling the trigger as fast as I can until I've emptied the clip.

When the firing pin clicks on the empty chamber for the third or fourth time I lower the gun. Only then do I realize no one is firing back and that the two flashlights appear to have fallen to the ground.

The sound of the wind and the distant surf reassert themselves. Clouds race in front of the moon.

Out of the renewed darkness, I hear a growl of animal rage. Even distorted by pain and anger, I recognize the voice of Captain Andriamana.

I stagger to my feet. Picard lies on his back, his arms splayed out. A glimmer of moonlight slips through the tattered clouds and I see his bulging eyes staring at the sky.

With the emptied gun in my hand, I walk across the clearing until I stand over the fallen policeman.

Andriamana writhes on the ground clutching his leg below the knee. I look around for the policeman's pistol and kick it away. The other policeman apparently dropped his flashlight and ran for the woods when he saw the Captain fall.

Like a wolf caught in the light of a campfire, Andriamana's eyes blaze in the moonlight. Choked, guttural curses escape his clenched teeth like a spray of bullets. By the rules of the world in which he lives, he understands his end has come. He shows no fear, only a bottomless indignation that this should happen to him.

I know I could, perhaps should, pick up Andriamana's gun and kill him with it. It would be a mercy to the community, a favor to anyone who might yet fall victim to his cruelty and ambition. A moral necessity.

I can't do it. It's not any sense of mercy or compassion toward a fellow human being. I simply don't have the right sort of resolve—the kind it takes to shoot an unarmed man for the sole reason that the world would be a better place with him dead—and I'm grateful for it.

In the glow of the Captain's discarded flashlight, I see something dark dripping to the ground—blood from my injured hand.

After a last look into the Captain's eyes, I put Esmer's pistol back in my remaining coat pocket, turn my back on Andriamana and walk away. The wounded man's incoherent raging follows me as I walk toward the shadowed monuments. I avoid the sight of Picard's body as I go by. My hand is beginning to throb and I feel lightheaded with shock.

"Robert…"

I spin around, my empty gun drawn.

"Robert…"

With a thrill of horror, I realize Picard is calling to me.

"What do you want?" I ask, like Hamlet speaking to the ghost.

"Robert…" Picard sighs. For a moment I think he's died. Then I hear him take a deep breath.

"*Vien ici* … come here, Robert." His hand twitches, beckoning me closer.

The Frenchman's eyes stare unblinking into the sky. He licks his lips and says something I don't catch.

Though revulsed at the thought of coming any nearer, a man's dying words demand a listener. I kneel beside Picard.

For a long time, he says nothing. His tongue licking his lips is the only sign that he's still alive. Finally, in a choked voice, he says, "Go see my daughter. Tell her how I loved her."

I don't have any choice. "I will."

"Martine Badaoui. Paris. Martine Badaoui."

I puzzle over her name. If she's unmarried, as Picard has said, why is her name different from his? One more thing I sense I'll never know.

"I'll talk to her. I promise."

"Tell her how I loved her," he says again. A few incoherent words escapes his lips before he says with sudden clarity. "Robert."

"Yes, Maurice."

"I always liked you." The moonlight illuminates a ghastly smile on Picard's face. He shakes his head gently. "And I…. I was never a colonel. Not even an officer. Just a sergeant."

"It's okay, Maurice. It doesn't matter now."

"Robert"—the same eerie smile—"your debts are all cancelled now, yes?"

"I guess so."

"And now I've paid mine too." Picard laughs weakly and closes his eyes. "Robert, don't let me die here. Take me with you."

"Maurice, I can't—"

"Take me into the cemetery with the others."

Which others does he mean, the living or the dead?

There is no way to refuse him. I grab the Frenchman's collar and try to drag him toward the cemetery, but with only one hand working, I can barely budge the big man.

Then Nirina is beside me. She grabs the shoulder of Picard's coat in both hands and together we drag the big Frenchman across the grass. As we grunt and tug and pant to get him into the cemetery I think I hear the old soldier of misfortune laughing.

We lay him among the shadows of the monuments. The big man looks around, sees he has come to a Malagasy cemetery and chuckles. Then he gives a long sigh and dies.

Walt, leaning against one of the monuments, looks at Picard. "Who is he?"

I consider the question. "A guy who said he was a friend of mine."

23

Speedy and I get Walt to his feet and begin walking toward the sound of the surf. We see no more flashlight beams. Despite Picard's praise of their skills, his two men seem to have wandered off and gotten lost.

Nirina is in front of us, standing at the top of a low rise, silhouetted against the rising sun.

When we catch up to her, we see the Indian Ocean before us, a cauldron of wind-whipped waves. The sun is peeking its head above the horizon.

A young man stands on the beach below us, a rowboat pulled up beside him on the sand. A couple of hundred yards offshore a fishing boat tosses on the waves.

Nirina introduces the man as her older brother, Monja. We lay Walt in the bottom of the rowboat and push it to the edge of the water, me shoving with my one good hand. Though the lightheadedness has passed, the pain in my hand hammers up my arm and into my head.

Nirina clambers into the boat. As she looks at me her brown eyes appear as bottomless as the sea itself. I look back toward the shore and think of Antananarivo beyond the hills, of the embassy and Lynn and Gloria. They'll be fine without me, probably better off. I climb into the boat beside her.

None of us has our bags, but we're not going to take the risk of going back to the car for them. Picard's men may still be around somewhere and might still feel duty-bound to kill us.

Monja takes the oars and begins to row toward the fishing boat.

Speedy, who has been pushing us deeper into the surf, stops, chest deep in the water. Over the sound of the waves he shouts, "Goodbye, Mr. Walt," and raises his hand in farewell. "Goodbye, Nirina." Then he turns and walks back up to the beach. I'm a little hurt he didn't include me in his farewells.

Within a few yards of shore the rowboat begins to take on water in the tossing waves. Monja shouts at Nirina and nods toward two plastic buckets in the bow. She hands one to me and we start bailing.

After struggling with our bailing buckets for maybe ten minutes, we come alongside the fishing boat. Monja calls to the crewman he left on the boat, "Rakota!" then makes a perfectly timed leap from one tossing boat onto the other. Both men reach out, pull me over the gunwale and throw me onto the deck like a landed fish.

Walt's next. He stands pale and unsteady on the rocking boat. Timing the rise, they grab him by his outstretched arms and pull him on board, with Nirina pushing from behind.

As they lay Walt on deck, propped against the gunwale, Nirina shouts something to her brother and braces to jump onto the fishing boat. A swell lifts the rowboat, then drops it just as she jumps.

Suddenly she isn't there.

There's no shriek, no sound at all. She's simply gone. Monja cries out to Rakota and points to a line lying on the deck. I grab it first, scrabble to the rail and look over the side. I see nothing but the empty rowboat and churning water.

For an instant I think of jumping in after her. Monja sees it in my eyes. "Don't be an idiot," he says in French.

I want to tell him it was too late for that. But I also know I'm too old to die for love.

With a splash, Nirina bobs to the surface, spitting water, gasping for air. Shoving past Monja, I reach over the side with my good hand and grab her by the hair. The water-slick strands slip from my grasp and she sinks again.

"Nirina!"

Nothing answers but the surge of the sea.

When I've given up hope, she pops to the surface once more, almost directly under the boat. Leaning over until I nearly fall in the water, I grasp her under one shoulder. Monja grabs her by the other arm and with a great heave we pull her over the side and onto the boat. She falls gasping onto the crowded deck.

Too shaken to speak, too uncertain of what we mean to each other to even smile, Nirina and I look at each other across the narrow deck.

Monja and Rakota pull the empty rowboat aboard and secure it to the deck in front of the fishing boat's small cabin, then pull up the sea anchor and get underway.

At the mercy of the churning sea, the fishing boat rises high on the crest of a wave. Its bow points into the air, then crashes down the back side of the wave as if we might go straight to the bottom. It's like a nightmare carnival ride, except our lives are at stake. Rakota, Nirina, and I frantically bail, but the boat rides ever lower as water crashes over the bow faster than we can bail it out. Walt lies on the deck, his eyes closed.

A wave crashes into the boat's cabin, breaking its window, scattering shards of glass like shrapnel. Unprotected now against the spray of the wind-whipped waves, Monja turns and shouts something to Nirina. She shakes her head and shouts back. He appears adamant and cocks his chin at Walt.

Nirina drops her bucket and crawls across the deck to me. "He says we are going to sink. He says Walt is bad luck, a curse on us."

I look at the old cowboy, white as a corpse. Whether he's bad luck or not, he can't take much more of this.

A ridiculous idea, but perhaps Nirina's brother has it nearly right. As the Malagasy professor said at dinner weeks earlier, maybe Madagascar is truly the last portal of the fantastic. The more implausible something appears, he said, the more imperative that it be true.

I shout to Nirina, "No. It's me! Tell your brother. I'm the Jonah on this boat. I'm not supposed to leave the island. Not yet." It is, I know, a fantastic notion and couldn't be true anywhere else. But here it's true.

Certain of what I have to do, I rise and stagger to the rail. I look into the churning water and know I can't throw myself overboard any more than I could let myself die for love.

"Okay, okay," I shout to no one, making one final bargain with myself. Everything I've done over the last night and a day and a night has come from a promise to act, to jump out of the long downward spiral that has become my life and do something.

I tell Nirina, "Tell your brother I have to go back. If you want to get away, you have to take me back."

Grasping the railing, she stumbles across the deck and shouts into her brother's ear. Waving his hands in the air, he shouts back, then grips the wheel again. She crawls back to me, cups her hands around my ear. "He says that if he tries to turn the boat will go crosswise to the waves and we'll sink."

"If I stay aboard we're going to sink anyway."

I look out over the stern and am surprised to see the beach no more than half a mile off, probably less. Nearer yet, perhaps fifty yards short of the beach, a line of breakers cuts a white gash across the line of the sea.

I stagger across the tilting deck toward the bow and begin working at the knots holding the rowboat in place. A wave crashes over the bow and I grab the line to keep from being swept overboard. Monja shouts at me, but I ignore him.

Nirina works her way up to the bow. For a moment, I think she's going to try to talk me out of it. Instead, she kneels beside me, working at the knots. Her hands are quicker and surer than mine and the boat is soon free.

I put a hand on her shoulder. "Say so long to Walt for me." I wonder what weight "goodbye" could carry? Or "I love you?" Or "I don't love you?" Words are no good. I pull her to me and kiss her.

The crewman, Rakota, comes forward. Shoving me aside, he throws the boat into the water. I reach out to shake his hand. He grabs it and throws me into the boat.

I land on my wounded hand and nearly pass out from the pain. Someone shouts to me from the fishing boat. I look up to see Monja throwing the oars to me. I set them in the oarlocks as our two boats drift quickly apart.

While the rowboat bucks on the roiling water, trying to toss me into the sea, I raise my head and look toward the fishing boat. The waves are driving me speedily toward land and the faces on board are receding, their forms wavering in the warm and humid sea air until they're no more than smudges against a blue background.

I set the oars in the water but the pain in my hand is too great to row. I turn around on the thwart, facing the shore, and take up one oar like a paddle, resting my injured hand lightly on the top, not needing to propel the boat, only working to keep my course straight.

The surging waves propel me rapidly toward the breakers. If I time my approach wrong they'll flip the boat and I'll drown. With the waves driving my quickly toward shore, I allow myself a last glance over my shoulder. For a moment I'm shocked by what I see, then I laugh out loud.

In the few minutes since I've left the fishing boat, the seas have turned calmer. The boat breasts the diminished waves, heading steadily east, toward Mauritius. I think I can see Nirina standing in the stern, looking back at me. I start to wave, but realize I have to turn and face the reckoning ahead of me.

While I've looked away, I've been driven almost to the line of the breakers. I'll have to pick a forming wave and ride it into shore like a surfer. If I go too fast, I'll get ahead of the breaker and flip the boat, too slow and the following wave will hammer me to the bottom.

I take a couple of quick breaths to quell the panic growing in my chest and try to back-paddle, buy myself a moment so I can time my approach. With the sea propelling me shoreward like a torpedo, I won't have much time to get it right.

Craning my neck to catch a glance over the top of the breakers, I see the beach glinting in the rising sun, not a hundred yards away. It seems a hundred miles. I wonder if I'll reach it alive.

My little boat begins to rise on a forming wave. I can see I'm coming in too fast. I dig the oar deeply into the water and pull back with all my strength. For an instant, I'm sure I've got it right. I'll ride the wave in and land soft as a feather on the sandy beach.

The oar breaks in my hands. For a stunned moment, I can only look at the broken shaft. Then I throw it into the water and grab the other oar. Too late. I've reached the top of the wave and the rowboat trembles on its crest like a bubble at the edge of a waterfall. Tossing away the second oar, I grab the sides of the boat and try to remember how to pray.

For an instant that lasts an eternity, I teeter on the edge of the cresting wave, then drop as if I've fallen from the sky. The rowboat tumbles as it falls, breaking my grip. I'm catapulted into the water. I manage to take a deep breath before I'm pounded straight to the bottom. I strike the sand hard and grunt out some of my precious air. Disoriented, I thrust out my arms and attempt to swim, but I've lost any sense of direction. Thrashing aimlessly, I try to swim to the surface, but feel weighed down. Something is dragging at me, knocking me off balance.

The gun.

My lungs feel ready to explode. Fighting the urge to open my mouth and breathe, I struggle out of my jacket, letting it and the gun drop away.

A new wave catches me from behind and shoots me forward, but I can't break the surface. Pressure is building in my lungs, the air desperate to get out. Again I hit the sandy bottom.

I lose all feeling except a sense of floating not through the water, but the air. This is death, I think. It feels rich and loving. With a shrug, I give myself up to it.

And in that moment of surrender, the water recedes from my body, leaving me lying face down on the sandy beach. I try to raise my head and breathe. I take in a mouthful of water and vomit it out. A new wave comes over me, small, almost gentle, only enough to cover me. Too exhausted to close my mouth, I take in more water. My head is spinning. With the blackness coming over me, I give up. It's all right. Everything's all right.

With a bone-jarring shock, my head and shoulders jerk into the air, dragging me from death back into life. Clean air rushes into my lungs. I'm being dragged across the beach and thrown onto the dry sand. I land face up, taking in the cool, delicious air. No beer, no wine, no scotch has ever tasted so good. I swear I'll never drink again, just breathe, only breathe.

I open my eyes to the great blue Malagasy sky. How beautiful it is, the most beautiful thing I've ever seen. My eyes get teary at its ineffable loveliness.

A new image comes into view. I blink to clear my vision. Of course. Speedy.

The young thief smiles down at me. "It's a good thing Speedy was here, don't you think?"

For the first time, I understand his smile. He's laughing at me. I amuse the hell out of him—all of us *vazaha* do—and he's laughing. And why not? Once the locals get over the idea that we're monsters or some separate kind of creature, they see us for what we are, a bunch of damn fools. Working for us must be like working for the circus. If I had any sense, I'd laugh too, but I'm too tired.

Unable to do anything but lie on the sand, I feel the delicious warmth of the sun. I close my eyes and sleep.

When I wake—an hour later? Two hours? Ten minutes?—I sit up and look for the fishing boat.

"It's gone, Monsieur Knott. Over the horizon."

Speedy sits next to me on the sand, his arms curled around his upraised knees.

I've never truly seen him because I've never tried. Gloria has been right all along. He's not Speedy. He's Dokoby and she knows it. Speedy is just a name we call him so we don't have to know him.

Do I know anyone? Is my cynical tough guy pose just a way to hide the fact that I don't know anyone, or anything? I grope for a question. "What are you doing here? Why …?"

"I knew you would be back. It wasn't time for you to leave. So I waited."

I remember how, as we got into the boat, Speedy said goodbye to everyone but me. He'd known.

"Besides, Monsieur Picard's car is blocking mine. And there's a police car too. I went back to look a little while ago and saw the cars and decided I didn't want to stay around. So I came back here to wait for you."

I close my eyes and laugh softly. That's all I need to do, see life as Speedy does, see it for the comedy it is. After a while I rise to my feet.

"You're strong enough to walk, Monsieur Knott?"

"Yeah, I think so."

"Let's go back and see if we can drive away now."

With Speedy leading me by the hand like a child, we make our way through the trees. They appear less tangled and dense than they had during the night.

Under blue skies and a warming sun we avoid the clearings, and the cemetery too. I have an eerie feeling that if we go searching for the graveyard this morning we won't find it.

By the time we come to the fallen tree and my battered Peugeot, everyone else has gone, Picard's men too. Speedy gets behind the wheel and starts the car on the first try. He sticks his head out the window. "Let's go home."

I shake my head. "Not yet."

Speedy looks at me, puzzled.

"I need to have my hand looked at, need to make a phone call."

"If we go into Tamatave, I think the police will shoot us."

"Not Tamatave. Someplace else. We'll be welcome there."

John Barrow tightens the bandage until I wince. The missionary looks at me as if trying to judge whether the pain is sufficient to do me any good.

"I've patched you up as best I can," he tells me. "The bullet went all the way through the hand, but it probably broke some bones along the way. You'll need surgery if you want it to heal properly."

I sit on the edge of the table in Barrow's little dispensary. My euphoria at surviving has faded, and I feel exhausted and depressed. "Okay," I say.

Barrow leans against a cabinet, crosses his arms. "You know, Robert, a few more inches to your left and you'd have been hit in the gut or the chest and we wouldn't be here talking to each other."

"Yeah, well, a few more inches to the right and he'd have missed me entirely." He doesn't laugh.

"I'm trying to tell you, you could've been killed."

I nod wearily. "John, I think I spent all last night trying to get killed. I managed to screw that up, too."

Barrow reaches out and turns my hand in his, inspecting the bandage "You got that other American out of the country. That's no small thing."

"If he's still alive."

Barrow waits a moment to ask, "What about the girl you were here with last time?"

"She's gone with him." I chuckle, though it sounds bleak even to me. "I'm the only one who didn't manage to get out."

"And now you'll have to face the music."

"If I'm lucky, the government of Madagascar will boot me out of the country."

"And what would bad luck look like?"

"I get booted out by my own government—and fired on top of it."

"Seriously?"

"My guess is that both governments'll be so happy to see me leave they'll go halvsies on the airfare." I blow out a breath. "Then I go off and try to start a new life."

"Born again?"

"Don't get the idea that you're going to baptize me, John. It's been done. Didn't take."

"You know what I mean."

"I do. Yeah."

"Why don't you and your friend spend the night? You could use some rest."

"No. Speedy's got someone waiting for him in Antananarivo. And Sarah has already dipped too far into her reserves of Christian charity to put up with me any longer."

"Won't the police be looking for you?"

"They'll be looking for me tomorrow, too."

We find Speedy in the living room, lounging in the best chair, a cup of tea in his hands.

Sarah turns to us, laughing. "Oh, John, Dokoby was just telling me the funniest story. He is the most charming fellow."

I smile at what a lucky guy I am to know him. "He is that, Sarah."

Speedy sips his tea and smiles.

"Come on, Dokoby," I tell him. "It's time to go home."

Barrow accompanies us to the car. "Thanks to your regular visits, I'm getting very good at treating gunshot wounds and looking after battered cars."

I regard my bashed and mud-spattered Peugeot. "I really have to knock this shit off, don't I?"

"Yes, you do." He puts a hand on my shoulder. "Will you join me in a short prayer before you go?"

"Do I ever?"

"No. But I keep asking.

"Say one for me."

"I will."

"You don't know how I count on it."

Speedy gets behind the wheel and starts the car. Waving goodbye, we make our way out onto the highway.

By the light of day, the damage from the tempest is less than I'd thought. The wind and rain have left little trace of their passage, as if the storm was nothing more than the product of our collective imagination.

Thoughts such as these have ceased to bother me.

24

Darkness has fallen by the time I drop Speedy at Gloria's and turn up the familiar driveway of my place in Ivandry. Razafy, a bandage around his head, gives me his customary tilt of the chin as I drive through the gate.

The house looks dark as a tomb. I enter through the kitchen, switching on the lights as I pass through each room. The few traces I've impressed on the house over my two years have been erased by the thorough clean-up, leaving it in the state I found it—anonymous as a waiting room.

A shriek from behind nearly pushes me across the living room.

"Hello, Jeanne," I manage to say after my heart restarts.

"Oh, Monsieur Knott, I thought you were a ghost."

"No. I tried my best, but here I am."

More out of relief than merriment, she put her hands on her knees and laughs. "You're right. A dead man would look better than you do."

Until this moment I'd never seen anything more than her mask. For an instant, she has let it slip and I have a glimpse, a revelation, of who she really is. Smart, funny. I like her very much. I wish I had known her.

She must have caught a glimpse of herself in my eyes because she immediately reassumes her ironic pose, again becomes a servant. "Miss Gloria has called three times today. I think she's very upset."

"It's all right. I just left her place."

Gloria nearly jumped into Speedy's arms when we came through the door, but managed to hold back, restraining herself until I left.

I asked her if anyone had been looking for me.

"Only everyone. Paul Esmer called, then the DCM, then the Ambassador. I don't know why they'd think I knew where you were."

"Because in fact you did."

The look she gave me wasn't pretty. "Not really, I didn't. Anyway, everyone's upset that Walt would take off like that." Like a pair of teenagers, Gloria and Speedy keep glancing at each other, then quickly away. "They don't know where he is."

"He's gone. With any luck he should be in Mauritius by now. And I suppose I'm toast for having helped him."

"That's the funny thing." And I could see that by "funny" she meant infuriating. "Everyone knows the whole thing smells to high heaven, but it doesn't seem to have occurred to anyone that you're connected with it."

"You're kidding."

"They have it from the Marine on Post One that he saw you in the monitor when you drove away. He says the others left in another car and in another direction. That's all they know."

I try to take it in. I'd hoped that the ruse with the cars would fool the cops outside the embassy. I hadn't anticipated that it would fool the embassy too.

"I suppose the Malagasy government is displeased," I said.

"Now *they* are madder than hops. They want someone's head on a platter."

"Mine, no doubt."

"The only betting at the embassy is whether they'll give you twenty-four or forty-eight hours to get out. And— What did you do to your hand?"

"Do you really want to know?"

She looked to Speedy for an explanation. The young man only smiled.

"Okay," she said to me, hands on her hips. "Why don't you just tell me that I'm too young to understand?"

"You're too young to understand."

"Anyway ..." She shook her head at me as if I were a naughty child. "I'm glad you're back."

"I think you want to be addressing those words to Speedy, don't you?" I said with a laugh. "Why, Ms. Burriss, I've made you blush."

She glared at me and took me by the arm. "Time for you to go home."

On the way out the door I turned and said, "Thank you."

"For what?"

"For not saying anything."

"Maybe it's only because no one asked me exactly what I knew."

"Yeah? Still, thanks."

So I left, wishing Speedy—Dokoby—a better night than the previous one, and drove myself the half-mile to my house.

Jeanne busies herself in the kitchen and finds something to fix me for dinner. She offers to return the money I gave her when I left.

"No, you'd better hang onto it," I tell her. "I don't think I'll be here very long."

The sizzle of a pork chop and the smell of roasting vegetables make me realize how hungry I am even as a wave of weariness comes over me. I decide to lie down on the sofa for a few minutes before dinner.

I wake to the morning light streaming in the window. Still groggy with sleep, I throw off the blanket Jeanne laid over me and stump around the house a bit. I eat the cold pork chop and vegetables she left in the refrigerator and go out through the French doors into the back yard. Despite my throbbing hand, I feel good, the sun is warm on my face and I enjoy the peace of a Sunday morning after a storm.

It's nearly ten by the time I get into the office the next morning.

"Where have you been?" Cheryl calls as I come down the hall. "People have been looking for you all weekend. They even called me—as if you'd be at my house."

I can't think of a suitable reply.

"Isn't it just beautiful out today?" she says, "Oh, did you know that Mr. Sackett just up and left Friday night?"

"No kidding."

"But I'm glad all those police are gone from around the embassy. I didn't like the way they looked at me." She glances at her notepad. "Paul Esmer says the government finally put the hammer down over the weekend and the riots stopped." Her eyes fall on my bandage. "What did you do to your hand?"

"Cut myself shaving." She doesn't laugh. "So, what's in the papers today?"

"Oh, there's a big story. In the *Midi. Le Matin*, too. They finally got that man who had been stealing kids. You'll never guess who it was."

It's a page one, above-the-fold story in all the papers, complete with photos of both Andriamana and Picard. A few breathless paragraphs describe how the intrepid policeman cornered the monster who had abducted dozens of children. In curiously identical terms that carry a whiff of government prose, the stories relate how Captain Andriamana attempted to arrest the kidnapper, but the degenerate *vazaha* fired at Andriamana, striking him in the leg. Ignoring his own wounds, the policeman stood like a rock and fired back, killing the brute, earning the thanks of a grateful nation and marking himself for greater things.

There are a few more paragraphs, but I stop reading.

"And that Mr. Picard sounded so nice over the phone." Cheryl shakes her head. "Oh, the DCM says you're to go to the Ambassador's office"

"Did he say why?"

"Some news he says he needs to break to you." She lowers

her notebook. "I hope your posting to Ouagadoodoo didn't fall through."

"Heaven forfend."

I meet Gloria in the hallway. She's been called into the meeting, too. I had expected it would be Trapp from Econ taking my place. He has the experience to fill in as political officer until my replacement arrives. I guess someone decided he has enough on his plate already. So it'll be Gloria. The irony doesn't amuse me.

Ambassador Herr sits behind her desk like a judge ready to hand down sentence. Pete Salvatore slumps in an armchair, his hands between his knees. Gloria and I take the sofa.

After a surprisingly warm welcome the Ambassador says, "As I'm sure you both know, we wish this weren't happening. We took a stand on protecting an American citizen and accepted the risks. But having one of our officers declared *persona non grata* is just wrong." She grits her teeth as if she can't bear to go on.

I'd have thought that having me thrown out of the country would put her in a better mood.

"I got the call at home last night," she continues. "The government of Madagascar will send over a Diplomatic Note this morning. Is that right, Pete?"

Her deputy nods.

She puts her hands flat on the desk. "Personally, I can't tell you how much I regret this. The embassy is losing a fine officer, one of whom I'm personally fond."

A valedictory is fine, but laying it on too thick robs it of even faked sincerity.

"Now, Robert, you already know most of the editors in town, yes?"

An odd question. "Yeah, I guess so."

"And I think you know Gloria's staff pretty well."

"Yes, ma'am. But what's that got to do with me getting PNG'd?"

Ambassador Herr looks at Pete Salvatore. "They just now got to the embassy," he says to her, then turns to me. "It's Gloria."

After the trials of the last few days, my shock absorbers are wrecked and I can't take it in. "What?"

"It's Gloria. She's the one they're throwing out."

Gloria looks at me, then the Ambassador. "Me?"

Ambassador Herr takes a breath. "The Malagasy government has made some trumped-up charge." She casts a baleful look at me. "They're saying that the events leading to Mr. Sackett's escape were precipitated by the story about the burglars. And they claim Gloria was the source of that story, when we know it was you, Robert. And they say that she helped a Malagasy criminal escape from prison. It's all … all so …" She gropes for the word. "… mendacious. But they claim they can back it up with witnesses, whom they've no doubt coerced into saying whatever they're told."

Pete gives us the details. The Malagasy government is giving Gloria seventy-two hours to leave the country. The embassy has already communicated with Washington. The Department will lodge a protest with the Malagasy embassy and consider expelling a Malagasy diplomat in return. Other than that, there isn't much we can do.

The Ambassador adds that Gloria needn't worry about what this might do to her career. She'll be fine.

Like someone who has been told of a terminal illness, Gloria looks from one to the other of us. "If I'm going to be so fine, why do I feel so bad?"

The mystery of Walt's whereabouts is resolved that afternoon when a cable comes from the tiny American embassy in Mauritius, stating that a man claiming to be an American citizen has turned up on the doorstep with a young Malagasy woman whose relationship to him is unclear. They say they want to go the United States as quickly as possible. Neither has any identification, baggage, or money. The little embassy's perplexity rises like fog from the brief cable, which concludes with a pathetic plea to "Please advise."

Lynn sits in my office, pen in hand, waiting for me to give her some notes for the cable to Mauritius she's been tasked with writing. I run my hands through my hair. "Well, I guess you can tell them that Walt's an American citizen who escaped imprisonment here—from jail or from the embassy, however you think it plays best."

She eyes me for a long time. "You had something to do with their escape. I'd bet my mortgage on it. And that's why you disappeared over the weekend."

"How much do you really want to know?"

"I haven't decided yet. And would you tell it to me straight if I asked?"

"I've never been rich enough, good-looking enough, or smart enough to stick to the truth."

The admin officer leans back in her chair and puts her pen down. "I'm not out to get you, Robert. That's going to be someone else's job. I want a lot of things for you. I want to see you kicked out of the foreign service. I want to slap you in the face. I want to see that you're not hurt. I want to take you to bed."

"But you're not going to do any of those things."

"Probably only one of them."

"Who gets to pick?"

She sighs. What a trial I must be.

"What do we tell them about the girl, Nirina?" she asks.

"Tell them that if they send her back here she faces imprisonment for helping an American citizen escape persecution. The USG should consider allowing her asylum in the United States."

"Just remember that you can't ask for the same thing for yourself. Everyone's tired of your act, Robert. Shape up, or you're going to be the next one out of here, and it will be the Ambassador who throws you out, not the Malagasy."

With that, she gets up to leave. Halfway across the room she relents and smiles back at me. "Hey, come here," she says.

When I get within arm's reach, she slaps me in the face.

Suspicions of misconduct swirl around my head throughout the following days, all the stronger for remaining unproven. I come up with a story of going down to Antsirabe for the weekend. No one can prove me a liar, but no one buys it and I'm cast once more into professional darkness. My phone has stopped ringing and no one comes by my office. Only Cheryl has anything to say to me, and then mostly to regret Gloria's departure, saying from time to time, "She doesn't deserve this." I don't miss the unstated implication that I do.

These lamentations hit a peak when, just before the close of business, Gloria stops by.

After Cheryl has finished making a fuss over her, I look up from the crossword in the *International New York Times*.

"I came by to say goodbye," she says.

"You may be the last person on earth still speaking to me," I tell her.

"I noticed there wasn't a line down the hall congratulating you on your great weekend." She leans in the doorway regarding me with a half-smile that suggests equal parts dejection and self-assurance.

If in very short order you take up your first major post, fall in love, decide to keep a dark secret from the embassy, and then get booted out of the country, maybe you gain a stronger sense of yourself.

She tells me, "I'm leaving tonight. I don't need seventy-two hours to pack out. You've seen my place. I never really unpacked. I'll be in Washington by tomorrow morning."

"Do yourself a favor. This time stay the night in Paris on the way. It's within the regs. Take yourself out to dinner or something."

She smiles and gives me that assertive nod of hers. "Maybe I will."

As she starts to go, I call after her. "Hey."

She turns in the doorway.

"Tell Annibal to just meet you at the airport. I'll drive you out."

25

As I get out of the car, Gloria waddles out her front door, an overloaded bag in each hand. She ignores my offer to help and makes it halfway down the walk before Speedy comes out of the house and silently holds out his hands to her. She looks into his eyes and sets the bags down. He picks them up. The everyday transaction holds an intimacy that makes me feel as if I should turn my head.

Speedy throws the bags in the trunk then comes back to Gloria, who is standing by the open car door. Watching her face closely, he puts his arms around her and kisses her briefly on the mouth. Gloria leans into him and kisses him twice, lightly, like a chicken picking at seed.

Emotionally exhausted, they both take a step back.

She speaks quietly. "The police will still be looking for you, Dokoby. You have to leave town as soon as you can."

"I have an uncle in Toliara, in the south. They'll never look for me there."

"Okay." Her eyes stay on his and she lays a hand on his shoulder. "Goodbye, Dokoby."

"Goodbye, Gloria."

Her eyes never leave him as she eases into the car like a sleepwalker.

As I drive away, Speedy spreads his arms wide and shouts, "One day, when you come back as ambassador, I will show you all of Madagascar!"

Annibal opens Gloria's door when we pull up to the terminal. "Good evening, Miss Burriss."

The air is thick with bus fumes and honking horns. Crowds of passengers and well-wishers flow like water around the piles of suitcases and cardboard boxes that fill the sidewalks.

Gloria takes a breath and clasps her hands in front of her. She suddenly looks very young and very small and I admire the hell out of her.

"So, what happens next in the 'Exciting Adventures of Gloria Burris, Girl Diplomat?'" I ask.

She smiles and gives a little jump. "Oh, I didn't tell you. I got a call at the house just before you came up. The Department's found a post for me. In Geneva."

"Geneva." I have to laugh. Twenty-four years in the foreign service and the closest I'll ever get to Geneva is a bar of Swiss chocolate. "You sure you'll be able to bear clean streets and phones that work?"

She looks around as if searching for the answer in the crowds of travelers in their brightly colored clothes, in the mellifluous and difficult language, in their very foreignness— and in hers. "I was so sure I wouldn't miss any of this. Now I'm sure I will."

I understand. She's fated for bigger things, tours in the great capitals of Europe and Asia, postings to the UN, policy positions in Washington. She might never again see anything like this.

Like a guy squinting through someone else's eyeglasses, I look around, trying to see all of it as a newcomer might, as something fresh and wonderfully strange, vibrating with possibilities all the more enticing for lying just beyond understanding. But I can't hold the sense of wonder I lost long ago. My years in Africa have robbed the scene of its novelty, of its ferment, the sense of community, the honest striving of a people not yet lost in empty individualism— still citizens, not consumers. For me, the novelty has been squeezed to death in the coils of the everyday. It's the United States that now seems to me like a strange and distant land.

With the end of my career only a couple of years off, I wonder if I'll ever accustom myself to my own country. Maybe I'd be better off doing as a few of my colleagues have done and find a large house in Zambia or Botswana, one I could never afford in the United States, hire a few servants, take up drinking again and live out my days in Africa, unable to go home, or, more truly, having no home. Just like Picard, but on the right side of the law.

I feel Gloria's eyes on me.

"You know," I say, "I've been thinking of this place as the end of the line for so long it never occurred to me that it could be the beginning."

She gazes at the scene a little longer, and with a perky tilt of her chin, says, "Maybe we'll get to serve together again."

Only a couple of years in the service and she's already picked up the clichés. The stated wish to serve together again is the most gracious way to say goodbye.

I shoulder my role in this little scene and deliver my lines with an easy naturalness. "When you make ambassador, pluck me out of whatever hole I'm living in and make me your DCM."

"Count on it." Gloria searches the crowds. "No photographer on the way out, I guess."

"Sic transit Gloria."

She holds out her hand as she had on the day she arrived, all business again. "Goodbye, Robert."

I shake her hand and nod toward the entrance. "You don't want me to come in with you?"

"No. Annibal knows how to see me through."

So, she's learned that too.

I drive through the open gate, acknowledging Monsieur Razafy's enigmatic tilt of the chin, the tug at the hat. Dinner will be waiting for me on the table.

The universe has been restored to its comforting order, though I continue to flounder within it. But, hey, I'm still alive, which is at least a start toward something new, something maybe a little bit better—if I'm willing to make it happen.

Rather than go inside, I stroll into the back yard, taking the evening air. I wonder if Bobby the Chameleon, securely hidden behind a bush or a rock, is watching me as I walk across the lawn toward the metal door in the garden wall.

As I pull open the door for the first time, it cries on its unoiled hinges like a newborn child. I walk toward the knoll and the tree that has always seemed to me the essence of the island's unknowable nature. It's closer to my place than I had imagined.

Under the rising moon I can see the rice paddies beyond the knoll and the purple line of distant hills that lay between Antananarivo and the coast.

I've seen it all so many times, yet I know it so little, have never allowed it to touch me. I've resisted Madagascar at every turn, cursed it, despised it, never understanding I was really cursing and despising myself. I need to reconcile myself to my own life. Once I do that, I can do anything.

I lay my hands on the strangely formed tree. Its texture is surprisingly soft. Yes, I'm sure it's my spirit tree and its roots go all the way to the center of the earth.

Up close, it appears more beautiful and less alien than I imagined, surprisingly like an evergreen. Timeless.

ACKNOWLEDGMENTS

Every book is a group effort. I want to thank my old friend and colleague from Madagascar, Annie Rajao for her help. My gratitude goes also to Virginia Kincaid and Patricia Alston for their sharp-eyed editing suggestions, to Veryl Behrens for his knowledge of firearms, and, as always, to my wife, Felicia, for her advice and support. Thanks, too, to my agent, Kimberley Cameron, and to all the good people at Blank Slate Press and Amphorae Publishing, including Kristina Blank Makansi and Lisa Miller. And my gratitude to J. David Ivester for his work on publicity and for his encouragement.

ABOUT THE AUTHOR

A native Oregonian and current Portland resident, Stephen Holgate served for two years as a diplomat with the American Embassy in Madagascar. In addition to his other Foreign Service posts, Mr. Holgate has served as a Congressional staffer; headed a committee staff of the Oregon State Senate; managed two electoral campaigns; acted with the national tour of an improvisational theater group; worked as a crew member of a barge on the canals of France; and lived in a tent while working as a gardener in Malibu.

Holgate has also published several short stories and successfully produced a one-man play, as well as publishing innumerable freelance articles. Also the author of *Tangier*, *Madagascar* is his second novel.